Stanley Morgan, author of the sensationally successful saga of Tobin, stud of the seventies, is also familiar to the public through his film acting career and voice-over recordings of many well-known television commercials. His sales in the Tobin series top a phenomenal million and his status is now assured as one of today's popular writers in Britain and the Continent. Mayflower will also publish his blistering new series of high-flying capers in supersonic jets – THE FLYBOYS.

Also by Stanley Morgan
in Mayflower Books

THE SEWING MACHINE MAN
THE DEBT COLLECTOR
THE COURIER
COME AGAIN COURIER
TOBIN TAKES OFF
TOBIN ON SAFARI
TOBIN IN PARADISE

OCTOPUS HILL
MISSION TO KATUMA

THE FLYBOYS

Tobin in Trouble

Stanley Morgan

Mayflower

Granada Publishing Limited
Published in 1974 by Mayflower Books Ltd
Frogmore, St. Albans, Herts AL2 2NF

A Mayflower original

Made and printed in Great Britain by
Hazell Watson & Viney Ltd
Aylesbury, Bucks
Set in Intertype Times Roman

ONE

You'd expect a feller with a name like Hi Low to be a bit of a nutter, wouldn't you? Well, Hi doesn't disappoint you.

He's the owner and barman of this hotel I'm staying at in Miami Beach, Florida. It's called the Hotel Splendide and the guy who thought up the name must have been either blind or balmy or is still splitting his sides laughing over the joke.

It's a run-down, paint-peeling hilarity just off Collins Avenue, and had I arrived in broad daylight I would've about-turned rather smartly and moved on up the Avenue to a more select hostelry. But I didn't. I fell out of the taxi four nights ago, weary unto death after two weeks in Nassau with that lecherous lay-about Stud Ryder, and cheerfully allowed myself to be steered into the Splendide by the cabdriver who, I have since discovered, is Hi's brother-in-law and undoubtedly hijacks patrons on commission. It was not, therefore, until the next morning that I discovered what a fleapit I'd been suckered into. And by then it was too late.

By midmorning I had succumbed to the kindly, generous, nutty, down-at-heel charm of the place and the characters it attracts, and now, four days later, would not swap it for a penthouse suite in one of the seventeen-star, thousand-room beauties further along Collins.

In those four days I have been investigated, accepted, feted and spoilt rotten by a host of crazy, lovable locals who have threatened to break both my arms if I make so much as a move towards my wallet to buy a drink. I calculate that my sojourn here has so far cost Hi and the Splendide half a season's profits and it's a good job I'm taking the midnight train to New York or the poor guy will be flat bust by the end of the week.

Hi is a middle-aged, paunchy, grey-haired chap with a propensity for loud bow ties, multi-hued waistcoats and spectacles as thick as jam jar bottoms. Without them he can't find the bar – even when he's standing behind it. A couple of nights ago, as he crossed the room, he took them off to clean them and walked smack into the jukebox, blind as a bat.

His wife Paula isn't much better. She works here too, helping him to lose money. She's a raven-haired, faded beauty, a one-time cabaret star with the lousiest voice imaginable, though she alone appears not to have noticed the fact. Up around midnight, with a dozen or so ginslings under her tightly corseted belt, Paula lets rip with a few heart-rending oldies like *Melancholy Baby* and invariably washes out her contact lenses with a flood of tears. Then the fun begins – everybody on the floor looking for Paula's orbs.

But, bless 'em, they are kindness itself, embarrassingly so in my case. And all because Hi was stationed in England during the Second World War. Apparently he was showered with affection by a mumsy widow while billeted in Liverpool and the mere mention that it was my home town released the flood of reciprocity in which I am currently bathing but from which I must soon escape if I'm ever going to make that midnight train to New York.

It is now five o'clock in the afternoon of the 20th day of December and the temperature on the beach today reached ninety-two fahrenheit. Which is what Miami in December is all about.

I enter the bar, staggering with thirst. It is darker than Grant's Tomb. One thing Hi can't stand is daylight. There isn't a window in the place. Hi is in his customary position behind the bar on the right, polishing a glass. Paula is tinkling away on a decrepit piano at the edge of a dance floor the size of your thumb nail. She is also singing.

Oh, boy . . .

There is but one other occupant – a young, handsome, rather dour looking lad at the far end of the counter, nursing a beer and humming along with Paula, staring into his glass in a thoughtful sort of way.

Hi senses me enter and peers myopically across the room. 'Who goes there – friend or foe?'

'Hi, Hi,' I greet him – a local joke. 'It's me – Ronald Colman.'

Paula thinks all Englishmen sound like Ronald Colman. She stops playing and lets out a whoop. 'Hello, Russ . . . !'

'Hi, Paula. Don't stop playing, it's lovely.'

'Hi – get Russ a drink, the poor guy's droppin'.'

'On its way, angel of light. What'll it be, Russ?'

I slid onto a stool, nodding to the young fellow and getting a nod back. 'The coldest beer you've got, Hi. The beach was murder.'

'Misery . . . pure misery,' he acknowledged, shaking his head while yanking a Budweiser from the cooler. 'Twenty-five years I've lived here an' never set a foot on that sand. I tell yuh – who needs all that heat when there's a good, dark, freezin' beer like this available? Russ . . . I want you to meet a good buddy of ours – Dave Brewer from Houston, Texas. Dave . . . say hello to a real nice guy from England – Russ Tobin.'

Honest – Americans really *do* talk like this.

The young fella got up and offered his hand, taking mine in a grip that could have crushed my knuckles to powder if he'd so desired. 'Howdy, Russ, glad to know yuh.'

'Dave here's a pilot,' explained Hi, pouring my beer.

'Oh, really? What airline, Dave?'

'Private. Small stuff. Anythin' from crop-dustin' to taxi service.' His manner was strange, not so much curt as clipped, perhaps shy; the sort of personality that pulls you up sharp as you detect hidden depths – possibly even violence. A weird, rather disturbing fellow.

'So you're from England,' he said, emptying his glass with a quick toss and nodding at Hi for another. 'On vacation?'

'Yes. Only four days, though I'm afraid – I'm catching the midnight train to New York.'

'Four days!' he grunted. 'Not much vacation. You need a lot more than four days to see Miami.'

He pronounced it 'Miam-ah' as most Southerners did.

'That's what I keep tellin' him,' protested Hi, pouring Dave a fresh beer. 'He ain't seen nothin' yet! Four days he's bin here and he ain't moved off that beach. He ain't seen Bayfront Park . . . or Biscayne Boulevard . . . the Orange Bowl . . . Vizcaya Palace . . . the Everglades . . .'

'Hi . . .' I interrupted, grinning, 'if I'd known the place was so beautiful I'd have arranged to stay for a month. But I'll be back, I promise.'

'You *have* to go to New York tonight?' asked Dave, sucking the froth off his beer.

'I'm afraid so. I'm booked on a two-centre tour with Sun Time. Four days here then six in New York. I've already paid. I really am sorry I didn't allow myself more time here.'

'Then you haven't seen Fort Lauderdale?' Dave queried, almost threateningly.

'Ain't I just told yuh . . .?' interjected Hi. 'He's bin lyin' on that beach since he got here. He ain't seen nothin'!'

'I was pretty tired,' I told Dave, with a grin. 'I've just spent two weeks in Nassau.'

'Oh,' he said, smiling for the first time, his face suddenly an unexpected boyish grin. 'Yeah, you would be tired after Nassau. Gee, it's too bad you haven't got more time. I'd have been glad to show you around.'

'Well, that's . . .'

'Ha!' It was Paula, still at the piano, knocking holes out of *Blue Moon.* 'Then thank your lucky stars you're leaving tonight, Russ. Get on the town with that one an' you'd likely end up in India or somewheres.'

I grinned at Dave. 'Now, that sounds interesting.'

He shrugged. 'She exaggerates. I never got further than Africa.'

'On a bender?' I laughed.

'Sure . . . why not. I was gettin' tired of the bars around here. Hi – give Russ here another drink . . . and have one yourselves.'

He dipped into the breast pocket of his oatmeal suit, which he was wearing over a natty brown cowboy type shirt piped in cream, and slung a bundle of greenbacks on the counter. There must have been a couple of hundred dollars there. 'An' keep 'em comin' till that's all gone.'

'Wey hey!' laughed Hi. 'The boy's got a thirst.'

'Well, hell . . . the least we can do is show Russ here a drink or two even if we can't show him around Miami.'

Oh, boy . . . I had the feeling this was going to be the start of something huge. Dave was not the sort of man to take refusal very happily.

'Well, that's very kind of you, Dave . . .' I began.

'Not even seen Fort Lauderdale,' he muttered, making it sound like I'd committed some heinous social boob – like strolling along Collins with me flies open.

'I told him!' seconded Paula, making a howling hash of a twenty-note ripple. 'Didn't I tell him, Hi – go see Lauderdale, I said . . . his first night here.'

'She told him,' confirmed Hi, sloshing slugs of gin into two glasses for himself and Paula. 'You surely missed something, Russ, so help me. That place is a sight for sore eyes. Yuh take a ferry boat ride from Bal Harbour, just down Collins here, through the waterways of Paradise itself. Some of those millionaires' homes frontin' that main stream take your breath away –

even more than Paula hittin' a top C – an' that's pretty breath-takin', believe me.'

'What yuh sayin' about me, yuh slob?'

'Nuttin', honey, Just tellin' Russ about Lauderdale.'

'Ah, what's the use of teasin' him – he couldn't go now anyways.'

'Yes, he could.'

This was a flat, emphatic statement from Dave Brewer. 'He could go tonight. There's one of them special champagne cruises . . . leaves Bal Harbour at six.'

'Huh!' humphed Hi. 'Fat lotta Lauderdale he'd see on one of them specials. Nuttin' but an excuse for a drunken orgy, them cruisers. I tell yuh, more gropin' goes on there than in the whole of London in a November peasouper.'

'Really?' I said, brightening.

'Sure, really,' said Hi, disgustedly, slipping me the wink because Paula was watching him. 'Yuh don't leave Bal Harbour till six so it's dark before yuh get to the end of the run. Then it's dancin' and boozin' all the way back.'

'And, er, what time would that be?' I asked nonchalantly.

'Around nine. Three hours' boozin' and dancin' . . . geez, that's awful.'

'Awful,' I agreed.

'Still . . .' said Dave, making thoughtful rings with his glass, 'he would see *something* of Lauderdale – before it got dark. And something's better than nothing, hmm Hi?'

'And he doesn't *have* to booze and dance,' continued Dave.

'Certainly he doesn't have to. He's a nice, quiet fella . . . there's nuttin' to say he can't just sit quietly by the rail and take in the beauty of the place an' just ignore all that boozin' an' dancin' and gropin' an' . . .'

'You're absolutely right,' said Dave. 'Nuthin' at all.'

'Er, how does one get *out* to Bal Harbour?' I enquired off-handedly.

'Take a bus right outside,' answered Hi quickly. 'Takes you straight along Collins . . .'

'Hey, now wait a minute, you guys . . .!' Paula murdered the end of *Smoke Gets In Your Eyes* with an excruciating *arpeggio* and spun off the stool. 'Now, don't you both forget Russ has to catch the midnight train to New York.'

'We ain't forgettin',' Hi told her. 'Heck, he'd be back here by nine thirty. Plenty of time to pick up his bags and get to the station.'

'Well . . . I dunno,' she said uncertainly.

'What's to don't know about it? He's a big boy now, he'll find his way back. All he's gotta do is stay on the ferry. Well, I reckon he oughta go see somethin' of Lauderdale before he leaves.'

'So do I,' nodded Dave, pushing the pile of money towards Hi. 'Come on, let's kill some of this, money makes me nervous.'

'Same again, Russ?' enquired Hi.

'Er, no thanks, I think I'll have a short. Two beers is about my limit. But, here, let me do this, it's my round . . .'

'No, sir,' rapped Dave, slapping the money with the flat of his hand. 'You don't buy a drink till this lot is gone. I made me some real money flyin' a rich cow-poke from Abilene to Miamah for the races and that sweet fella put a C-note on a wild outsider for me that slid home at forty to one.'

'For . . . forty to one!' I gasped. 'But that's . . .'

'Four thousand semolinas,' he nodded. 'And as Hi will tell you, I never go home until I'm broke.'

'True enough,' confirmed Hi, reaching for the vodka bottle and throwing about half a pint into a glass. 'Er, touch of tonic, Russ?'

'A smidgin, Hi. Well, thanks, Dave . . .'

'De nada. Make yourself at home an' drink hearty – this is on Danny Boy, field-flattener of the three-thirty.'

I took a gulp and shuddered. 'Wow!'

'You'll need that,' said Dave. 'Gets a mite chilly out there on the Bay.'

'Gets a mite chilly in here, too,' grinned Hi, pouring three more gargantuan slugs for them. 'Well, here's to Russ – proud carrier of the British flag . . . a noble emissary in a foreign field . . . and also one of the nicest guys it's ever bin our pleasure to meet.'

'I'll drink to that,' Paula said sweetly, raising her glass. 'Make sure you come back real soon, y'hear?'

'I'll be back,' I promised, then we all drank to Tobin.

'And here's to you two,' I said. 'To two of the kindest people it's ever been *my* pleasure to meet.'

'Hear hear,' said Dave, and we all drank to Hi and Paula.

'Can't leave Dave out of this,' insisted Hi. 'Hell, he's our best customer.'

'Here's to you, Dave,' said Paula. 'Many more trips and always happy landings.'

'By golly, I'll second that,' Hi said earnestly and threw another gulp down.

After that we found twelve other things to drink to and by half-past-five we were all well and truly pissed.

* * *

'Listen . . . if I'm going to fatch that ce . . . catch that ferry, I'll have to go,' I said, feeling that if I didn't climb off that stool in the next five seconds I'd keel off it like a felled redwood.

'Don' worry 'bout a thing,' Dave reassured me. 'We can do Bal Harbour in fifteen minutes easy.'

'We?'

'Sure, we. You don't think I'd let a buddy ride a bus out there, do you? I'll drive you out. Take us fifteen minutes.'

'Well, that's very good of you, Dave . . .'

'Don' keep sayin' that, it's my pleasure. Wha's the time, somebody?'

Hi peered at his watch, holding it first out at arm's length then up under his nose. 'It's . . . twenty-five after six,' he slurred.

'Ya nut – it's half five,' said Paula. 'Time you guys were goin'. And, Dave – don't speed, the cops are hot here on the Beach.'

'Wha' – me?'

He gave a silly grin and his elbow fell off the bar, slopping his drink. 'Ooops! OK . . . well, maybe we'd better go at that. Hi – start pourin' another drink . . . I'll be back before you reach the top. Come on, Russ, let's go.'

'I'll see you folks later,' I told them.

'We'll be here,' Hi assured me. 'Heck, we've bin no place else in twenty-five years, have we, gal?'

'You're damn right,' sneered Paula, changing it into a smile for me. 'Take it easy, come back in one piece. And Dave – you take care of this boy, now, we love him.'

'I'll keep it down to thirty,' he grinned. 'Just like always.'

We went out to the street to where Dave's rented Oldsmobile convertible graced the curb. It was good to be out in the fresh air although the brightness of the sun was quite obscene.

Suddenly he was gone from my side and with a wild whoop leapt clean over the side of the convertible and landed with a bounce in the driver's seat.

'Let's go, buddy! Come on, jump in!'

I accepted the invitation, took a flying leap, caught my toe in the folded hood and finished in a heap in the back seat.

BAARROOMM!!

'YAAAHHHOOO!!'

To the squeal of tortured tyres we swerved away from the curb, played chicken with an oncoming bus, ran for fifty yards with two wheels on the pavement, then shot across an intersection against the traffic lights. And I was still in the back!

'This heap's a real dog,' he complained, turning round at fifty to peer into the back. 'Hey, ain't you coming up front?'

'When I get a chance. Dave . . . the truck!'

'Mm? Oh, yeah.'

With a flick of his wrist he swung the Olds round the rear end of a pick-up upon which we were advancing at terrible speed, then swung back into line, missing the truck's front end by three-eighths of a bee's ball. Thank God he wasn't flying me! Though I reckoned that was only a matter of time.

I got one leg over the front seat and then we encountered the traffic lights. Whatever possessed Dave to obey them, God knows, but he did and I finished up draped over the windscreen.

'Ain't you ever gonna sit down?' he grinned, then gunned the Olds again as the lights changed, flinging me back into the cushioning.

On we shot, straight down fabulous Collins Avenue, passing countless, towering white hotels gleaming in the setting sun, the narrow waters of India Creek on our left and glimpses of the Atlantic Ocean on our right and who gave a stuff!? All I was concerned with was reaching Bal Harbour alive.

'Great place, huh?' he remarked, horn-blasting a pink Cadillac that was crawling along at a mere sixty.

'Wonderful,' I gulped.

'You should see it from the air.' In *his* plane! 'Great sight.'

'Yes, I'm sure.'

Goodbye New York, I thought, shutting my eyes as he swerved round the rear end of a car backing out onto the Avenue . . . farewell London . . . Mum . . . Dad. I could see the headlines now – 'TOURIST TOBIN PULVERIZED IN PILOT'S PILE-UP' . . . 'CRAZY DAVE CLOBBERS COMRADE IN COLLINS CRASH.'

'And . . . here we go!' he cried exultantly, throwing the Olds hard to the left, off the Avenue and into an enormous parking area that reached right down to the harbour, three hundred yards away. Across it he zoomed, finally skidding to a slithering halt only inches from the little wooden ticket office situated right on the quay.

'That's it,' he said, pointing to an open-decked ferry boat moored at the wharf. 'Have a ball, baby. See you back at the hotel. I'll take you to the station 'bout eleven thirty.'

'Th . . . thanks very much,' I stammered, stepping out on rubber legs. 'Thanks a lot, Dave.'

'De nada, amigo. Adios!'

With a whoop and a wave he was gone in a cloud of dust and a zizz of scattered gravel, sweeping out onto the highway into the path of a rushing bus, then gunning it back along the Avenue, tyres squealing horrendously.

As I reached the ticket office the window slid back and an old guy in a peaked sailor's cap muttered through a curtain of cigar smoke. 'What's with Ben Hur – he get caught short or sumpn? He drives like he's gotta club foot.' He ripped off a ticket and slid it across. 'That'll be a hundred and ten dollars . . . ten for the cruise and a hundred for the gravel.'

I grinned and gave him ten.

'OK to go aboard?' I asked.

'Sure it's OK. Yuh see more that way.'

I picked up the ticket and walked across the wharf to a gangway, at the side of which a billboard proclaimed the wonders of the trip. 'Special champagne cruise to luxurious Fort Lauderdale – the Venice of America' it said in radiant orange day-glo, so bright it hurt the eyes. 'Magnificent homes fronting on beautiful landscaped boulevards. See the wonders of the New River by night. Dancing. Free champagne! Ferry leaves 6.30 p.m. prompt.'

Six thirty! I had half an hour to spare.

I crossed the gangway and had my ticket severed by a long-haired youth in gold velvet jeans and an admiral's hat. The boat appeared totally deserted.

'Anybody else coming?' I asked him.

He nodded, then spat with formidable accuracy through the three-inch gap between boat and quay. 'They'll be along.'

'Can I sit anywhere?'

'Anywhere but the ladies' can and the engine room.'

'Thank you.'

I sauntered across the deck, the delicious ferry boat smell

conjuring up memories of my Liverpool youth, mounted a flight of stairs and emerged onto the upper deck at the stern.

As I said, it was an open-decked boat, its upper deck almost totally filled with two very wide rows of wooden seats separated by a centre aisle, there being two other aisles down the sides. A canvas canopy covered the entire boat, offering protection from the killer Miami sun, and amidships stood the captain's cabin and wheelhouse.

As I reached the top of the stairs, the view of Biscayne Bay was revealed. Evening calm had flattened the water into a sheet of blue steel, and far off down the coast the city of Miami glowed radiantly in the pink of dusk. Out on the Bay a hundred sail boats dipped and tacked in the gentle ocean breeze and here and there a speedboat tore across the top of the water with exuberant verve.

Peace. The smell of salt and the warm December breeze against my cheek. Hard to realize that New York and London were freezing to death, clawed by winter. I must be mad, I thought, leaving all this for snow. But I had to see New York before making my way back home. All things come to an end – including the Tobin bank balance. Come in number six, your time is up! Time to get back to work.

Thoughts of Nassau and the high old time I had with Stud had me grinning. Wonderful holiday. But in six days time – back to earth with a thump. I'd have to give some real thought to my next job – and not only what but also where I wanted to work. There were so many places I hadn't seen yet – the Middle East . . . the South of France . . . Scandinavia . . . yes, Scandinavia, now there was a thought. All those long-legged, blonde-haired lovelies . . .

A blast of motor horns ruptured my reverie and into the parking area swept two . . . three . . . four big coaches, packed to the gunwales. The first one drew up by the ticket office, its doors opened with a hiss, and out poured eight thousand jubilant souls, all laughing and poking and wearing funny hats.

Like a swarm of multi-coloured locusts they surged towards the gangway, their courier heading for the ticket office with a bouquet of tickets. The boat rocked, shuddered, sighed and settled, surrendering itself to the inevitable. The peace of the Bay was irrevocably shattered and the evening of gaiety had begun.

* * *

'NOW . . . SETTLE DOWN PLEASE, FOLKS, AND HEAR THIS . . . ! FOLKS . . . WOULD YA KINDLY SETTLE DOWN!'

Ooh, the agony of it. I was standing in one corner of the deck, leaning against an iron pole that supported the canvas canopy, when a loudspeaker, mounted six inches above my unsuspecting head, exploded into life.

'Folks . . . could I have a little hush for just a minute, if you please . . .'

Gradually the furore – emananting from a million and a quarter people all trying to grab the best rail seats, died.

'Well, now, that's just dandy . . .' continued the tannoy. 'Folks . . . this is your captain, Bud Grover, speakin' and extendin' to you – to one and all – a sincere welcome aboard this cut-down version of the *Queen Elizabeth* (trickle of laughter) and promising you an evenin' to remember as we meander slowly along the magnificent waterways of fabulous Fort Lauderdale.

'Perhaps some of you on board are first-time visitors to Miami, and to you, on behalf of the company, I extend an extra special howdy, nice indeed to have you with us, and be assured we fully intend to send you on your way with nuthin' but the fondest memories of our beautiful land.

'In just a few moments now we'll be castin' off, so get yourselves settled all comfy cozy and prepare to see some of the most beautiful homes in America – an' don't you worry none about that ole sun goin' down, because after dark most of these homes will be lit up like fairy palaces. OK, now . . . here we go.'

Down on the quay a bell clanged and was answered by one from the bridge control. The engines started, sending a shudder through the boat. Then a rumble signified the retraction of the gangway and immediately the boat began moving away from the quay, heading into mid channel.

The packed crowd were, as always, a motley lot – short, fat, thin, long, some pale, the majority tanned to chestnut brown. Many were dressed in their Saturday night finery, others relaxed in shirts and slacks.

A group to my left were rattling away in Italian, all talking at once, and elsewhere I picked out Spanish, German, Yiddish, Bronx and Boston. On a couple of occasions I even heard English! Hip flasks abounded, priming the wicks of jollity, and the Italian family, naturally, were already tucking into garlic sausage and red wine.

Yes, it had all the makings of a merry, rowdy, bawdy, beautiful evening – provided you could find room to lift an elbow.

'ALL RIGHT NOW, FOLKS . . .!' It was that bloody tannoy again. 'For a little while we'll just be putterin' up this main channel with not too much to see exceptin' water . . . so I'll take this opportunity to tell you a little of the history of Fort Lauderdale . . .'

The Italian lot were still rabbiting on, going like Bren guns, not taking a blind bit of notice of Grover.

'Sssshhh! Silencio – por favor!' hissed a Spaniard, a young lad, one of a group of five or six who were obviously out on a stag night. He got a stream of abuse in Italian for his trouble.

Aye aye, I thought. Champagne, dancing *and* a Mafia versus Inquisition double-header as an unexpected bonus. Nothing like a good earthy punchup to round off the festivities.

The Spanish lot responded with appropriate snarls and indelicate gestures and everyone settled down to listen to Grover – at least for the time being.

'Well, now, way back in 1910 . . .' he drawled, his tone rich in studied, squirmy folksiness, '. . . a bunch of public-spirited businessmen got together an' organised a Board of Commerce in order to develop a community that would attract the kind of business and the class of tourist that they *themselves* wanted as business and social neighbours. Starting modestly, with a population, in 1920, of only 2,065, today Fort Lauderdale is one of the fastest-growing communities in the United States – with a population of around 130,000. *And*, because it possesses more than 270 miles of waterways within its city limits, Lauderdale has now become known as . . .. The Venice of America . . .'

A chorus of dutiful 'ohhhs!' greeted this revelation, then Grover continued. 'Very shortly now we will be cruising slowly along some of these wonderful waterways, and passing very close to some of the loveliest, most lavish homes in the land which front onto quite breathtaking, landscaped boulevards . . .'

On he droned, extolling the beauties of Lauderdale, but I was no longer listening. Something other than beautiful landscaped boulevards had suddenly caught my attention – a group of girls who had just emerged from the lower deck and were now standing at the top of the stairs, looking around for seats.

There were four of them, all in their early twenties. Mmm – things were beginning to look up. Naturally I'd been casing the crowd ever since they got on for young unattached talent but up to now hadn't seen anything that wasn't either firmly attached to a fella or surrounded by family. So I abandoned Grover and concentrated on this lot.

As is, for some unaccountable reason, always the way, two of the girls would not have raised a beat on a shipwrecked sex-maniac. They were short and plump and blondish, one dressed in a green trouser suit, the other in blue, and so alike they could've been sisters. On second thoughts they weren't so much 'dressed' as taking their clothes for a walk, but, from the way the other two were laughing at them, it was obvious they were the 'characters' of the group and it wouldn't much matter what they looked like.

A third girl was sort of in-between – tallish, slimmish, not-badish, a brunette with spectacles and a studious air, though when she smiled she showed very nice teeth. A distinct possible at a push.

But it was the fourth little bird that had it all – face, figure, the lot, such a chic, sexy creature it amazed me she was knocking around with the others. But there you are, that's how it goes.

Dressed in a yellow silk creation that clung to her lithe, full-breasted figure like a second skin, she stood there straight and proud, her hair a swathe of gleaming chestnut, burnished to gold by the setting sun, falling in a soft wave across her cheek then tumbling about her shoulders in a shining mantle. Lovely eyes, grey, I think, set above high tanned cheekbones, peered at the crowd with quiet interest while her wide, full lips smiled dutifully at something one of the chubby blondes had said.

Slowly she covered the crowd and it was only a matter of time before they reached me, standing perhaps ten feet to her right. On they travelled and then . . . shot back.

Zing! Our eyes met . . . and continued meeting. I felt myself face flush, my heart leap under her bland yet smouldering gaze, and for a small eternity I remained paralysed, her prisoner, finished for the evening. Finally, with no semblance of a smile or encourgement, other than the duration of the gaze itself, she coolly turned away and continued her inspection of the crowd.

Well, that was me completely discumknockerated for the night! In a wink I had lost all interest in fabulous Fort Lauderdale with its 270 miles of waterways, fabulous homes and breathtaking boulevards, in Captain Bud Grover and his folksy, yukky commentary, and in the ferryboat ride through Paradise. All I wanted now was to get to the end of the run, turn around and start dancing – with her. Everything else was a heinous waste of time.

I began to plot, plan, scheme – how to get close to her, talk to her. Once the dancing started it would be easy, I'd simply go up and ask her – provided I wasn't killed in the rush. But the competition around there was too fierce to wait that long. Already I could see Italian and Spanish heads turning, Latin eyes lighting up lasciviously, elbows nudging, and as any of you fellas who have spent your hols in Italy or Spain know, these lads are not exactly backward in coming forward when it comes to pursuing a bird – even another guy's wife! Any minute now, I thought, she's going to be inundated and that will be that.

So, in something of a quandary about how to make the approach, I was standing there mulling over the possibility of pretending I recognized her as Dave Brewer's sister, when good old Captain Bud Grover inadvertently came up with the answer by announcing, 'An' now, folks, we are approachin' the first of the fabulous homes we promised you. There on your right . . . the palatial summer residence of Willis P. Loudermilk II, chairman of the Loudermilk Truss and Corset Company, whose daddy up an' died three years back and left young Willis, aged only twenty-two, close on one hundred million dollars . . . (gasps from the crowd) . . . and if I were to say that of "corset's" a heck of a lotta money to "truss" to young Willis. I'm sure I'm only reiteratin' your feelings. Just take a look at that *fabulous* house, would ya . . .?'

They did. Groaning at his awful pun, four billion souls made a sudden rush to my side of the boat, caught me up, swept me to the rails, my back to them so I couldn't even see the flaming house!

Pressed in on three sides, drowning in garlic fumes and deafened by gabbling Spaniards, I was about to start swinging when suddenly . . . she was there! Only inches away, so close that with the slightest lean forward I could have kissed her lovely face. Now, in extreme close-up she was even more desirable, her skin flawless, her eyes warm and passionate. The perfume of her hair reached me, clouted me in the head, knocked me dizzy. Then, incredibly, someone pushed from behind and with a cry she fell against me, treading on my big toe.

'Ugh!' I went, as her hands drove into my chest.

Her eyes swept up, wide with apology. 'Oh, I'm *sorry* . . .!'

'Entirely . . . my pleasure,' I smiled, through gritted teeth, as she shifted weight from toe to instep.

'OH!' she exclaimed, as another push from behind drove her harder against me.

I couldn't believe it. She was here – in my arms! All soft and warm and smelling like Harrods' perfume counter. Wonderful.

'Oh . . . I'm *so* sorry,' she grimaced, pushing against me manly chest. 'They're . . . pushing . . .'

'Good for them. I really don't mind . . . at all.'

I smiled down at her and the sexy warmth returned to her eyes. 'But I'm standing on your foot!'

'You are?'

'Ah!' The breath was driven from her fabulous bosom by another surge from the rear. 'Oh, this is awful . . .!'

'You must . . . forgive me if I disagree,' I grinned, then gasped as the rail found my kidneys.

'You're . . . very gallant,' she panted, surely aware by now that the white hot press of her thighs was beginning to drive me potty. I mean, we couldn't have been closer if we'd been at it.

'It's . . . the way we Britishers are taught . . .' I gasped. 'Chin up through all adversity.'

'OH!' she gaped, as my leg slid in between her thighs.

'Sorry . . . I was doing my best to avoid that,' I said, trying unsuccessfully to take it out again. 'I hope you believe that.'

'Could you . . . sort of turn sideways . . . so's I can get to the rail?' she pleaded, attempting to slide round me.

'I can . . . try.'

Crushed together unmercifully – and utterly delightfully – I edged round, feeling the warmth of her breasts and thighs every delicious inch of the way, now across my back, her arms around my waist.

'How're you doing?' I grinned over my shoulder.

'Nearly there . . . uh!'

A final, excruciatingly beautiful squeeze and she was at my side, sighing, 'Oh, this is terrible . . . I detest crowds.'

'Me, too – normally. I had no idea it would be like this.'

'Me, neither.' She shook her head, pushed her hair from her face, lifting an eminently kissable profile against the setting sun. 'The evening has hardly begun and I feel a wreck already.'

'Needless to say, you look anything but. Would a cigarette help?'

She gave me a smile that started my motor running again. 'Thank you.'

I gave her one and lit it, cupping the lighter in my hands, delighting in the purse of her mouth as she drew on the cigarette and exhaled downstream. 'Thank you very much.'

Meanwhile, Bud Grover was going on with himself, '. . . note the incredible roof of matched Italian marble slates, folks . . . every single one imported by Willis at the total mind-boggling cost of . . . wait for it? . . . of three . . . hundred . . . thousand dollars . . .' (another appreciative gasp from the mob). '. . . and you may well be thinkin' that Willis musta lost a few of his *own* slates, spending all that money just to keep out the rain!'

The girl at my side joined in the laughter, revealing beautiful teeth.'

'A lovely place,' I said, nodding at the house. 'Though I imagine you're used to seeing all this by now.'

She shook her head. 'No, I haven't seen it before. This is my first cruise to Lauderdale. I've only been in Miami a few weeks.'

'Oh, really? Where were you before this?'

'California . . .'

'Hey, Evie . . .!'

A shrill voice deafened me from the rear and the girl I was talking to gave a start, looked behind me, then gave a grimace that said 'God, what a crowd'.

'You all right?' called the voice.

I turned. It was one of the little blondes, the one in green. She was standing on tip-toe, her hand on a Spaniard's shoulder, with a querying expression in my direction which disappeared as I looked round.

'Fine,' Evie answered. 'How're *you* doing?'

The blonde gave a sexy grin. 'Terrific! His name's Alphonso. See you later, hm?'

She dropped down, disappearing from sight.

Evie turned back to the rail, smiling. 'Well, looks like Annie's fixed up for the trip.'

'Yes . . . those Spanish lads don't waste much time.'

Again the smile. 'Do the English?'

I laughed. 'Contrary to popular myth, some of them do have their moments.'

'I haven't met one yet that didn't.'

'Oh? You've met a lot of Englishmen?'

She smiled evasively. 'A few.'

'In California?'

'Mostly in London.'

'Ah, you've been to London.'

'Been – and stayed. I lived there for a few months.'

'Really? When was this?'

'Oh . . . up to a few weeks ago. I've only just got back.'

'Well, well. Were you working over there?'

'Mm . . . sort of. More accurately I was . . . studying.'

'Oh?'

I waited, but nothing more came.

'So . . .' I said at last, 'you know London pretty well. Where did you live over there?'

'The Hilton.'

'Naturally,' I grinned, reflecting that it costs a packet to live in the Park Lane Hilton for a few months and beginning to wonder what sort of a girl this was I'd fallen in love with. Well, figuratively speaking fallen in love with. For the time being let's just say fancied like mad, particularly the way she was leaning over the rail right now and showing me almost all of a fabulous pair of breasts, size fortyish, and undoubtedly knowing exactly what she was doing.

'So your name's Evie,' I said. 'May I know the second half?'

'Shumaker. Spelled with a "u" – not an "oe".'

'German?' I ventured.

She nodded. 'My father was German, my mother French.'

'And whose eyes did you inherit? Your mother's, I'll bet.'

She laughed. 'Fortunately, yes.'

'Very. You've got wonderful eyes, Evie.'

'Thank you.'

'And . . . may I say, wonderful everything else.'

She didn't reply, just smiled. 'And . . . what's your name?'

'Tobin. Russ Tobin.'

'Russ . . . Tobin,' she repeated, slowly, as though trying it for sound, then, after a small pause. 'Are you here on vacation?'

'Yes, I am – or rather was. Unfortunately this is my last day here. I'm off to New York on the midnight train.'

She looked at me, frowning slightly, as though I'd just said something of significance to her. 'Midnight?'

'Yes. I'm booked on a two-centre tour – Miami and New York – and sorry I am, now . . .'

'Oh?'

I smiled. 'I've been here for four days and hardly moved off the beach at the hotel . . . hardly spoken to a soul. Now, when I want to stay longer, it's time to move on. It's always the way, though, isn't it? Holidays always get interesting on the last day.'

'And . . . what has suddenly happened to make you want to stay longer?' she asked, knowing damn well but playing female games. Right, I thought, I can play, too.

'Well . . . I met this girl, you see . . . she's *very* beautiful . . .'

'Oh?'

Hee hee, I swear her face fell. Not much, just a touch.

'Yes . . .' I continued, dolefully. 'On my very last day.'

'Where is she?' she asked, slightly puzzled.

'Oh, right here – on the boat.'

'Oh?' Now she was really puzzled. 'Then . . . why aren't you with her?'

I grinned and flicked my cigarette stub down into the water. 'I am.'

She stared at me for a minute then broke away, smiling to herself.

'Sorry . . . very presumptuous of me,' I said. 'But time is very precious. And there's far too much competition on board to allow for subtleties. There's absolutely no guarantee, of course, that you would want to spend time with me . . .'

'None at all,' she said, playfully aloof.

'Even supposing that *you* are alone . . . that there isn't somebody, say, downstairs . . . a husband, even . . . in the gents . . .'

She nodded. 'That's possible . . . though there isn't.'

'Thank heaven for that. Not, mind you, that it still means very much. You might still prefer to take off as soon as this crowd clears.'

'Mm . . . that's possible, too.'

And the cat left it at that.

Right, I thought, well at least she can't make a move until the crowd goes back off, so make the most of it. *You have about one minute in which to make her want to stay, starting from . . . now.*

I couldn't think of a thing to say.

But Captain Bud, bless his heart, once again came to the rescue.

'And now, folks, comin' up on the right, one of the most fabulous homes in all Lauderdale . . . the gracious villa of Marion Georgina Slatt . . . founder of Mother Slatt's Pinkie's for Pale and Poorly People – those little pink pills we swallow in their billions to cure anythin' from belly-ache to bunions. Note particularly the ancient statuary embellishing Mother Slatt's gracious, sweeping lawns. Each and every piece is a treasure of antiquity garnered from the four corners of the world by Marion's private army of collectors and flown here in one of her six private jet planes. Whoever would have thought there was so much money in plain ole belly-ache. (Laughter) Well, if any of you folks present have ever bought a box of Mother Slatt's Pinkies, one thing is sure as heck certain – "stat-*you*" have helped to buy every one of those priceless pieces. Now, don't *that* make you feel better?' (Crowd-sized groan).

'Isn't he awful?' chuckled Evie.

'Dreadful. About as subtle as a kick in the stomach. Tell me . . . why did you come on this trip? I could've sworn it wasn't your scene somehow – hanging over a rail, being flattened by a crowd.'

'Ha! If I'd known it was going to be like *this* . . .' she shrugged, . . . 'well, maybe I'd still have come. The girls wanted to see Lauderdale and . . .'

'Do you work with them?'

She shook her head. 'No . . . but close to them. We all work in shops in Miami. We're kind of neighbours.'

'You work in a *shop*?'

I tried to keep the surprise out of my voice, fearing offence. But she just didn't look like a girl who worked in a shop.

'Sure,' she said, teasingly aggressive. 'Why not?'

'Oh, no reason at all . . . very honourable calling. What . . . sort of shop is it?'

'It's . . .' she gave a little laugh, 'a *super*market.'

She delivered the *super* in a very mysterious way, pursing her lips, making it sound . . . well, super! I put it down to her jokey way of telling me it was super because she worked in it. Or something.

'Uh huh . . . and what do you sell in this . . . *super*market?'

'Oh, all sorts of goodies,' she teased. 'It's a great pity you won't be able to see it. I'm sure there are *lots* of things in there you'd want to buy.'

'Oh?' I said. 'What . . . sort of things?'

'All sorts,' she chuckled, her manner whimsical, to say nothing of downright naughty.

'You mean . . . as presents?' I said, going along with the game.

'Mm . . .' she nodded. 'I suppose you could look upon them as presents.'

'Evie . . .' I said warningly. 'I've got a sneaky feeling you're pulling Russell's leg . . .'

'Oh, now would I do a thing like that? I hardly know you. And I don't go around pulling strange men's legs.'

'No? Mm . . . well, anyway, how many of you work in this *super*market?'

'Just me,' she said, off handedly.

'Just you! Then it can't be much of a supermarket . . .'

'It's not a supermarket. I told you – it's a *super*market . . .'

'Yes, well, I can see I'm not going to get any more out of you on this subject.'

'Mm . . .' she went. 'Well, you never know.'

Something awfully funny was going on here. She probably didn't work in a shop at all and was just enjoying herself ribbing me. I just couldn't see a bird like her working in a supermarket or any other sort of market. Photographer's model, yes. And executive's secretary – sure. But she was certainly no shopgirl.

I let it go for the time being, thinking she'd probably confess when we started dancing – if we ever *did* start dancing, that is. It now seemed as though we'd been pinned against the rail for four hours. Another couple and they'd have to carry us off stiff as Mother Slatt's statues.

But, would you believe, at that very moment Captain Bud once more came to our rescue.

'And now, folks, comin' up on the *port* side . . . that's the *left*-hand side of the boat this evenin' . . . the exquisite colonial-style mansion of Arthur Z. Claphanger, who, like his father before him, built an empire out of timber . . . a real "chip off the old block" you might say . . .' (Abundant groans). 'The feature of this magnificent property is the cascading fountains set amidst the emerald lawns, a sight that is alone *really* worth takin' this cruise to see . . .'

Suddenly Evie and I were alone. En masse the crowd charged from the starboard rail to the port rail as though the boat had hit a rock and keeled over that way.

'Ugh!' I gasped.

'Phew!' she breathed, rubbing her delectable stomach. 'I'm going to bear the imprint of this rail for ever.'

'You . . . sure you don't want to see Arthur Z. Claphanger's cascading fountains?'

'I think I may just be able to resist the urge. What I do need right now is . . .'

'. . . and one more time on the *starboard* rail, folks . . .' Bud Grover blurted, '. . . is the enchanting split-level villa of Doctor Benjamin Bilgedauber, the inventor of boil-proof knicker elastic and the Bilgedauber bicycle clip . . .'

We made the stairs with not a split second to spare and fell down them, laughing.

'Look out!' cried Evie, grabbing my arm, as the crowd turned as one and surged towards us on the run.

'You were . . . about to tell me . . .' I gasped, '. . . that what you need right now is a . . .'

'I need a drink!'

'Right – follow me!'

We found the bar tucked behind the funnel housing, deserted but for a lugubrious barman who looked something like Phil Silvers but with even less hair. I gave him a friendly nod. 'How d'you do?'

'We're closed.'

'Oh.' I turned to Evie. 'He's closed.'

'Oh,' she pouted. 'And what time do you open?'

'When we get to the end of the line, lady. If we opened now half of 'em wouldn't *get* to the end of the line. Used t'be we opened up as soon as we cast off at Bal Harbour, but we had ta fish so many of 'em out of the Bay before we hit Willis P. Loudermilk's joint, we changed the rules.'

'Oh,' Evie said again, pouting even more beautifully. 'Oh, that's too bad . . . we were hoping for a . . . for a quiet drink together . . .' she raised soft, adoring eyes at me and gave a wan smile. 'You know . . . before the crowd came down.' She turned the smile on Phil now, who gave a cough and scratched his polished head.

'Yeah, well . . . I'm sure sorry, Miss, but . . .' he cleared his throat. 'Look . . . what was it yuh wanted anyways . . .?'

'Oh, anything,' she beamed.

'Vodka tonic?' I suggested to him.

'Vodka tonic . . . yeh, well . . . look, tell you what I'll do . . .' He gazed around, furtively. 'Here – come in here, quick!' He pulled open a door behind the bar and flicked on the light. It was a tiny storeroom, half-filled with cases of bathtub champagne and other booze.

'Kinda crowded,' he apologized, 'but at least you'll be alone. I'll be right back wid the drinks, make yourselves to home.' Then he closed the door.

Evie looked at me and burst out laughing. I shook my head at her. 'What a way you have with men. Here . . . have a seat.'

We sat on two cases of champers, facing each other, our knees almost touching. 'Well,' I said, looking round, 'not exactly the London Hilton, but at least it's all ours.' I looked at her and had to laugh. 'Crazy! Eighteen thousand miles I travel to see fabulous Fort Lauderdale and end up in a ferryboat stockroom.'

'Do you mind?'

I grinned. 'Do I mind? The view's nicer in here than out there.'

She inclined her head. 'Thank you.'

'You obviously enjoy doing daft things, don't you?'

'So, obviously, do you,' she smiled.

'Mm . . . with the right person. Funny, isn't it . . . half an hour ago I didn't know you existed. My life was all neatly planned for the next few hours. I'd see the sights, maybe have a dance or two, force a glass or two of this dreadful champagne down, pick up my luggage and board the train. Now look at me – sitting in a stockroom and having a terrific time.'

'Are you?'

'Certainly I am. Wouldn't swop this for Las Vegas . . .'

The door opened. Phil handed us in two glasses filled to the brim, saying in hushed toned, 'Take yuh time, no one'll disturb you . . . just keep your voices down, hm?'

'Ah, this is wonderful of you,' said Evie. 'What's your name?'

'Mine . . .? Er . . . Frank Hubbard, miss.'

'Frank . . . you're awfully sweet. Thank you very much.'

'Nah,' he grinned. 'You two have a nice time.'

He shut the door.

I raised my glass. 'Evie . . . to you. I think you're terrific.'

'Thank you. And here's to you . . . have a great time in New York.'

'I'll try.' I took a sip. 'Oh, brother . . . that brings tears to your eyes. Phew! It's at least a sixple.'

'Lovely,' she said, taking a swallow.

I put my glass down and got out my cigarettes. 'Here . . . let's go the whole hog – perdition or bust! Tonight I feel evil.'

She laughed and took one. 'What a lovely thought.'

As I lit her cigarette I looked at her, I mean *really* looked – seeing her as an entity rather than a collection of beautiful bits and pieces, realizing I liked her very much. Good looking girls are reasonably plentiful, but to find one like Evie, beautiful and chic but prepared to sit in a crummy stockroom having a giggle is a rare and lovely thing. And I told her so.

She smiled. 'Maybe this is what comes from having four brothers. They were always into all sorts of trouble and if I couldn't keep up I was left behind, so I made certain I did.'

'Well, you've certainly grown up to be a nice-lookin' fella. Where was your home, Evie?'

'Texas. Dallas.'

'Sounds very romantic . . . longhorn cattle . . . the Texas Rangers . . .'

'Sorry to disappoint you. Father owns a gas station. Where were you raised?'

'Cheshire, mostly – though I spent a lot of time in Liverpool.'

'Now that *is* romantic . . . the Beatles . . . all that wonderful talent . . .'

'Most of us have left,' I grinned.

'Oh?' She raised a naughty brow. 'And . . . where do your particular talents lie?'

My heart gave a kick. 'Mine . . .?' There was no doubting the direction the conversation had just taken. 'Ooh . . . here and there . . .'

'Nicely evasive – you must be a politician.'

'God forbid.'

'What *do* you do?'

'Ooh . . . difficult to answer, Evie – I'm not sure I even know myself. I've done a number of jobs . . . died the death in offices . . . sold sewing machines . . . collected debts . . . been a courier for a travel firm . . . and I've just finished a season in Africa as a courier on photographic safari. Well, a couple of weeks ago – I've been in Nassau for a while . . .'

'Oh? Doing what exactly?'

'Ohh . . . sort of "investigating life", you might say?'

'Sounds delicious,' she laughed. 'And what did your investigations reveal?'

I laughed. 'That both the sun and the women out there are

pretty hot – and that over-exposure to either can be *very* debilitating.'

She laughed aloud, but cut it short, glancing at the door. 'Oops! Well, sounds like you had a ball. Do you . . . always enjoy yourself wherever you go?'

'I certainly try: I once heard a man say that we begin dying the moment we're born – so I'm trying to pack a fair amount in before I pop off.'

'Sound philosophy,' she agreed. 'So now you're off to New York to do some more "investigating". Then where?'

I shrugged. 'Don't really know. Probably back to London for a while, and then . . .' I shrugged again. 'I really don't know. I'll have to see what comes.'

'How marvellous – working your way around the world.' She gave a small thoughtful pause, took a drink, then continued with a rueful grin. 'Do you meet many interesting . . . people on your travels?'

'Evie . . . what you mean is – do I meet many interesting *women* on my travels . . .'

'Something like that,' she chuckled.

'Mm . . . yes, I've met . . . one or two.'

'Possibly three or four?'

'Well . . . yes . . . *possibly* three or four.'

'How about five or six?'

I had to laugh. 'Hey . . . why the interest in my love life?' My heart was at it again, sensing what was coming. She kept homing in on sex like ground-to-air missile.

'No,' she said, changing her mind. 'Let's have a discussion.'

I laughed. 'All right . . . what on?'

'Sex.'

Just like that – straight out. Oh, these emancipated American women can really sock it to you. Actually it's very nice. And it does save *so* much time.

'All right,' I grinned, tickled to death. 'Fire away.'

'OK. Now . . . for the sake of experiment, I am regarding you as a typical Western male, chosen at random from half a boatload of typical Western males, who has been brought up in typical Western tradition with regards to sex . . . right?'

'Right.'

'I mean you didn't have a Japanese nanny or spend your formative years in Sumatra or anything like that, did you?'

'Er . . . no.' I had to think about that one.

'Fine. So therefore you learned about sex in the typical and traditional Western fashion – illicitly – via school rumours and furtive exploration with any little girl who would let you have a look? No sex tuition from your parents – right?'

'Wrong.'

'Oh.'

'When I was sixteen my father coughed, turned bright pink and muttered. "Son . . . it is generally regarded as being clever to stick your hand up girls' clothing – but believe me it's not." '

'That's all?'

'That's it.'

'And what did you deduce from that?'

'That the old man must have missed a heck of a lot of fun in his life.'

She laughed aloud and again had to staunch it. 'All right . . . that incident sets you up perfectly as a typically sex-tuition-starved Western male. Now for some questions . . . you're sure you don't mind?'

'Not in the least.'

'And you'll answer honestly?'

'Scouts honour.'

'Hm . . . were you ever *in* the Scouts?'

'No.'

'Never mind, I trust you . . . you're obviously enjoying this too much to lie. Right . . . Question One . . . do you primarily see the sexual role of the male as that of "hunter" and that of the female as the "hunted"?'

'No.'

'In that case, do . . . hm?'

'No, not at all. They each have a perfect right to make the going – right down the line.'

She looked at me, suddenly disheartened, and released a sigh. 'Oh, hell.'

'What's the matter?'

'You've just ruined the game. You're not typical at all. What a lousy thing to do.'

'Oh, I'm sorry . . .'

She sighed again, pretending deep dismay. 'Huh . . .! Just my luck . . . half a boatload of male chauvinist bulls up there to chose from – and I had to pick you!'

'Oh, I *am* sorry, Evie. Look . . . tell you what, let's pretend I haven't answered yet and I'll change my plea. Yes, dammit, I *do* believe that man is the hunter, the aggressor . . . and that women should be prepared to lie down and take it at the drop of a trouser . . .!'

She was shaking her head. 'It's no good, I can't believe you . . .' Then . . . she brightened. 'All right . . . then tell me *why* you think women have an equal right to make the going!'

'Mm . . .? Well . . . because they're human beings.'

Her eyes narrowed cunningly. 'But surely women aren't blessed with the same spontaneous sexual *urge* as men? A man's up and coming before she's even got her mind off the shopping.'

'Well . . . yes, that's what they say.'

'Aha! That's what *who* says?'

'Well . . .' I shrugged. 'It is said.'

'By men!'

'Mmm . . . yes, possibly. But you do read these letters in the women's magazines . . . "Dear Mary, my husband is a beast. He comes in two minutes flat and leaves me yearning and frustrated. I have never had an orgasm and . . ."'

'Ah! Now what conclusion does that lead us to?'

'That . . . a woman takes a lot longer to come than a man . . . and therefore is not blessed with the same spontaneous sexual urge . . .'

'In other words – she hasn't got the same sort of equipment as a man and therefore he can never *really* enjoy the same exploding emotion as a man . . .?'

'Well . . .'

'Wrong! She is even *better* equipped to enjoy sex than a man!'

'Really?'

'Infinitely! Her equipment is far more advanced.'

'Get away.'

'Truly. I suppose you subscribe to the popular belief that the clitoris is merely a feeble imitation of man's mighty penis?'

'Well . . . Freud said so . . .'

'Freud was wrong.'

'Oh.'

'The fact is – that the clitoris is only the iceberg tip of a vast internal system of *very* sexy tissue . . . which, as far as sexual enjoyment is concerned, can leave the penis *standing* . . . I mean . . .'

We both roared with laughter.

'Well, you know what I mean,' she chuckled.

'Go on – this is terrific.'

'You didn't know all this?'

'No, I didn't. Where did you learn about it?'

She smiled, evasively. 'I told you – I studied in London. Anyway, this intricate system inside a woman, compared to the more simple penis, is one reason why she takes longer to warm up and reach a climax – but once you get her going – watch out! Her capacity for sex is so prodigious . . . well, when fully extended it is truly unbelievable. For instance – did you know that a man reaches his sexual peak in his late *teens* – then quickly runs downhill?'

'Oh, my God.'

'How old are you?'

'Twenty-six.'

'Huh! Over the hill.'

'Eh?'

'Finished! – at least compared to a woman. *She* has barely started at that age. And if it's allowed to, her capacity will grow and grow . . .'

'Allowed to? Who's going to stop it?'

'You! You men!'

'*What* . . .?'

'Men stop it. They're afraid that if they please their women too much she might get to like it too much and become unfaithful – or at the very least neglect her housework.'

'Aw, come on . . .'

'It's true! You've just quoted those letters to the women's magazines – "my husband comes in two minutes flat and leaves me frustrated". And haven't you ever known a woman who's *never* experienced an orgasm with her husband?'

'Oh, yes, sure. I mean . . .'

She laughed, catching me out. 'But you gave her one?'

I grinned. 'Well . . .'

'Sure you did – because you behaved like a lover, not a husband. He couldn't care whether she came or not – so long as she had his dinner ready. But I'll bet if he had a girlfriend on the side, he'd make sure *she* had one – or she wouldn't be his girlfriend for long.'

'Yes, I guess you're right – exceptions excepted, of course.'

'Yes, of course. Oh, there are plenty of exceptions . . . there's a Polynesian island, for instance, where *no* woman is frigid, because it's socially obligatory for a man to make his woman come two or three times to his once. And if a young man seduces a girl who doesn't reach a climax, he has to keep going back until she does!'

'Wow! How much is the fare?'

She laughed. 'Russ, do you have another cigarette?'

'Oh . . . sure. Huh, I'm so engrossed I'm forgetting to smoke.'

'The . . . subject interests you, then?'

'Sure it does.' I lit her cigarette. 'Very much.'

'Hm . . . hm. Why?'

'Mm . . .? Well, for one thing I find it very exciting talking to you about it . . .'

'And for another?'

I shrugged. 'Well . . . I like to think that . . .'

'You like to think that you're a good lover?'

'Sure . . . don't all men?'

'All of them may *think* it . . . but very few are.'

'Oh? I wonder why that is?'

'For the reasons stated – they're too impatient, don't give the woman time to warm up.'

'Strange isn't it – you'd think it would come most naturally to us.'

'I think what *does* come, comes naturally to you men. It's the woman's role that isn't natural.'

'I'm not sure I follow . . .'

'Monogomous marriage has forced woman to hold back her vast sex drive, I really believe that.'

'Really? And can she *do* that?'

'Much more easily than a man. A woman can live virtually without sex if the circumstances require it. You must know some women who live without it, surely?'

'Oh yes – one or two back home . . . relatives . . .'

'But . . .' she smiled, 'at the *other* extreme, once a woman starts letting herself *enjoy* it, there is quite possibly no upper limit to the amount she can take – short of physical exhaustion.'

'Really? And . . . how much are you talking about?'

'Well . . . it's my belief that the more a woman does, the more she can, and the more she can, the more she wants to. Six . . . seven orgasms during intercourse is really quite modest . . .'

'Oh, sure.'

She paused, grinning at me cunningly. 'You agreed with that statement much too quickly, Tobin . . .'

'Well, I . . .'

'As though you yourself had witnessed similar occurrences.'

'Well, I . . .' I shrugged and laughed.

'Well, good for you,' she said earnestly. 'My, my . . . what *have* we come upon . . .?'

'You were, er, saying, Evie . . .'

'And modest, too . . . how rare.' She took a drink, still looking at me, things going on in that head that had my stomach in granny knots. The question was equally apt from my direction – what had I come across? The obvious answer had my throat so lumped-up I had to clear it to speak.

'You, hm, were saying, Evie . . . about a woman's capacity for orgasm . . . six or seven being really quite modest.'

'During intercourse,' she reminded me. 'Up to fifty have been recorded with a vibrator.'

'You know, I heard that. Is it true?'

'Perfectly.'

'Good God. Makes us fellas seem a bit puny, doesn't it?'

'What have I just been saying?'

'But . . . if a woman is so inherently sexy, how come so many of them don't appear to know it? I mean, how is it that so many of them don't even experience *one* orgasm?'

'Well, there are two theories to explain it – one we've already covered – that men have purposely suppressed women's sexuality over the ages in order to keep them at home. The other theory is that women *themselves* have purposely suppressed it – out of need for protection from one man – and in order to protect the family group.'

'Yes . . . I can see that's possible. Blimey, it's a good job they did suppress it, isn't it?'

'A very good job,' she laughed. 'Can you imagine what would happen to the world if all the women suddenly realized their sex potential and decided to investigate its upper limit! Every woman being capable of enjoying it twenty . . . fifty times a day – leaving a trail of exhausted males in her wake!'

'Lord, what an orgy!'

'But . . . think ahead! – to the time we're making babies in laboratories and women have become redundant as mothers – and therefore *don't* need the protection of one man!'

'Yes . . . I can see it! Packs of sex crazed women roaming the earth, hunting us poor males down for a bit of the other . . .'

'For a great deal of the other! Remember . . . fifty times a day!'

'Oh, Evie, stop! You'll put me off for life.'

'Fat chance,' she grinned.

'Hm . . .? How do you know?'

'Call it . . . women's instinct,' she grinned, finishing her drink.

I drained mine and stood up, then, with my hand on the door handle, turned to her. 'Just . . . one thing, Evie – why this discussion . . . and why with me?'

'Because I'm very interested in the subject of woman's sex potential. And I questioned you simply because you're a man and therefore think as men do.'

'Not *all* men.'

She smiled. 'Obviously not – I'm delighted to discover.'

'And . . . what particular aspect of woman's sex potential interests you most?'

She smiled wickedly, placed her hand over mine on the handle, and said, very close, 'Its uppermost limit. I want to find out just how much a woman can take . . . before exhaustion brings her to a halt.'

I gulped. 'I see. With . . . or without a vibrator?'

'Both,' she grinned, and opened the door.

TWO

We emerged from the storeroom surprised to find the boat lit up, the world outside in darkness.

'Jurst turnin' now for the trip back,' Frank Hubbard informed us. 'You folks sure didn't see much of Lauderdale, but then . . .' he cackled a laugh, ' 'spect you had yuhr own fun goin' for ya. You two young folks married . . . engaged?'

I glanced at Evie, finding her grinning. 'No, Frank,' she answered, 'we're sort of . . . business partners.'

I frowned but she avoided looking at me.

'Thanks very much for the use of the room,' she said, 'it was lovely.'

'Ah, you're welcome. When it gits too crowded I hide in there myself. A body's gotta be able to get away from all this hoo-ha sometime.'

I paid Frank for the drinks, and, taking Evie's arm, led her to the rail. 'So that's what we are, hm – "sort of . . . business partners"?'

'If you want to be,' she said lightly.

'And what sort of "business" are we in exactly?'

'We're . . . private investigators,' she grinned. 'It should be right up your street – seeing you spend most of your time investigating life.'

'All right,' I agreed, 'we're partners. When and what do we start investigating?'

She grinned. 'You'll know when we do.'

'I see. Well, one thing I've learned about you so far – nobody gets to know anything about anything until you're good and ready to tell 'em.'

'Oh, Russ . . .' she laughed, 'just look at that mansion all lit up.'

'Yes, beautiful.'

'Well, you could say it with a touch more enthusiasm.'

'How can I care about anything when you've got me so knotted up I can't think straight?'

She looked up at me, fluttering her eyes with mock innocence. 'I have?'

'You have and you know it.'

'Yes,' she said, suddenly serious. 'And I'm the same.'

'You . . . are?'

'Russ . . . look . . . you haven't much time, have you – before your train leaves?'

'No, not much. By the time we get back to Bal Harbour it'll be nine thirty . . . then I have to collect my luggage and . . .'

'Russ . . . are you *really* keen on dancing?'

'Hm . . .? Well . . .'

'I mean – are you really keen on this champagne bit?'

I laughed. 'Heck, no – not at all. I wouldn't drink this stuff anyway, it'll be paint remover.'

'Well . . . if we could get ashore – now – and catch a cab to Miami, would you . . . would you want to?'

My mouth opened a couple of times but nothing came out, which she took as a negative response.

'Oh . . . you wouldn't want to . . .'

'Oh no, Evie . . . I do! I mean, sure . . . but how?'

She was away, heading back to Frank Hubbard who was setting rows of champagne bottles on the bar top. She smiled at him, said something to him, and now his mouth was open.

He looked across at me, frowned, did some heavy thinking, then, nodding uncertainly, plonked down the remainder of the bottles and disappeared round the funnel.

A few minutes later he was back, nodding to her and grinning, drawing a wide smile from her, then she was scurrying back to me, beaming.

'He's had a word with the captain. There's a landing place about fifteen minutes down river. He can't stop exactly but he'll draw close to it so's we can jump ashore. He says it's highly irregular but in the circumstances he'll do it.'

I frowned at her. 'Er . . . in what circumstances, Evie?'

She gave a quick, guilty grin. 'I . . . told him we were in a great hurry to get ashore . . . to get married.'

My mouth was at it again, gaping like a goldfish. 'Get . . . you didn't.'

'I did.'

'Married!'

She shrugged. 'Well, he wouldn't have stopped for anything less.'

At that moment the music struck up, taped mayhem coming over the tannoy, and with a wild whoop eighty thousand people poured down the stairs to get at the champagne.

'OK . . . OK!' yelled Frank, 'there's plenty for everybody . . . you don't have to rip my arms off! Get back there . . . you ain't allowed round heh! Hey, come outta that stockroom!'

A barrage of corks went off and the party had really begun.

'Well,' said Evie, 'we've got fifteen minutes. Would you like to dance?'

'Why not?'

Then we were in the thick of it, jigging around to a souped-up version of *Does Your Mother Come From Ireland* by Mickey Splitz and the Ripped Jeans, hemmed in on all sides by glass-toting, bottle-waving, champagne-guzzling merrymakers, all determined to have a good time even if it killed 'em.

'Oh, there are going to be some lulu hangovers in the morning!' I shouted to Evie. 'This stuff is *murder*!'

'How d'you know if you haven't drunk any?'

'I don't have to! They serve exactly the same bilge in Spain! Take a tip from a courier – whenever you see "free champagne" – run . . .!'

Suddenly I wasn't dancing with her anymore. One of the Spannish nutters, a tall, darkly handsome lad with an obvious skinful and a leer of pure Latin lechery, had side-stepped between us and dropped his eyes down the front of Evie's dress. She frowned at him, annoyed, and moved sideways to get back to me, but again he nipped in front of her, grinning like an idiot.

She flashed an appealing look at me and I tapped him on the shoulder. 'Mind if I cut in and dance with my girl?'

He ignored me absolutely.

'Hello, baby,' he slurred. 'Who's a big girl, then?'

Evie's eyes flashed. 'Do you mind?'

'Not at all. Any time you like . . .'

Biff! I hit him on the shoulder with the heel of my hand. 'Move it, Pedro . . .'

He staggered back, floppily, then rounded on me. 'You hit me?'

'Not yet. But I will if you don't clear off.'

'Russ . . .' It was Evie, getting all worried – though not half as worried as I was getting because I could see his mates moving close, watching the action. 'Russ . . . let's sit this one out, hm . . .?'

'He's going, Evie,' I said pointedly, hoping awfully hard he would.

Finally, with a murderous, mischievous glare, he did – straight to his pals, and I wasn't at all happy with what I read in their faces.

'Trouble makers,' said Evie, coming close and hooking my arm. 'Everywhere you go there's trouble.'

'Yes, they come on these trips looking for it.'

'Let's get out of their sight. I must find the girls and tell them we're getting off or they'll think I've fallen overboard.'

'All right.'

We found our way out of the crowd and found room to breathe at the rail. We'd no sooner got there when Evie went up on her toes and said. 'Oh, there's Annie now – right in the middle. You stay here, I'll go and tell her.'

In a moment she was out of sight.

It was a couple of minutes later I heard her shout, 'Russ!' even above the din. My stomach lurched. She sounded in trouble! I went up on my toes but still couldn't see her, so I climbed up on the rail and spotted her immediately – surrounded by a ring of grinning Spaniards, all linked together, their arms around each others shoulders, dancing around her, holding her prisoner. She looked close to tears with anger.

I jumped down and on trembling legs pushed into the crowd, wondering how I was going to handle this. Though I am not entirely averse to having a go on the spur of the moment – if sufficiently provoked – fisticuffs is not primarily my metier, and the odds of six-to-one did very little to encourage a current change of heart. Still, something had to be done.

Authority – that was the tack!

I pushed my way through and with quaking spirit reached the ring of grinning, prancing idiots.

'All right, break it up, you fellas . . .'

'Russ!' it was Evie, in a bit of a state.

'Come on now . . . break it up! Let her out of there!'

I grabbed an arm and wrenched it from the adjoining shoulder . . . and in the next instant I was staggering backwards, pushed hard in the chest.

A roar of laughter from the Spanish bunch and a howl of protest from the people I'd barged into.

'Hey, watch it, mac . . .!'

'What's wid him – he drunk or sumpn . . .?'

I regained my balance, anger now coming to a boil. Russell was really getting his paddy up, because if there's one thing I can't stand more than drunken horseplay it's bird-pulling. Lining up on the next guy round, I plunged into the fray, grabbed a great handful of his thick black hair and yanked it backwards very hard. With a yell he shot backwards, throwing his arms high, breaking the ring.

Biff! His windmilling fist smacked me right on the nose.

'Russ!' it was Evie again, thinking I was being murdered. Out of the ring she ran, hurling another Spaniard backwards with a thump in the chest. Back he staggered, tripped over his own feet and sat on his arse with a bump. Another one immediately tripped over him, then a third went down. I could just about see all this through the tears that ensued from the thump on the nose.

'Russ . . . you're hurt! Come on – let's get out of here!'

Clump! Something very like a fist clouted me between the shoulder blades, then Evie was lashing out at whatever hit me, fetching someone a terrible kick on the shin.

'Leave him alone . . . stop it!'

'OW!'

'Hey . . . get off . . . get off!' this was one of the guys on the floor, watching his fingers being stomped to hamburger.

'What's going on!' someone shouted.

'It's a fight . . . it's a fight!'

'Yiiipppeee!'

'Hey, fellas, there's a fight!'

There must have been at least two million people now crowded into a space the size of a shower stall, a good dozen of them on the floor, curled up into balls, their hands protecting their heads, yelling as the crowd stomped all over them, kicked them in the kidneys, trod on their legs. And all this time Evie was pulling on my arm, pulling me out of the maelstrom.

Suddenly we were out in the open, face to face with a gawping Frank Hubbard. 'What in hell is *happenin'*! Christ, we got a riot!'

'It's that Spanish lot,' I told him. 'You ought to chuck 'em off – or better still – overboard.'

'Right,' he nodded. 'Hey, you two had better get over to the port side, we're comin' into that landing.'

Instantly we heard bells and felt the engines cut. 'Go on – off you go!'

'Thanks for everything, Frank!'

'Lot's o' luck to yuh!'

We ran off, round the funnel housing and along the port side, spotting the wharf not ten feet away and closing. Eight feet . . . six . . . we drifted closer. And then, suddenly – a shout behind us.

'Aqui! . . . aqui . . .!'

I shot round, heard pounding. It was three of the Spanish punks, coming to see us off – with champagne bottles!

'Quick . . . over the rail!' I grabbed Evie's arm and urged her over, then in a wink I joined her, standing on a tiny ledge.

Four feet . . . two feet . . . almost there.

A shout in Spanish, 'They're getting away!' and the thunder of feet along the deck.

'Jump!' I shouted.

We hit the wharf and started running.

Fzzzzzzz . . . an empty bottle missed my head by a hair.

Crash! Another shattered into the wharf immediately ahead of us.

Thump! The third one got me between the shoulder blades.

And all the time Bud Grover's voice was booming over the tannoy, 'There they go, Folks . . . the happy bride an' groom to be . . . with champagne to send them on their way! Let's given 'em a cheer to wish them Godspeed and all the luck in the world . . .!'

A desultory cheer went up from the boat but we were God-speeding it across the wharf as fast as our legs would carry us.

Tooowwwooo . . . wooh!

With a burst on the ship's horn, the engines rumbled into life and as it headed back towards mid-stream, we heard Grover announcing, 'OK, folks . . . now on with the dancin'. Are we all havin' a good time . . .?'

'YYEESS!'

Evie and I slowed, then halted, gasping, falling against one another, catching our breath, then looked at one another and collapsed with laughter.

'God . . . how awful!' she laughed. 'What a *dreadful* boat! Are you sure you're not hurt?'

'Positive. Come on – let's find a taxi.'

Arms around each other, we walked down the street leading up from the quay and came out on the main avenue, finding a taxi immediately.

'Boy, oh, boy . . .' I laughed, closing the door, 'can I find it. No – correction, can it find me!'

'What – trouble?'

'Evie, I really am the most peace-lovin' fella, but, by golly, you wouldn't know it. I must have one of those faces that people love to punch.'

She snuggled closer and pecked me on the cheek. 'Well, I think you were very brave. You know, that's the first time I've ever been fought over? It was lovely.'

'Brave,' I chortled. 'I was scared witless.'

'Well, that makes it even braver. I thought the way you grabbed that Spaniard's hair and pulled him backwards was just beautiful.'

I grinned. 'I couldn't think of anything else to do. You know, after a scuffle like that I'm always determined I'll rush off to the nearest gym and learn karate, so that next time I can leap in and decimate them with a few well-chosen chops, but I never do. I just can't be bothered. It's far less trouble just to run away.'

'Anyway . . . thank you for coming to my rescue, it was very sweet.'

'Huh! I couldn't let them do that to my partner, could I? We've got a lot of work to do . . . whatever it is.'

'Yes,' she chuckled, snuggling closer. 'We have.'

The taxi rejoined Collins Avenue and sped south along the Miami Beach peninsula to the Venetian Causeway, one of the five bridges that link the Beach with Miami proper. Crossing it, Biscayne Bay was quite a sight, the city ahead a riot of lights, the Beach behind us an endless necklace of multi-coloured jewels.

'A beautiful city,' I observed. 'I was crazy not to see more of it.'

'I wish you had more time, I'd love to see it with you. There's an awful lot to see . . . Vizcaya Palace, the Everglades, Disneyland . . . you're sure you can't stay any longer?'

'I'm afraid not, Evie.'

'Well . . . maybe you'll get back again one day.'

'I feel I should. Great pity not to see it all.'

We had now entered the city, its streets bright as day lined with handsome shops. For a while we stayed with them, turning occasionally, then finally turned into a narrow service road, little more than an alley, at the rear of a row of two-storeyed shops, set back beyond enclosed yards.

'Two-two-oh-seven,' the driver announced.

We got out, paid him and he drove off. Evie fumbled in her purse for a key, angling it towards a distant wall-light, finally located it.

'You live here – over the shop?' I asked her, indicating an apartment visible over the yard wall.

'Yes.'

'Handy,' I said, still finding it hard to believe she worked in a shop but now very curious to find out what sort of a shop it was. 'Not too many rush-hour traffic problems. I take it.'

'Not on the stairs,' she laughed.

Opening the door, she led me into a long narrow yard, and while she was re-locking the door I had a peer around, looking for clues – packing cases, old advertising material, but the yard was immaculate, done out very nicely with a patio and a swinging sun-seat.

'Is this where you get your tan?' I asked her.

'One of the places. When the shop's closed I usually head for the beach. I water-ski a lot.'

We walked up the yard and she opened a second door and ushered me into a narrow hall. In it was the door that obviously led into the shop and a staircase. Snapping on lights as she went, she took the lead up the stairs, unlocked yet another door, pressed a switch and waved me into a lovely modern apartment.

The lounge was big – a good thirty feet to the opposite wall which was nearly all window and obviously over-looked the street. The entire floor was covered in beige carpeting, its deep, curly pile inviting you to take off your socks and walk barefoot through it, which Evie promptly did. There was a comfy looking couch and a couple of armchairs arranged in front of a copper-canopied stone fireplace, a glass-and-chrome dining suite and, on my left, a long white wall unit containing books and stereo equipment.

As I stood there looking around, the lighting suddenly dimmed to a rosy glow and I turned to find Evie with her hand on a dimmer switch.

'It's lovely, Evie . . . did you decorate it?'

'Uh huh. Take your coat, off make yourself at home. You'll find drinks in the unit – right-hand cupboard. Why don't you make us one, I won't be long.'

'All right.'

'And find a tape while you're at it.'

'Roger.'

She disappeared through a door on the right. I crossed to the fitment and got out the drinks, then riffed through a stack of cassettes and selected something, late-night and stringy, and as the music oozed through, gazed half-curiously along the books to see what she was interested in. I quickly found out. The subject was sex. Sex and Love . . . Freedom In Sex . . . Deviationism . . . Fetishism . . . The how, why, when and where-ism. Now I became aware of other sex orientated objects around the room – the pictures and prints around the walls, some of them beautiful watercolours of women in the noddy, bathing, grooming themselves, simply reclining. Over here – a porcelain study of a naked, embracing couple, tenderly holding one another . . . and there – an abstract sculpture representing a naked, splendidly endowed fella.

I was studying this when the door behind me opened and she said with a laugh. 'Jealousy will get you nowhere.'

'Poor devil . . . fancing having to . . .'

I turned . . . and caught my breath. She had changed into a full-length kimono in peacock blue, edged in gold, with long, drooping sleeves. She looked wonderful, her hair brushed out around her shoulders, gleaming in the lights.

'Evie . . . you look fabulous.'

'Thank you sir,' she said, dropping a curtsy, then turned in a swirl of hair and headed for the drinks.

I joined her, nodding at the books. 'Part of your studies?'

'All of them.'

'You know, you intrigue me, Evie . . . no you don't, you downright puzzle me. Just what were you studying in London?'

She smiled teasingly. 'I told you – studying.'

'Sex?'

'Why not? After self-survival it's our strongest emotion. Terribly important, you know. Did you know that a man thinks about sex every seven minutes of his life?'

'Which man?'

'Every one of you, you dirty devils.'

'Every seven minutes, hm? I didn't know I took that much of a break.'

'Oh, there *are* extremists who *never* think of anything else.'

'Ah, that's more like it. But . . . having studied it, what do you *do* with the knowledge?'

'Well . . .' she said, turning away to the couch and settling into the cushions, 'it helps me in my search, for one thing.'

'Your search,' I said, joining her. 'You mean . . . for women's limit of enjoyment?'

'Mm,' she nodded. 'The "Inth", as I call it.'

'The "Inth". Sounds very appropriate.'

'Tobin . . .' she said, very softly. I looked up at her, surprised by her sudden change of tone and hypnotised by what I found there in her eyes. She had changed in a moment. Now I sensed a . . . a radiation emanating from her, like heat from a hot boulder. Her smouldering, half-smiling eyes bore into mine, passing a message that set my pulse pounding, my blood racing through my veins.

'Y . . . yes?' I croaked.

'We're wasting time . . . we have so little.'

'Yes.'

'Come.' She took my hand and got up from the sofa. 'I want to show you something.'

She opened the door she had previously gone through, revealing a gorgeous bedroom, furnished in white and dominated by a huge bed covered in white silk. With her arm around me she moved into the room, then, by the bed, suddenly turned into me, her hand snaking behind my head, and brought her mouth to mine.

Moments later we were lying across the bed and I knew I'd caught me an alligator. Her passion was almost frightening. Writhing, grinding, groaning, she didn't just kiss she devoured! . . . took huge sucking bites out of my mouth and face, voracious as a starving lioness. Suddenly she stopped. I eased away, fighting for air, my heart thundering in my chest, and looked up to find her laughing!

'Oh, you'll do . . . beautifully,' she chuckled. 'Come . . . I want to show you something else!'

She was up and away, pulling me after her, jubilant, like a child who's just found a new playmate and can't wait to show him her toys.

Out into the lounge we went, then out into the hall and down the stairs. At the bottom she produced a key from her pocket, opened the door to the shop, reached in for the light switch, and said, 'Close your eyes!'

She guided me through the door and far into the shop, then stopped. 'Right, open them.'

I did.

'Well,' she chuckled, 'what d'you think?'

I blinked, aware of a modern, well-appointed shop with numerous display racks around the walls, yet unable to make out what was actually being displayed. I turned to the nearest rack and peered at it, at dozens of closely packed cartons, then picked one out and read it, my heart exploding again as I read: 'Eternity – analgesic spray for men. Prevents premature ejaculation in the hyper-sensitive male. Enriches love-making by ensuring the loved one has ample time to achieve personal satisfaction, so often curtailed by premature ejaculation . . .'

Evie moved to my side. 'You should see your face.'

I laughed aloud. 'It's . . .' I looked around the shop.

'Yes – a sex shop . . . like I said – a *super* market. I've just opened it.'

'You . . . run it all by yourself?'

'I own it all by myself.'

'Really?'

'Shocked?'

'No . . .' I laughed. 'Just a bit surprised. I didn't know they had them over here.'

'Of course. Were you ever in one in London?'

'Oh, yes. They caused quite a stir when they first opened . . .

we just couldn't believe that Merry England had sexually stepped into the twentieth century.'

'Did you ever *buy* anything in a sex shop?'

I shook my head. 'Nope, never did. I just went in out of curiosity. I'd probably have been too shy to buy anything even if I'd wanted something.'

'Well, they do take a bit of getting used to. But you don't have to be shy now. Let's have a look around and see what there is.'

'Love to.'

With my arm around her, ever conscious of the warmth of her body beneath the flimsy gown, we moved along the racks, pausing to inspect the products, some so hilarious we burst out laughing. There were creams for women, lotions for men, tablets and pills and capsules, all promising enormous vitality, increased sensitivity, decreased sensitivity or irresistible attraction. And some of the product names were a riot in themselves.

There was 'Kum-fort' . . . and 'Slo-go' . . . 'Thryce-times' . . . and 'Bull', 'Stallion' . . . and 'Frenzy' . . . 'No-jac' . . . and 'Full'.

Now we left the creams and lotions and got onto the hard stuff, if you'll pardon the expression. There were vibrators in white and in black and in three different sizes – normal, huge and Jeezuskrist! Dildos of all shapes and sizes, some inflatable to pander to the current moment's whim. There were phallic candles with ridiculous wicks sticking out of the end and a whole range of weird-looking sheaths bearing the oddest rubber protrusions, all designed to thrill the ladies.

'Incredible,' I laughed, picking one up that resembled a dinosaur's backbone. 'Do they really work, Evie?'

'I . . . don't know,' she answered, in that soft, quiet voice that had rocked me upstairs. 'But I need to find out.'

'You . . . do?' I gulped, strangled again.

'I need to know just how effective these things are . . . what they can really do for women. I feel a responsibility selling them. Also . . . I feel they may help me in my search for . . . the "Inth".'

'Yes . . . I can see that.'

'But, of course . . .' the smile smouldered in her incredible eyes, 'I need help.'

'Yes . . . of course.'

'I can't try them by myself.'

'No, I can . . . see that.'

'I need . . . a partner.'

I swallowed hard. 'Indeed you do, Evie.'

'So . . . how about it . . . partner?'

I wreathed a grin. 'Which of these are you most interested in?'

'The lot!' she growled, and began loading stuff into my arms.

* * *

There was no doubt about it, Evie was an artist, a thorough professional, from the top of her glorious chestnut hair to the soles of her pretty little feet. From the word go she applied herself to the subject at hand with the sensitive dedication of a master craftswoman, leaving nothing to chance, allowing no unsubtlety to mar the moment, employing tact, charm and an abundance of awareness every step of the way – which is certainly not to say her performance was in any way mechanical or clinical, it certainly wasn't. It was simply her way of doing things and very nicely she did them, bless her.

'Come,' she said taking one laden arm, giving it a squeeze and leading me out of the shop, pausing in the corridor to smile impishly and ask, 'Excited?'

'Evie . . . any minute now my heart is going to burst right through my chest.'

'Good.'

Up the stairs we went and into the bedroom. Crossing to the bed, she turned a switch on the wall at its side and the lights dimmed to a cozy glow.

'The right lighting is so important. Don't you agree?'

'Absolutely.'

If only people would realise it there'd be far fewer sexual hangups and problems in the world. A few dollars spent on a dimmer switch would halve most people's sexual troubles. Making love in absolute darkness or in glaring light – particularly glaring light – can be equally disastrous.'

'I agree – totally.'

'Here – let me take those things.'

She put the gadgets on the bedside cupboard then went back into the lounge. A moment later the reverse side of the cassette filtered through from speakers hidden in the room, then she returned.

'Music – not absolutely essential but a pleasant adjunct.'

'Lovely,' I nodded.

She cocked her head on one side. 'Would you like a shower?'

'I'd love a shower.'

'This way.'

The bathroom was fabulous, turquoise and gold, with a large separate shower. Drawing the curtain, she turned on the tap, adjusted the temperature and gestured me in. 'There – help yourself, I'll go and get the drinks.'

'Right.'

Grinning to myself, I stripped, stepped under the spray and closed the curtain. Ah, wonderful. Incredible what a warm shower can do for you.

I stood there soaping myself and having a quiet chuckle, thinking about life, marvelling how it can change course completely in a moment. One minute you're taking a quiet cruise through Lauderdale, thinking of nothing but the prospect of looking at a few lovely houses, and the next minute you're standing in a beautiful bird's shower, contemplating a wild and woolly evening. Who says travel doesn't broaden the mind? Fascinating, really . . .

'How're you doing?' she called from the door.

'I'm doing just lovely.'

'Care for some company?'

'I . . .' oh, boy . . . 'well, certainly.'

Swwiisshh . . . back went the curtain and there she was, naked as sin but for a shower cap, cool and calm and unselfconscious as her biblical namesake, Eve, the first of the great strippers, tanned all over to a rich honey gold, slender and as perfect as it is possible for a bird to be and the owner of the most beautiful boobs I've ever seen.

I gaped at the sight of her, water running off the end of my nose and into my open mouth. And she in turn had a damn good look at me, covering me from head to toe and nodding with amused approval at the Equator.

'Quite a fella . . .'

In she stepped, not touching me, drew the curtain closed and reached for the soap. 'Turn round.'

I turned my back to her, now certain my heart was going to burst through my ribs any second, and heard her work up a lather. Then she touched my shoulders and began working in lazy featherlight circles across them and down my spine, making me shiver as she hit nerves and chuckling as I jumped.

'Nice?'

'Wonderful.'

'No better way for two people to get to know each other than this.'

'Very true.'

'You have a lovely, firm body, Russ. Do you play sports?'

'Snooker,' I laughed.

Round and round . . . down and down she went, her delicate touch sending shivers all through my body and up into my scalp. Now she reached my waist and began tentative, teasing explorations round the sides, advancing, then retreating, venturing a little further each time, driving me cuckoo as she got nearer and nearer to Herc who by this time was standing up proud and perky, rock hard and rigid, somewhere up around mid-chest.

Swish . . . swish . . . closer and closer came the silky suds and then . . . bullseye!

She struck. I jumped. She gasped . . . turned me round . . . and gasped again. 'Oh . . .!' her breasts rose and fell as she stared with mock horror. 'Oh, you *naughty* man!'

I burst out laughing.

'Woolworths. Christmas sale last year.'

'I should be so lucky! Oh, he is . . . beautiful.'

She touched him, almost tentatively, making me jump. 'Hey . . . you'd better be careful. Much more of that and I cannot be held responsible for what might happen.'

'Good,' she exclaimed, staring at him like a child looking upon its first birthday cake.

'Give me the soap and turn round,' I said.

She handed it to me, 'Just one last look.'

'Just one.'

'Oh, Russ . . .'

'Go on, round you go. You'll damage your eyes.'

With a laugh she turned, and now I worked up a lather and began soaping her shoulders, very gently, delighting in the satin texture of her skin . . . in the long, slender line of her spine and the exquisite curve of her splendid bottom.

'So *I* play snooker,' I said. 'What's your excuse for a perfect body?'

She shrugged. 'A bit of swimming and water skiing. I don't go big on violent exercise.'

'Keep it up, it's working beautifully.'

'Russ . . .?'

'Hm mm?'

'Do my front.'

Oh, boy.

She turned to me, unsmiling now, her expression urgent, impatient. Standing almost at attention she offered herself to me, shoulders straight, her full breasts thrusting. I took them in my hands, gently, and began to caress, fondle, squeeze, capturing her hard, erect nipples between thumb and finger and drawing them out . . . drawing them out. A spasm took her, buckling her knees. 'Oh . . .' Her hands came up and caught my waist for support. 'Oh, Russ . . . that is beautiful . . . oh, God, that is wonderful!'

Her breathing became more erratic and now she began to squirm, to cross her thighs and squeeze, eyes closed, face contorted . . . now murmuring in a plaintive gasp, 'Oh, Russ, I'm coming . . . God, I'm *coming* . . .!' Breath broke from her in ruptured gasps, as though she was lowering herself into ice-cold water. Her fingers clutched my body. 'Oh . . . oh . . .' she cried, building, faster and faster and then . . . 'OH!' a tormented cry and she flung herself hard against me, her face buried in my chest, and there she clung, jerking, hugging me hard.

I put my arm around her and held her close, stroking her shoulder, enjoying the soapy silkiness of her skin. After a moment she eased away and looked up at me, blowing like a surfacing grampus, eyes shining.

'Wow!'

'Well . . . how was number one?' I laughed.

With a groan and a grin she came back to me, face buried in my chest. 'Need you ask?'

'That didn't take long.'

'It's you.'

I jumped. 'Hey . . . what you doing down there?'

'Just . . . stroking him.'

'No kidding?'

'I think he's *very* lovely . . . lovely enough . . . to eat!'

Down she went, taking me in her hot, moist mouth, sending me straight up the shower head. 'Evie . . .!'

'Mmmm?'

'Oh, girl, what you doin' to me?'

Her answer was unintelligible. A while longer then up she came, splattering me with a big wet, warm kiss. 'Come on, let's get out of here, we're getting waterlogged.'

She reached behind turned off the water, kissed me again and threw back the curtain. A moment later we were drying each other with big, hot fluffy towels.

'You're *very* lovely, Evie,' I said, smiling at her.

'Thank you. I'm certainly *very* clean.' She took off the shower cap and shook out her hair, then stood brushing it in front of a mirror, offering me a wonderful sight.

'Do you ever go in for beauty competitions?' I asked.

She laughed and shook her head. 'No.'

'You ought to – I reckon you could walk away with the Miss America title. Everything you've got is perfect . . . legs, body, face, hair . . .'

She put down the brush and came to me, wrapped her arms around me and gave me yet another kiss. 'I'm very glad you approve. Feel like a drink?'

'Gasping.'

'Come on.'

We went into the bedroom and lay on the cool silk coverlet, our backs to the padded headboard, and toyed with the drinks we didn't really want, listening to the music and allowing the moment to come in its own sweet time. I put my hand on her thigh and began a gentle caress, going nowhere in particular, just stroking.

'That's nice . . .' She put down her drink, slid down the bed and began kissing my stomach, bringing Herc to attention in an instant.

'Hmm,' she laughed. 'Doesn't take *you* very long, either.'

'What do you expect – doing that?'

Now she reached over to the bedside cupboard, brought back the 'Eternity' spray and read the label. 'D'you suppose this really works?'

'I've never tried any.'

'Meaning you've never needed to?'

I grinned. 'Not recently. But it might be a good time to try it.'

'Oh?'

'You've got me mighty sensitive.'

'All right . . .'

She opened the box and took out the small aerosol container. 'Ready?'

'Fire away.'

She took aim . . . and fired.

'YOOOWWW! It's freezing!'

She laughed but kept on squirting.

'Hey, I think that's enough! He'll be so anaesthetized he'll drop off.'

She stopped and put the spray back on the cupboard. 'Anything happening?'

She reached out and tickled him under the chin. 'Feel that?'

I jumped.

'Obviously,' she said. 'We'll give him a few more minutes.'

'You sound like he's cooking in an oven.'

She grinned. 'He will be – in time.'

'Naughty.'

She lay on me, her cheek against my chest and gave me a hug. 'I think you're lovely . . . and I think *I'm* very lucky. The odds against me finding somebody I could do this with must be enormous . . . I mean, do it *exactly* like this with . . . serious yet great fun.'

'Love making has to be fun, doesn't it, Evie? It has to be relaxed and unembarrassed and . . . well, fun! You have to be able to prance about with each other, naked . . . and take your time about it . . . doing what the other one wants, and, well, making a loving game of it.'

'Yes . . . that's what it's all about – doing what the other wants.'

'You know you have the most delicious skin?' I said stroking her shoulders and running my hand right down her spine. 'It is pure sun-tanned velvet. I could eat you.'

She looked up then, smiling impishly. 'Go ahead then.'

That did it.

That was the whistle for go. One shrill blast and the game was on, players in position, adrenalin pumping. She fell upon me, smothering me in kisses, her devilish tongue, probing exploring, now retreating, kissing me all the way down until she found what she was looking for and swallowed me.

'Evie . . .!'

Kisses, pecks, nibbles, joy, her excitement matching my own, then suddenly superseding mine in a sudden and totally unexpected orgasm that curled her into a tight ball across my thighs. A few moments pause, then on she went with breathless impatience, pulling me over her and urging me down, wordlessly telling me the things she wanted me to do.

'Oh, God . . . Russ!' was her continuous cry as she reached

and passed each climax, each one, incredibly, not diminishing in intensity but if anything improving on the one before. She was a volcano of passion, pouring out a white-hot capacity for enjoyment that seemed endless. I gaped, frequently, with astonishment as yet another explosion took her, feeling that this, surely, must be the last, then gaping anew as she began again.

'Oh, Russ . . .' she laughed, drowning me in kisses.

'Are you sure you're all right, Evie?'

'Wonderful . . . fabulous! Try this . . . that . . . everything! They're all . . . *super*!'

'Anywhere near the "Inth" yet?'

'God no! I could go on *forever*!'

And, by gum, it seemed like she was going to, but then, suddenly, heaven knows how long after we'd started, she looked up at me, her eyes wide and ecstatic, and murmured fervently, 'Russ . . . I *want* you . . . just you . . . nothing else.' And I joined her for the grand finale.

To claim that almost instantly she experienced the biggest and the best of the night might seem immodest on my part, but it certainly sounded like it. She let out one deafening howl and took me with her in a devastating explosion, then wrapped me around with legs of iron and held me captive while she shook and jerked and twitched to a final halt and then . . . she collapsed.

'Ooooo . . . OOOOHHHHH!!'

I mean really collapsed.

* * *

It was a good ten minutes before either of us stirred and she started it with a chuckle that shook me up and down. I raised myself up and looked down at her and slowly she turned her head and half opened her eyes, grinning at me.

'Oh . . . you . . . *naughty* man,' she groaned, and I laughed. 'Oh, you naughty . . . super . . . lovely . . . beautiful . . . fella.'

'How do you feel?'

'How do I *feel*? I feel *fucked*, that's how I feel! Positively, gloriously, totally and comprehensively *screwed*!'

I roared with laughter

'God Almighty, I have never . . . never . . .' she shook her head bewildered. 'Well, I just *haven't* and that's all there is to it. I am . . . numb! . . . paralysed! . . . pole-axed!'

'Would you like a drink?' I grinned.

'Drink! I couldn't raise my head off the pillow to swallow! You'll have to feed me.'

'Intravenously?'

'Oh, God, don't . . .'

'OK. I'll get it.'

'Now . . . watch how you go, huh? This may be kinda tricky.'

'All right, easy does it . . .'

Slowly I backed away, chuckling at her expression of grief. 'Oh, boy . . . oh . . . *boy*! UH! Oh, my legs! Oh . . . aaah! . . . awww . . .!'

I left her attempting to straighten her legs and slid off the bed, chuckling, collecting the drinks and the cigarettes, then lay down beside her, lit a cigarette and fed it to her. She drew on it deeply and exhaled with a long drawn-out sigh. 'Oh . . . heaven!'

'Think you can manage a sip?'

'Only if you lift my head.'

I did so. She took a gulp and collapsed again, flopping her arms onto the bed. 'Let me die . . . let me die . . . let me die.'

'That's your trouble, Evie – no staying power.'

'Just dig a big hole and drop me in . . .'

'A mere twenty-seven orgasms and you behave as though you'd had a five-star orgy or something.'

'Let me close my eyes and . . .' Her head came round, suddenly alert. 'How many?'

I shrugged. 'Twenty-seven . . . twenty-eight. I lost count. It could've been thirty.'

'You lie!'

'No.'

'Aw, come on, you're kidding! Twenty . . .'

'No, really, I mean it. For the sake of the experiment I felt it appropriate to *try* to keep count but I'm afraid I got lost somewhere around sixteen.'

'Aw, now, Russ, come on . . . I *couldn't* have.'

'Evie, I'm afraid you *did*. Well, not afraid – you just did.'

Frowning, she lay back against the pillows and stared at the ceiling. 'Good God . . . you know I had no idea. All I can remember is that it was absolutely fantastic and after you came I couldn't have had one more to save my life.'

'Is it any wonder? Obviously it's a good thing that exhaustion stepped in and stopped you . . . otherwise you might have killed yourself.'

She laughed, joyfully. 'But what a fabulous way to go.'

'How do you feel now?'

She turned to me, the light of fresh devilment growing in her eyes. 'Recovering . . . fast.'

'Oh, my God.'

'And I suppose you, the poor male chauvenist slob, are finished for the night?'

'Hey listen . . . we may be temporarily out of action but give us another few minutes.'

'God, I believe you, you devil,' she laughed and threw herself on me, kissed my chest. 'You were wonderful, you know that? Simply wonderful. I shall never, ever forget you.'

'No I you, Evie. And I'm *very* grateful you chose me for the experiment.'

She frowned. 'Experiment? You know, I didn't give a thought to that experiment the entire time. I was far too busy enjoying you. And you know something else . . .?'

'What's that?'

She smiled warmly. 'Not one of these gadgets means a damn thing unless the right fella is using it . . . and not one of them comes anywhere near the feel of a real live man. You – just you – were beautiful, right there at the end. Then I *really* flipped.'

I grinned. 'So I noticed.'

'Pig.'

'So . . . what about the gadgets? Think you can sell them with a clear conscience?'

'Oh, sure – they're OK – provided the customer doesn't expect any improvements on a real hot fella. They're great for a bit of fun . . . or for a change, variety *is* the spice of love, after all. But tell me, how did you feel about using them?'

'Me? Evie as long as you were enjoying them, they were fine. No point to them otherwise, is there?'

'No,' she said, giving me a hug. 'Thank you, Russ . . . for everything.'

'And I thank you. Evie.'

She smiled and nodded. 'OK, we thank each other. And now . . . I've got something very sad to tell you . . .'

'Mm . . .?' I said, alarmed. 'What is it?'

'The clock over there says it's five minutes to eleven . . . and if you're going to catch that . . .'

'Eleven! It can't be!'

She chuckled. 'I'm afraid it is. Believe it or not, Tobin, we have been screwing one another for nearly three hours!'

'I . . . good God. Oh, Evie . . . oh, buggerit!'

'Come on, get dressed. I'll drive you to the hotel and then to the station.'

'Evie, I do *not* want to go.'

'And so help me I do not *want* you to go, but you're booked through and it'll cost you a lot of money if you don't go. Come on, get dressed.'

* * *

She dropped me off at the hotel and I shot up in the lift, packed in three minutes dead, raced down to the bar and shocked poor old Hi and Paula with the imminence of my departure. Dave Brewer was nowhere to be seen.

'Going? Now!' cried Paula. 'Oh, baby, have a last drink with us – please!'

'Paula, I can't. I'd love to but I can't – my train leaves in fifteen minutes.'

'Russ,' said Hi gravely, offering his hand. 'It's been a real, real pleasure. Come back real soon and next time stay longer, huh?'

'We'll both miss you, ya big hunk,' said Paula, throwing her arms round me and wetting my suit with tears. 'Take care, now, and do as Hi tells yuh – come back real soon.'

'I will, I promise. Goodbye, Paula . . . Hi . . . and thank you for everything.'

I exited slowly, not wanting to hurt their feelings, waved a last goodbye from the door, then hared down the corridor and out to the car.

'God, how I hate goodbyes,' I told Evie. 'If only there was some other way of leaving without going away.'

'Yes,' she nodded. 'Darned if I know why, but it seems we have to pay for everything pleasurable – as I am about to find out.'

I looked at her and she smiled. 'It had to be today that we met, huh, Tobin? I mean, I couldn't have bumped into you like four days ago when you first arrived! Four days you've been lying on that beach all alone and the same four lousy days I've been keeping shop not two miles away. Tobin, you're a heel . . . why didn't you let me know you were in town?'

'I'm sorry, Evie,' I said, squeezing her thigh affectionately. 'Next time I sure as heck will.'

She gave a glance, then returned her attention to the road. 'Could there *be* a next time?'

'Everything is possible, Evie.'

'I'd like to think there could. Oh, I won't be waiting for you to walk into the shop, it doesn't work out that way . . . but if you can . . . well, you know I'd love to see you.'

'Thanks, Evie.'

'Well, here's the station. I . . . won't see you off, I'm not too fond of goodbyes myself, so get out quick and don't look back – OK?'

She brought the car to a halt then turned to me. 'One thing I learned about the "Inth" tonight . . .'

'What was that?'

She leaned close and kissed me, very tenderly, on the lips. 'With the right man there just ain't no such thing . . . because there's really no end to it. What there is . . . are pauses to catch your breath, and a lucky woman can go on forever. Now – go!'

Before I'd reached the station doorway she was off with a scream of tyres and a farewell blast on the horn, waving out of the window, then out of sight around the bend.

I stood there for a moment, watching the last glimpse of her tail-lights, and was about to become very dejected when a voice from within shouted, 'You for the New York train, sir?'

I gave a start and turned, seeing a stout porter hurrying towards me.

'Er . . . yes . . .'

'Then if you wanna catch it yuh'd better skip along – it's pullin' out any second now? Here – gimme those cases . . . go on – get goin' through there! What compartment number you got?'

'Er . . .' On the run I fumbled in my inside pocket, pulled out the ticket, peered for the compartment number. 'It's . . . number ten.'

'Ever' car's got a number ten! What's yuh car number?'

'Nine-oh-nine-oh.'

' 'Kay, get movin'!'

Across the foyer we shot, through a door and out to the back and the tracks, hearing already the dreaded, 'Aaaalll 'booaarrdd!'

'Hold on, there, Jason!' gasped my porter. 'We gotta live one here!'

'Hurry along there, then Willerby.'

'What in tarnation d'ya think I'm doin'? Heyah . . . here yuh go, young fella – up yuh get an' I'll pass these up to yuh.'

I scrambled up the steps, turned and took the case and the grip from him, slipping him a dollar.

'Much 'bliged. OK, Jason, get this thing rollin' – yuh're late!'

Willerby disappeared down the tracks, puffin and chuckling to himself, and I entered the coach, feeling strange yet elated to be on my first American train.

Now . . . number ten. I walked down a long centre corridor, finally reaching compartment ten on the right-hand side, about four from the end. Drawing back the sliding door I climbed two steps into a completely self-contained and beautifully appointed couchette, a tiny sitting room with a double seat, cupboards, toilet and fold-away washbasin, the wall behind the seat, which was on the left, folding down to form a bed when needed.

Closing the door behind me, and enjoying the feeling of the self-contained privacy, I stowed my cases on the overhead rack and began investigating the room, opening cupboards, dropping the aluminium washbasin, fiddling with the air-conditioning, then had to make a grab for the luggage rack as the train jerked into motion.

Sadly now, thinking of Evie, I watched the rail yard slide past the window, its lights becoming fewer and fewer until at last they disappeared and darkness filled the glass.

With a sigh I slipped off my jacket, filled the washbasin with hot water and bathed my face, more for something to do than out of need of a wash, God knows! – not after *that* shower! Then I sat down, head back against the cushioning, and stared sightlessly at the room's reflection in the window.

Thoughts drifted idly through my mind . . . of Nassau . . . and Stud Ryder . . . then of Miami . . . and Evie . . . thoughts that became more and more interwined, less and less collected as exhaustion, aided by the drum of the wheels and the gentle sway of the train, took me.

Finally I fell asleep, into deep, untroubled sleep, little realizing, poor idiot, that in a matter of only a few more minutes life would take yet another devastating veer from the norm and plunge me into an adventure so weird that even now I can hardly believe it happened.

Well, I have certainly learned one thing out here in the big, wide world – and that is – if you stick your nose into it, investigating life, one day you're liable to turn round and find to your dismay that life is investigating you!

I found out at the very next station.

Oh boy.

THREE

Picture, if you will, my state of mind when it all began to happen. I was unconscious. And now recall, if you will, your *own* state of mind if you have ever been very rudely awakened from a deep, untroubled sleep by a loud crash, bang or wallop, as the case may be.

Confusion.

Crash! The door flew back so hard I'm surprised it didn't finish up in the next coach.

I shot awake, the room whirling, nothing making any sense – and there was this fellow, leaning into the couchette, prodding my arm and gasping. 'Miami . . . Miami?'

'Er . . . yes!' I muttered, thinking – I'm here! I've arrived! I'd nearly overslept!

'Listen . . .' He jerked back into the corridor, glancing furtively along it . . . no, not furtively – *fearfully* along it, then plunged back again at me, clutching my arm. 'Now, listen . . . listen!'

'I'm awake! I'm listening!' I protested, wondering what the hell was going on.

Thump! A brown paper package was dumped into my lap, narrowly missing doing me a very serious injury. 'They're onto me!' he gasped, white as a sheet. 'Tell Kokheimer this has gotta be the last . . . you understand?'

'Kok . . . heimer,' I repeated, staring down at the package. 'But . . .'

'Ssssh!' Out into the corridor he went again, this time giving a terrified start and slamming the door closed.

Well, I just sat there, staring at the door, then down at the package, then finally I got up and opened the door. Nothing. The corridor was empty. So I closed the door and sat down again, utterly and totally perplexed.

'Kokheimer . . .' I repeated.

Suddenly – a movement outside the window, drawing my attention to the fact that the train was stopped in a station. Shows you what a state I was in, I hadn't even realized we had stopped! And there, racing across the tracks and heading for the station exit was the chap who'd just left me. Out he went, disappearing through the doorway, then ten seconds later two other guys ran from the direction of the train, going like the clappers and obviously chasing him, and also disappeared through the doorway. And that was the end of that. A moment later the train started and Tobin was left knee-deep in bewilderment.

Well, I thought, this is rum. He'd obviously mistaken me for someone else and lumbered me with this package of whateveritwas. I turned it over, looking for a name . . . an address, but the paper was completely blank, then I weighed it in my hand, smelt it, shook it gently, and all this time my imagination was working overtime. What*ever* was in the package, it had to be illicit . . . like heroin or . . . well, I mean his whole demeanour had been so . . . so . . . OK – take his dialogue for a start! 'They're onto me! Tell Kakhammer . . . no Kokheimer this has got to be the last!' Just reeked of criminality.

And who the fuck was Kokheimer when he was at home?

Well, by now I'd begun to wake up a bit and my first instincts were – right, Tobin, you've got to hide the parcel! If it does contain Big H the last thing you ought to be doing is waving it around in public. So – into your grip with it!

I stood up and, you know, I'd just got that package out of sight when –BAM – the door flew open again and there stood the most devastating piece of dark-skinned crumpet I have ever clapped eyes on. Beautiful! Draped in a leopardskin coat with a cute little hat to match.

I just stared, speechless . . . and she just stared, but not so speechless.

'Who in *hell* are you?' she demanded.

'I . . . hm?'

'What you doin' in my couchette, mister?'

'I . . . hm?'

'Compartment ten – this is mine! You got balled up somewheres?'

'Well, I . . . well, no, I don't think so.'

She looked away down the corridor and bellowed, 'Steward!'

'Yes, Ma'am . . . I'm comin'.'

'There's a guy here in my couchette – reckons it's his!'

'Comin', lady.'

Up he trundled, a grey-haired guy, nice as pie. 'Well, now, what seems t'be the trouble?'

'He's in my couchette,' she rapped. 'Number Ten – says here on mah ticket, don't it?'

He inspected her ticket. 'Sho' nuff does, ma'am.' He looked in at me, smiling. 'May I jurst see your ticket, sir?'

'Certainly.'

I gave it to him.

'Ah, well, now . . . right here is where we find the answer to the problem. You're in the right couchette sir . . . but you sho' is in the wrong rail car. This here says nine-oh-*nine*-oh . . . and this here car is nine-oh-*five*-oh. You belong about six cars along – towards the locomotive.'

'Oh . . . Miss, I'm sorry. You see, I got on in a big hurry and . . .'

She gave a sniff. 'OK.'

'. . . well, the porter back in Miami put me in this . . .'

'I said OK, mister! Just move out and lemmi in there, will yuh?'

The old steward stepped in, winking at me. 'It's all right, sir – out you go an' I'll bring your baggage along. Head down to the right, I'll catch up with yuh.'

I stepped down, swept past the girl, who was tapping her foot impatiently, and started walking along the corridor, smarting at her tone. One thing I cannot stand is stroppy birds. I mean, there was just no need for her to blow up like that.

On and on I walked . . . through the diner and out the far end, finally coming to car nine-oh-nine-oh where I waited for the steward.

'Here yuh go, sir – number ten. Don't think you'll be disturbed any more. Like yuh bed made up now?'

I thought about it. It had been a long, hard day and it was getting late – too late for much to be happening on the train in the way of entertainment (not, of course, counting strange men who burst into your compartment and throw mysterious packages in your lap!), so I said, 'Yes, I think I will, thank you.'

'Done in no time.'

And it was. I've never seen anything so slick. He released two catches and the panel behind the seat dropped forward, revealing a ready made bed that almost completely filled the tiny room.

'There yuh go, sir. Sleep well.'

'Thanks very much. I've a feeling I just might.'

I climbed in, finding it a tight squeeze now the bed was down, and closed the door. Feeling a bit like Houdini escaping from a straight-jacket, I got undressed, then reached for my grip which contained my toothbrush and stuff and put my hand on . . . the package.

I took it out, sat on the bed, and looked at it, shook it again, weighed it again in my hand, and picked thoughtfully at the binding of heavy Sellotape, very *very* tempted to open it. And what, asked the voice of reason, if it's a bomb?

Mmmm.

Well, I sat there for a long time trying to decide what to do with it. Throw it out of the window? I rejected that thought the moment it came. Say – just *say* there was a thumping big reward for it! Say I decided to hand it over to the New York police and it turned out to be counterfeit money plates or something . . . and it led to the capture of a gang and there was a huge reward . . . well, OK but why not? There were such things as gangs and counterfeit money plates and rewards.

No, I could *not throw* it out of the window. What then? Well . . . I didn't know, I'd have to think about it, sleep on it. But instinct told me that if I did I ought to hide it. There was something mighty mysterious about this package and it would not do to just leave it lying about. So, after I'd cleaned my teeth I emptied the little washbasin, dried it off, put the package in it and raised the bowl securing it by its catch to the wall. Out of sight, out of mind. Then I got into bed and despite all the excitement and mystery, was fast asleep in minutes.

But not for long.

Some time later, perhaps an hour, I was brought to the surface again by the tap . . . tap . . . tap on the door. I sat up, confused again, and fumbled for the light. Oh, God, was I never going to get any sleep?'

'Who, . . . who is it?' I croaked.

'Open the door!' a voice whispered. A bird's voice!

'Who . . . who is it?'

'Open up, honey . . . it's me!'

Honey!

I slipped the catch and eased back the door, then nearly died of heart attack. It was her! . . . the gorgeous, rude, beautiful, stroppy negress, still swathed in leopardskin though she'd taken off the hat.

'Hi!' she grinned, her teeth gleaming in the faint cabin light. 'Mind if Ah slip in fo' a while?'

Eh!

'Er . . .'

'Ah jurst got a liddle bit lonesome up there and thought you might like some . . . *company* fo' a while.'

She gave a sexy chuckle and pushed the door further open.

Oh, man!

She didn't give me time to say yes or no, she was in! Door closed behind her.

Now, there was nowhere else to sit but on the bed, so that's where she sat, filling the room with her sexy perfumed presence, very close to me, leaving me breathless. I mean, this was *all* woman, a flaming tigress, radiating sin and the innate ability to destroy a legion of lovers in a single night with the crush of those naked thighs, most of which I could see right now because the leopardskin coat had fallen open, just like she wanted it to, and as she leaned languidly towards me, coming to rest on her elbow, the coat fell open just that little bit more and all I could see before my very eyes was a pair of enormous brown boobs and it was heart-stoppingly obvious that she hadn't got a damn thing on under that coat.

'We kinda got off on the wrong foot, didn't we, sugar?' she cooed, her tone pure dripping syrup. 'Ah shoulda known by your accent yuh didn't know your way around these trains. You're English, ain't yuh . . .?'

'Yes,' I squeaked, my throat choked tight by the way her big, brown beautiful eyes were caressing my naked torso, as though gauging it for staying power.

'Ah'm sorry Ah lost mah temper back there. Things went a bit awry tonight an' I only just made the train by the skin of my teeth.' She smiled, showing me all four hundred and sixteen of them.'

'That's . . . quite all right,' I croaked.

'An' when Ah got settled in I got to thinking 'bout you . . . such a nice-lookin' fella, Ah said to mahself. Miami . . . you oughta be ashamed, speakin' to a nice English guy like that – snappin' his head off just because someone put him in the wrong couchette. Now why don' you go along an' apologize . . . see if there ain't *some* little thing you can do to make it up to him . . .' she grinned outrageously, 'know what Ah mean, honey?'

. . . A hooker, I thought. She's on the blinking game! She plays the trains, picking up the suckers on the overnight runs.

'Well, I . . . yes . . . I . . . is that your name – Miami?'

'Sure. Miami Jo Dell. And what's yours, lover?'

'Er . . . Tobin. Russ Tobin.'

'Russ Tobin,' she sighed, really pouring it on. 'Gee, that's a nice name. Tell me . . . are you goin' all the way to New York, Russ?'

'Eh . . . well, yes, I am.'

'Now ain' that a beautiful coincidence, so am I. I reckon it's lucky, bumpin' inta you. Twenty-four hours on a train can be *very* borin' without some kind of . . . recreation, don't you think?'

I had the greatest difficulty thinking anything because her coat had parted yet another few inches and I could now see *everything*! And she knew it, because she was grinning at me like a lynx, and now moved even closer, dragging the coat wide open . . . so that without even moving I could have reached out and grabbed one of her big, brown, beautiful boobs.

'You . . . think Ah'm beautiful, Russ?' she whispered, her voice hoarse with passion.

'Yes,' I piped, my heart murdering my ribs.

'You're kinda beautiful yourself, big boy . . . and Ah jurst *bet* you've got nuthin' on under them bedclothes . . .'

'No,' I gulped, watching her advance, helpless as a bird hypnotised by a snake.

'So, why don't Ah stop wastin' precious time an' slide in there beside you . . .'

In one fluid movement she stood up, dropped the coat to the floor, whipped back the sheets and was in! . . . her scorching, naked flesh hard against mine, her hot tongue lancing into my ear and her hand snaking down to grab Herc.

'Oh, baby . . .!' she gasped. 'Oh, he is . . . *beautiful*! Man. Ah was not wrong about *you.* Ah tell yuh, the moment Ah opened that couchette door an' saw you standin' there at the rack, tall . . . an' *strong*-lookin' . . . Ah said to mahself now there is a fella who's jurst gotta be *built*! Now, Russ, he really is *somethin'* . . .!'

All the time she was talking in this low, breathy whisper she was raining kisses on my face, ear, neck and working her way further and further over me until now she was almost straddling me, massaging me with her hot, silky flesh, working her thigh in between my legs and really socking it to Herc.

'Ah, sho' am a lucky girl,' she chuckled, 'findin' a man like you in mah couchette. Were you . . . in there long, honey . . . before I arrived?'

'Not . . . too long,' I gasped, sweltering in her steam heat. 'I . . . got on . . . at Miami.'

'Did you now,' she whispered, pausing to do some incredible things with her tongue, then continued, very casually, 'Tell me . . . did . . . anything happen – jurst before I arrived?'

'H . . . wow! . . . happen . . .?'

'Yes, you know, like...did anyone...open your door by mistake . . . talk to you . . . ask any questions . . .?' A studied pause, then, 'Give you anythin,' maybe – like a package or somethin'?'

Under no circumstances did I think it possible for my heart to thump any harder than it already was thumping but somehow it managed it. So *that's* what this little interlude was all about! The bloody package! She was no more interested in screwing me than playing hopscotch – she was after the loot!

But *why*? Who was she? A policewoman? Ha! – hardly. Even in the line of duty I think the average female cop would have tried a *few* straight questions before leaping into bed starkers with me.

No – Ding Dong Dell, here, was up to no good. This sweetness and light routine was all a big come-on, if you'll pardon the expression. She was making amends for the rude start, softening me up (ha!), breaking me down so's I'd spill the whereabouts of the goods. Well, now, that little ole packet was becoming more intriguing by the minute. If she was prepared to go to these lengths (ho!) to get it, it must really be valuable – to say nothing of dynamite!

But what the heck was I to *do*? Did I give it to her right now – or wait a little? It seemed indecent to break off now when things were going so well – particularly as she was going to so much trouble. Or would I not give it to her at all – the package I mean.

Secure in the knowledge that I was in control of the situation, I just lay back and enjoyed the rewards of power, determined to squeeze the very last atom out of the situation before I either did or did not reveal to her the whereabouts of the package, depending on how I felt at the time.

But – never underestimate the persuasive powers of a red-hot momma when she's pulling out all the stops. A few more tickles and licks and a sneaky hand up the inside of me leg for a quick squeeze and I was spilling the beans before you could say sniff.

'Well . . . ooh! . . . yes . . . as a matter of fact a . . . cor! . . . funny thing *did* happen . . . early on . . . oh, brother . . .'

She stopped what she was doing instantly, raised herself above me, her big, brown eyes alive with sudden interest. 'What?' she demanded, almost forgetting herself, then softening up immediately, cooing, 'Tell me, baby . . .'

'I . . . I was fast asleep . . . and suddenly the door flew open and this chap was shaking me, saying "Miami . . . Miami" and then he slung a package at me and ran off . . .'

Her manner changed with alarming suddenness. She was up on her knees, gripping my arms, breasts heaving. 'Where is it, honey? That package was fo' me! He was askin fo' me! Fo' "Miami" . . . Miami Jo Dell . . .!'

'But . . . if he knew it was for you, why did he give it to me?'

'Because he doesn't *know* me! He was told to deliver it to "Miami" in compartment ten, nine-oh-five-oh and . . . look! what the hell am Ah explainin' it to *you* fo' – where *is* it?'

She loomed above me, eyes flashing angrily, a *very* strong bird, looking not only very capable of ripping out my throat with those flashing choppers but just about to do it.

Almost subconsciously my eyes went to my grip, up on the luggage rack behind her, and then she was on to it in an instant. She whipped round, then back to me, grinning jubilantly. 'Your grip! You were standin' up at the rack when I opened the door!'

She was off the bed in one leap and standing up there, a study in hard, rippling black muscle.

'Now look here . . .' I began, throwing back the blankets.

'Shut up!' she snapped, then, hearing my movement on the bed, turned towards me, bent down, caught hold of the end of the bed and yanked it up. Up it went, clean as a whistle, taking me with it, legs in the air, head bent to my chest at an excruciating angle, expecting to hear the awful crack as my neck broke.

And then the lights went out. Or so it seemed. What had happened was that all the blankets had fallen down into the crevice and were now very effectively smothering me.

'Miami!' I yelled.

I felt a thump, as though she'd jammed something under the bed to prevent my pushing it down.

'Miami! I'm suffocating!'

'So long, sucker!' she laughed, 'Jezus, what a crumb!'

I heard the door swish open and then she was gone. Gone! How in hell was I going to get out! Another few minutes and . . . my God, it was murder in there . . . like an oven . . . not a breath of air.

'Help!' I yelled.

Pathetic. In that position, covered by the blankets and by the train noise it was little more than a squeak.

'Heeeelllppp!' I tried again.

Terrible.

I was trapped, totally, couldn't move a muscle, flattened like a bug in a book.

Well, whether it was pure good fortune or she'd timed it that way. I don't know, but a few more seconds and the train began to slow, another few and we were stopping at a station and I reckon that stop saved Tobin's life. The air was getting so thick in there my head was spinning and at a conservative estimate Russell would've been a goner in another ten minutes.

'HEEEEELLLLPPP!!'

'Anyone in 'ere?' a voice enquired, unmistakeably Australian, and even in my state I managed surprise.

'Yes! Behind the bed panel! Can you pull the bed down?'

'Eh? Blimey . . . yes, hold on, mate. Bloody hell, how on earth did you get in this mess?'

I heard the obstruction being dragged away, I presumed it was my large case, and then the bed was rushing down, I was falling down, rolled across it and fell with a thump on the floor.

'Jeezuskrist!' someone gasped, and then began to laugh. A broad-shouldered blond lad, dressed in dazzling blue pyjamas and a disbelieving grin. 'What were you doin' in there – practicing yoga or something?'

I heaved a huge sigh of relief and shook my head. 'No, I was suffocating . . . *boy*, oh boy . . .' Shaking like a jelly I got up off the floor, flopped on the bed and began massaging my screaming neck muscles.

'But . . . how the 'ell did you get in there?' he repeated. 'Did the thing fly up on you?'

I shook my head. 'No . . . hang on a minute, I feel a bit dickey.'

'By God, you look it too. Got any booze with you?'

'No . . .'

'Hang on, I've got some brandy across the way. Back in a jiff.'

He went out, closing the door behind him. Realizing I was naked, I pulled my trousers off the hanger and had just climbed into them when the door slid open again and in he came, carrying a bottle and two glasses.

'Here you go . . . a shot of this will soon put you right.' He half-filled a glass and handed it to me. 'Very nasty that . . . being trapped in there. You might have suffocated.'

I took a swallow and made a face, enjoying its firey glow, then took a couple of deep breaths, another good gulp and began to feel better.

'Ah, coming on a treat.' I sighed.

'I'll join you – feel quite shook up meself,' he grinned, swallowing a good gulp. 'By the way, the name's Malone . . . Buzz Malone,' he extended a huge paw, 'from Sydney. You're English aren't you?'

'Yes, Pom through and through,' I grinned, liking him immediately. 'Mine's Russ Tobin – from Liverpool, London, and more recently the edge of the grave. Thanks a lot, Buzz, I reckon I owe you my life. Another few minutes and I'd have been past calling for help. It was getting a mite close in there.'

'I'll take a bet. But . . . how did it happen? And how in hell did your case get under there?'

I heaved a sigh. 'Buzz . . . how's your credence quota? This you're just *not* going to believe.'

'If you tell me – I'll believe it,' he said with touching charm.

'Well, that's very nice of you.' I took another swig, reached for my cigarettes and offered him one. 'Buzz, you've obviously knocked about the world quite a bit – well, you're certainly a long way from home.'

'Oh, sure,' he said, taking a light. 'I'm in the tennis racket . . .' he grinned. 'I'm a pro – just finished the Miami circuit, then on to Canada for a tournament. Sure, I've covered most of it.'

'Anything . . . *weird* . . . mysterious ever happen to you on your travels?'

He frowned. 'How weird d'you mean?'

I sighed and took another swig. 'Well, a month ago I finished a season in Africa as a courier with a photographic safari firm, and I thought I'd take a few weeks off and see a bit of the world – particularly the Bahamas . . .'

'Smashing,' he grinned. 'Stupendous sheilas over there.'

'You dig?' I laughed.

'Dig. I certainly wouldn't do all this runnin' around just for the flamin' tennis.'

'Well, now, that makes this story a bit easier. Shake hands with a fellow student. I love the little darlings – with the possible exception of those who jam me in fold-up beds and rifle my lug . . . gage . . .'

I was staring at the baggage rack.

'What's the matter?' asked Buzz.

'Jesus . . . she's pinched my grip.'

'Eh?'

'She's pinched my grip! Taken the lot!'

'Who . . . who's she? A bird?'

'A bird? A bird and a half, Buzz – you should've seen her! A coffee-coloured knockout with a pair of t . . . but . . . back to the story.'

'If you insist.'

'You're not going to believe it.'

'Try me.'

'OK, God's honour this is the truth. I got on the train at Miami – I'm on a two-centre holiday – Miami and New York . . .'

'Goodo,' he nodded. 'This sounds promising. Go on.'

'Well . . . for one reason or another,' I grinned, 'I was pretty knackered when I got on the train . . .'

'And who needs two guesses why.'

I laughed. '. . . and I fell asleep as soon as the train started. Then, a few minutes later, the train stopped at a small station and suddenly the door flew open and there was this guy shaking me awake and jabbering, "Miami . . .? Miami . . .?" at me. Well, just waking up like that, I was going confused and I thought he was asking me if I was going to Miami! And in my stupor I answered "yes". Then he ducks back into the corridor, gives a very scared look down it and comes back into me, white as a sheet, and says, "Listen . . . they're on to me! Tell Kokheimer this has got to be the last?" – thumps a package in my lap and runs like hell!'

Buzz's mouth was open. 'Yeah?'

'God's honour. Well, I was still half asleep, hadn't a clue

what was happening and was sitting there wondering what had hit me, when suddenly, through the window, I see this guy haring across the tracks and out through the station door. Then, a few seconds later, I see two other guys run across, obviously chasing him, and they disappeared through the station door. Then the train started and that was that.'

'Blimey. I must say nothin' like that's ever happened to me.'

'Hang on, that's only *half* of it – and the least interesting! Well, I had a think about this package . . . it was quite small, very light, covered in plain brown paper . . .'

'No writing on it?'

'Nothing – except thirty-six miles of Sellotape – impossible to open without ripping it to pieces. Well, naturally, I sat there wondering what was in it. Could it be drugs . . . counterfeit plates – you know how your mind works?'

'Sure,' he grinned. 'You *want* it to be drugs or counterfeit plates – it's no fun otherwise.'

'Right,' I said, knowing now I'd found a soulmate. '*Or*, I wondered, could it possibly be a bomb!'

'Yeh,' he pondered. 'There's an awful lot of them knocking about these days.'

'Quite. Well, I sat there wondering what to do with it – throw it out of the window . . . hand it over to the New York cops . . . Anyway, I decided to keep it for the time being and was stowing it away in my grip when the compartment door flew open and there stood this fabulous negro bird swathed in leopardskin fur . . .!'

'Holy mother . . .!' he gasped. 'Some guys get all the flamin' luck.'

'Well, not this time, Buzz. She lay back and gave me a right old mouthful – told me I was in the wrong compartment and looked ready, fit and able to throw me out bodily there and then!'

'Great,' he chuckled. 'And *were* you in the wrong compartmen?'

'Right compartment – wrong car! I only made the train by the skin of me teeth and in the confusion the porter had put me in nine-oh-five-oh instead of this one, nine-oh-*nine-oh*. She was dead right – it was her compartment. So I got out and came up here. Now . . .' I took a swig of brandy and gave him a wry grin, '. . . now comes the really hard to believe part.'

'Go on, you're doin' fine. We've got a saying back home,

"there's nowt so queer as folk". And there are some pretty rum buggers about, I can tell you.'

'Well, we've got precisely the same saying and I agree entirely. There're a heck of a sight more nutters running around loose than locked up – as one day in London will testify. Anyway, credibility established, here's the truth, Buzz. The porter made my bed in here and I fell asleep almost immediately . . . only to be awakened about an hour later by a knock on that door. Buzz, so help me, it was her – the negress, nice as anything, really giving me the come-on, calling me "honey" and telling me how lonesome she was and how she'd like to have a chat with me . . .'

'Good God.'

'Then – before you could call "fault!" she was in here, door closed, lying across the bed in that leopardskin coat, telling me how sorry she was for being rude . . . and what a handsome guy she thought I was and wasn't there something we could do together to pass the time all the way to New York . . .'

'Bloody hell!' he gasped.

'But hang on! All the time she was talking, she was inching further and further up the bed and as she came towards me that damn coat was opening, Buzz . . . and may I be stricken dead right now if I lie, but she was as naked as Sunday underneath . . . not a damn stitch on!'

'Jezus wept . . .'

'And seconds later she stood up, dropped the coat and was in bed with me, making like she'd missed dinner and was determined to make up for it!'

'No!'

'Gospel!'

'Holy . . .'

'Buzz, she was going at it like she'd just discovered it . . . grinding all over me and grabbing handfuls of anything that caught her fancy . . . when suddenly she started asking questions! Well, before I knew it I was telling her all about the package and when I threw a glance towards my grip, up on the rack, she put two and two together, figuring I'd put it in there and the minx changed completely. She was up out of that bed, lifted it up and jammed me against the wall, pinched my grip and was gone!'

'But . . .'

'Buzz – her name was "Miami" Jo Dell! That package was

for her! *She* was the "Miami" that guy was looking for! He didn't know her by sight. He'd been told to deliver the package to "Miami" in compartment ten, car nine-oh-five-oh – and he gave it to me! Now, what d'you think of *that* little lot?'

'But . . . I . . . she . . . Jezuschrist,' was what he had to say. 'And she's pinched your grip? Why the . . .'

'Buzz, I had some presents in there from Miami – you know, bits and pieces to take back home. She probably didn't know what the package looked like, so she took the lot. Besides, she was in a hell of a hurry. She couldn't afford to hang around with me yelling my lungs out.'

'Good God . . . but . . . do you think she's still on the train?'

'I doubt it very much. I'll bet she got off at the station we'd stopped at when you heard me shouting. I've got a feeling she even timed it that way – so she could nip off with the package.'

'Yeh, quite likely. What else was in the grip – anything valuable?'

'No, not really, razor . . . socks . . . couple of books.'

'And the package,' he said dolefully. 'By heck, I'd give a month's pay to know what was in that thing. Must have been something pretty hot to make her act like that, Russ.'

'That's what I think. I'm obviously very curious myself as to what was in it – but I don't know about a month's pay. The money you fellas earn it could cost you a small fortune.'

He shrugged and grinned. 'About three thousand bucks. But I still reckon it'd be worth it.'

'Huh huh,' I nodded, getting off the bed and heading for the washbasin. Releasing the catch, I lowered the basin, took out the package and threw it into his lap, making him jump. 'That's three grand you owe me, Buzz. If you're short of cash I'll take a cheque, you've got an honest face.'

You should have seen his honest face!

'I . . . you . . . crafty . . . bastard!' he gasped, staring down at the package, then up at me, then exploding with laughter. 'Well, I'll be buggered.'

FOUR

Time: Fifteen minutes later.

Place: My compartment.

The bed was made, the compartment tidied, I was fully

dressed, and the package lay before us on the smoothed-out blanket, simply throbbing with mystery.

In the past few minutes we had shaken it, smelled it, listened to it, weighed it and minutely inspected it, finally coming to one very firm and mutually agreed conclusion – we hadn't a clue what was in it.

Now we simply stared at it, as though willing it to give up its secret, drinking enjoyably from Buzz's bottle and working up a good thick fug of smoke as we contemplated.

'You think drugs, hm?' he said, breaking the momentary silence.

'A possibility. I know nothing about them but from what I've read it could be a few ounces of heroin and therefore worth a fortune.'

'Mmm,' he mused. 'You also mentioned counterfeit plates. Don't you think it's a bit on the light side for that?'

I shrugged. 'I don't know. Possibly not if they were made out of aluminium or something.'

'Mmmm,' he went again. 'How about diamonds?'

'Could be . . . wrapped in cotton wool so they don't rattle.'

'Mmmm . . . a drop more red-eye, Russell, if you please.'

I slurped in another shot, saying, 'Aren't you supposed to be in training?'

'Yes,' he said, swallowing a good belt. 'I am. This is the first since last night.'

'Oh.'

Once again he picked up the package and shook it gently, sighing with bewilderment. 'It's got to be something hot, Russ. I mean – the bloke who gave it to you, he was really running scared, hm?'

'Terrified.'

'Well . . . let's go over what he said once again.'

'He said "They're on to me? Tell Kokheimer this has got to be the last!" That was all.'

'Tell Kokheimer . . . I wonder who the hell Kokheimer is? Unusual name that, sounds German doesn't it? I wonder how you spell it . . . C-o-c-k . . . K-o-c-k . . . K-o-k . . .? Question two – *where* is Kokheimer?'

'Presumably New York. At least that's where Jo Dell said she was heading. Mind you, that could've been a load of bilge – all part of the come-on.'

'Mmmm, possibly. I wonder who that guy was running away

from . . . who those guys were that were chasing him. Obviously they were the people who were on to him – but what had they caught him doing? Pinching the stuff from them and feeding it to Kokheimer? But if he'd done it before – why didn't he know who "Miami" was?'

I shrugged. 'Maybe he hadn't done it before. Granted he said, "Tell Kokheimer this has got to be the last" – but that doesn't necessarily mean this wasn't the first package, does it?'

'No,' he agreed.

'And as far as him not knowing "Miami" – maybe Kokheimer uses a different pick-up courier every time. Maybe this was Miami's first go.'

'Yes,' he said, then heaved a sigh. 'It's a heck of a mystery, Russell, but undoubtedly most of the answer lies . . . right . . . in . . . there!' He prodded the package irritably.

'Buzz . . .?'

'Mmm?'

'I've just had a nasty little thought. Supposing those guys caught the bloke who gave me the package . . . and they made him tell them where he'd dropped it! They could be . . .'

'Following the train right now,' he finished for me, frowning with some concern. 'And just supposing they caught up with the train – which they could do with a good fast car – they would . . .'

'Make a beeline for compartment ten in car nine-oh-five-oh and . . .'

'Find it empty,' he said with relief. 'Russ . . . how would you like to go and check – just to make *sure* she got off the train? If she did – the trail ends right there. They couldn't possibly know *you've* got the package . . . could they?'

I thought about it, the first stirrings of real discomfort nagging me, my sixth sense mechanism telling me that, fantastic or not, we were about to be caught up – were already caught up – in something potentially very nasty. And I could tell from Buzz's manner that the same realization was simultaneously dawning upon him.

Somebody was *very* desperate to get their hands on that package. Miami Jo Dell had been prepared to commit manslaughter for it. So the two men who were chasing the guy who gave it to me would also be pre . . .

Suddenly it struck me – the one thing that was wrong with Buzz's supposition about the trail ending with Jo Dell.

'Buzz,' I said, with growing anxiety, 'if those two men *did* catch that guy and did wring the information out of him – he would tell them that he delivered the package to a *man* in compartment ten, car nine-oh-five-oh, right?'

'Yes . . .' he said uncertainly. 'But if it's empty now . . .?'

'If it's empty now they're going to question the steward . . . ask him what happened to the man that was in there! And he's going to tell them about the mix-up in compartments and he's going to tell them he moved me into this one and they are going to come looking for me so fast . . .'

He was on his feet, picking up the package, plucking my case off the rack. 'Come on! Over to my place . . .!'

'Hell, Buzz, d'you think . . .?'

'Yes! I think! I'd forgotten all about that bloody steward! Sure he'd tell them . . . come on!'

With jangling nerves and thundering heart I grabbed the booze, my toothbrush, half shoved my feet into my shoes, wrenched my jacket off its hanger, clouted my shin on the corner of the bed, tripped over the trailing blanket and fell on my face on the bed.

'Ssssh!' Guardedly, Buzz slid back the door and peered out into the corridor. 'OK! Come on,' he whispered.

Over he went, opened his door, I was across with one leap, slamming the door behind me.

'Buzz, it's damn good of you . . .'

'Nuts,' he grinned. 'This is more fun than I've had all year.' He slung my case on the rack. 'Make yourself at home – and pour us another shot, I reckon we need it.'

'Buzz . . .' I said, feeling a touch safer now, 'we're presuming an awful lot, aren't we? I mean, that guy might have got away for one thing – and then they wouldn't even know he delivered it to the someone on the train.'

'True,' he nodded, taking his glass from me. 'But we're forgetting one other thing aren't we, old son?' With a superior smirk he took another gulp, waiting for my answer, which didn't come. 'We are forgetting the beautiful and treacherous Miami Jo Dell! It is now . . .' he looked at his watch, '. . . something like . . . half an hour since she got your presents and discovered the real package is missing!'

I gaped at him. 'Oh, blimey . . . I'd forgotten all about her!'

'So – where does that leave us, Russell?'

'Right up it. She'll be spitting blood! She's probably telephoning Kokheimer right now with the news that some English bloke copped the packet and still has it – on the train!'

'Correct! So I would say, what with one thing and another, and all things being taken into consideration, that any minute now this car is going to be swarming with all sorts of interested parties, hammering on your door and generally desiring you hand over a certain little package, and all prepared, or so it would seem, to cut off your goolies and use 'em for golf balls if they don't get it!'

Aghast at the prospect, I sank down on the bed, seeing the scene as a real likelihood.

'But . . .' he continued, discerning my need for comfort, 'provided you stay out of sight in here, they're not going to find you. They can't possibly go right through the train tearing every compartment to pieces looking for you, can they?'

'Can't they?'

'Well . . .' he gave a cough. '*But* . . . safe as you may be in here, we still have a problem – because if the two parties concerned are as desperate to get their mits on that package as they appear to be – then they will simply bide their time and grab you when you get off at New York!'

'Eh! Oh, Jezus . . . but . . . how can they be sure I'm still on the train?'

'For the simple reason, old lad, that none of the train staff will have seen you get off! You don't just nip off these trains like you do at home, you know – out onto the platform and away. There aren't any platforms over here! You climb down steps – and there's always a steward on hand to help you. And he'll tell them you didn't get off!'

'Oh, my sainted aunt . . . hell, Buzz, it looks like I've really fucked it up this time.'

'Looks rather like it,' he grinned.

'But I've dragged *you* into it! Look, I'd better get out of here before . . .'

'Siddown!' he commanded, chuckling away. 'Look, I told you, this is more fun than I've had for ages. You've no idea how bloody boring playin' tennis can be. No occupation for a man anyway. Nah, this is great – gets the adrenalin flowin'.'

'Maybe your blood, too,' I said miserably. 'All over the floor!'

'Forget it. Look, you stay put – I'm going to take a peek at that bird's compartment in nine-oh-five-oh . . .'

'Buzz . . .'

'Relax – no one down there knows me. I can just be takin' a stroll, lookin' for a beer. One thing about bein' Aussie over here, they think we're all crazy – an' looking for a beer at two in the morning is normal practice. Pour yourself another coupla fingers and keep staring at that package, maybe somethin' will come to you.'

'It already has,' I said glumly.

'Oh, what's that?'

'I should've chucked it out of the window right away – and forgotten to let go!'

'Nah,' he grinned, then slid open the door, peered out, and was gone.

No sooner had he departed than the train drew into yet another station, probably the fifth or sixth since Miami Jo Dell had sealed me up behind the bed, and before it had stopped I was kneeling at the window peering through a gap in the curtain, seeing a couple of people get off and a dozen or so get on, yet realizing I could see only a small part of the traffic boarding and disembarking along the great length of train.

Time went by, the station cleared, and the train started again. I closed the curtain and sat on the bed, wondering just what sort of mess I'd got myself into, and, more importantly, how I was going to get out of it! Thank heaven for Buzz. I didn't feel so bad with him around. But even with him, how was I going to get off the train at New York without being spotted?

I looked down at the package, cursing the damn thing, realizing it wouldn't do me a bit of good if I threw it away now. If anything, I'd be better off with it. If – or rather when – the two interested parties came looking for it, at least I'd have something to bargain with. Perhaps I could just hand it over and they'd let me go and who the heck was I trying to kid? Just knowing about the packet was probably enough to earn me a cement overcoat and a midnight plunge into the Hudson!

Nah, I told myself, don't be ridiculous. Good God, this wasn't the 1920s, there were laws about these things . . . and police to enforce them. People just couldn't go around dumping other people in rivers when they felt like it. Besides, I was British and they can't *do* things like that to us.

I'd just made up my mind that everything was going to be all right when the door flew open and in shot Buzz and ruined the whole damn thing.

'Blimey!' he gasped, slamming the door behind him, panting like he'd just run up from Miami.

My heart erupted. 'Wha . . . what's the matter?'

'Mate – it's them! In her compartment! . . . two of the toughest-looking bastards you ever laid eyes on! I mean, really *mean*, Russell . . . one guy's only got one ear . . . and the other . . . well, someone musta stitched his face together with baling wire!'

'Oh, Jesus . . .!'

'They were standing there, looking at the compartment when I passed the open door. Man, they looked at me like I was a stink-bug. It's got to be them, Russ . . .'

'Buzz, I will kill myself, right now. I will throw myself off the next viaduct and save everybody a great deal of trouble.'

'Russ . . .'

'Mmmm?'

'I've been thinking . . . I think . . . we ought to open the package.'

I swallowed hard. 'You do? But . . . there's no going back after we do. We can't parcel it up again like . . .'

'I know. But if what we think is in there *is* in there, I reckon we ought to get in touch with the cops right away. I'll get word to the conductor and he can call 'em at the next station. What d'you say? Man, I don't think we ought to mess around with these guys, they look mean enough for anything. God knows what we've got into, but one look at them and I want out. What d'you say we open it?'

I looked down at the package, picked it up and for the nineteenth time weighed it in my hand. Then I made my decision.

'Yes.'

He was at the bed in one stride, opening a penknife with his teeth.

'Please God don't make it a bomb,' I pleaded. 'We're both too young and good looking to die.'

He took the package from me, inspected the binding, then slid the blade under the Sellotape.

Snip.

It parted.

Again . . . snip.

Slowly, with the tenderness of a mother unbandaging a boil, he peeled away the tape . . . and the outer covering of brown paper fell away, revealing . . . another layer of brown paper, also bound with Sellotape.

Snip . . . snip.

That layer of paper fell away, revealing . . . a white cardboard box, bound in more Sellotape.

'Jezus,' he muttered. 'How much more?'

Snip . . . snip. Now all the bindings were gone. Gently he eased the lid from the box, not yet raising it, just making sure it was free. Then, with a grin, he looked up at me.

'Any last bets?'

'My money's on drugs.'

'Huh huh . . . and I say . . .'

He didn't say anything. At that moment there were voices out in the corridor and someone was knocking on my door. Buzz gaped at me, I at him, then, box abandoned on the bed, we were on our feet, ears pressed to the door, listening like we'd never listened before.

'Er, Mister Tobin . . .' called a voice, a gruff gravelly voice, trying awfully hard to be genteel and failing.

Tap . . . tap . . . tap.

'Maybe he's asleep, genl'men, he wus mighty tired when I made up his bed.' That was the quiet gentle voice of the old steward. 'Ah don' really know that I can allow you . . .'

'That's OK, pop, he won't mind. We've got some important news for him. Now, why don't you just run along an' do what you have ta do . . .?'

'Well, now, Ah . . .'

We heard the rustle of paper, like bills being peeled from a wad. 'I'm sure you've gotta nawful lot ta do back there, pop . . .'

The steward gave a chuckle. 'Well, now you come t'mention it . . .'

'Off you go, then.'

A moment passed, allowing the steward to leave, then we heard the door slide open.

'Empty!'

'Fuck!'

'Hey, steward . . .!'

'Yassir?'

The old man came trundling back.

'He's gone!' growled the gruff voice. 'He's not in here . . . no baggage.'

'Not in . . . well, he sho' didn't get off the train, gents.'

'And you're positive this is the compartment you brought him to?' asked a lighter voice, lighter but just as mean.

'Sho' Ah'm pos'tive – number ten . . . car nine-oh-nine-oh.'

'Well, he ain't here now. Tell us again what he looked like . . . give us more detail, pop.'

'Well, now, Ah just don' know as Ah should be givin' out . . .'

Again the rustle of bills. Pop was doing very nicely.

'Height?' the gruff voice demanded.

'Oh . . . 'bout six foot . . . no small fella but a bit on the slim side . . . 'bout a hun'erd and seventy pounds . . .'

'Hair?'

'Kinda brown and kinda long on the collar, like these young fellas wear it.'

'Clothes?'

'Er . . . fawn suit, kinda snappy, with brown stitchin' . . .'

'And he was English, huh?'

'Oh, yassir, no doubt about that.'

'Great, pop . . . anythin' else you remember? Baggage . . . baggage labels . . .?'

'Yep, always check the labels, though Ah don't *read* 'em y'understand – just the surname so's I can check it against the couchette bookin'. He was travelling Sun Time and the surname was Tobin. R. Tobin, yassir . . .'

'Pop, yuh did real great. OK, you can blow.'

'Anytime, gents, anytime.'

Another pause. 'Tobin, huh . . . travellin' Sun Time. Wonder where the punk is now?'

'Maybe he found a lay,' suggested the deep, gravelly voice. 'Maybe he's shacked up somewheres?'

'With his baggage? No, he's layin' low, Charlie.'

'I just don' figure this, Frank . . .'

'Think about it. When Bellamey handed this creep the package he musta told him we were after him – right?'

'Right.'

'So maybe he figured we'd catch Bellamey and get onto him – Right?'

'Right. So maybe he's taken a powder . . . slipped off the train already.'

'Maybe – but I don't think so.'

'Why not?'

'Because I don't think the jerk knows what's in that package, Charlie. He was in the wrong compartment – right?'

'Right.'

'Pop moved him out when that coloured broad arrived on the scene. I reckon she was the pick-up, not the creep. So what happens then?'

Charlie, who didn't sound all that bright, had a think. 'Er . . . she comes here after the package!'

'Right – but somehow I don't think she got it . . .'

'Oh, why not, Frank?'

'Because the creep ain't here, is why. If she'd relieved him of it, he'd still be here. If he's a guy on vacation, would he move outta his compartment after he'd lost the package? No, he would not. He'd go back to sleep wonderin' what it was all about. We know the dame got off the train an hour back, but I gotta feelin' she did not have that package – and, Charlie, I wanna know why.'

'Maybe the creep wouldn't give it up . . . maybe he got suspicious?'

'An' the dame went for reinforcements? Charlie, yuh mighta put your finger on it. OK, supposin' you're right . . . that means the creep *and* the package are still on the train somewheres, which also means . . .'

'He's gotta get off!'

'He's gotta get off . . . so we pick him up in New York. OK, we stay in here, courtesy of the creep . . .'

We heard the door slide closed and for a long while after, Buzz and I remained frozen, staring at one another, then slowly straightened and let out breaths we must have been holding for ten minutes.

'Oh . . . brother!' I gasped. 'Buzz . . . this can't be happening!'

'It's happening,' he assured me.

'No, no . . . it's a nightmare . . . I'm really fast asleep over there in number ten and, Buzz . . . pinch me and . . . ouch!'

'Ssssh! Well, you did ask.'

'Buzz . . . we have got to give them the package – somehow! We'll leave it outside their door, knock, then nip in here quickly. Once they've got it they'll leave me alone . . .'

'Which only leaves the other gang to contend with when we get to New York, hm?'

'I . . .'

'*And* nothing to bargain with.'

I let out a groan. 'Buzz . . . couldn't we . . . cut it in half?

Buzz, how am I going to get off this train! These blokes will be watching out for me like hawks . . . and the other gang . . .'

'Never mind, we'll think of something. Right now I am just bursting with curiosity as to what this fuss is all about. Russ – the box!'

Once again we sat on the bed, staring at the wretched thing, quite hypnotized by it, and by now . . . afraid of it.

'Maybe . . . it's better not to know, Buzz. Maybe it would be better just to wrap the thing up and . . .'

'Eh?' he said, cocking a disbelieving eye at me. 'You mean to say after all this you could just wrap it up without having a look inside?'

I managed a grin.

'Russell,' he said solemnly, 'to the end of your days you'd be driven mad, wondering what was inside this box. Look at it . . . the lid is loose . . . all we have to do is raise it up . . . two or three inches . . . and have a peep inside.'

This time I laughed.

'OK – open the bloody thing! On the count of three – OK?'

'OK.'

He reached out . . . picked up the box . . . got his fingers over the lid. 'Ready.'

'Right . . . one!'

'If it blows up, Russell, our worries are over . . .'

'Two . . .!'

'Just one big bang and peace for everyone . . .'

'THREE . . .!'

'Goodbye, Russ . . . it's been great knowing ya! VOILA!'

With an expansive gesture he swept the lid high . . . peered into the box . . . and gasped, his face crumbling with utter disgust and unmitigated horror. For a long, tortured moment he remained rigid, frozen in terror, then with an anguished cry flung the thing onto the bed, desperately got rid of it, and as it hit the blanket the contents bounced out, leapt in the air – and landed right on my hand.

I bloody near died.

Horror seized me . . . and with a yell they must have heard in the Bronx I leapt off the bed, my skin crawling, nerves screeching, and hit the door with a hell of a thump, for there, sitting on the bed, looking at us with its forty-seven pairs of the most evil glassy green eyes, was the biggest . . . fattest . . . blackest . . .

hairiest . . . most vile . . . despicable . . . sickening *spider* it has ever been my gross misfortune to behold.

'OH! . . . My sainted bloody aunt!' I gasped, stomach heaving and the gall rising in my throat. 'Godallbloodymighty, did you ever see anything li . . .'

But Buzz wasn't listening.

He was stretched out on the floor, eyes closed, mouth open, sleeping like a babe in a dead faint . . . and if it hadn't been for the thought of that dreadful bloody thing crawling all over my unconscious body, I'd have joined him!

FIVE

'Buzz . . . Buzz! Come on, wake up . . .'

'Errruuummmwwwooozzzaaammm . . .'

'Come on, drink this . . .'

'Mm . . .? Waarriissiitt . . .?'

'Water?'

'Eh?'

Then, suddenly remembering, he shot to his feet, knocking the glass all over the place, flattened himself against the wall and stared in horror at the thing on the bed.

'Russ . . . get rid of it! I can't stand them! I hate them . . . loathe them!'

'Me, too, buddy,' I panted. 'Always have, I nearly joined you on the floor. I've aged ten years in the last five minutes. But, Buzz . . .'

'What?'

'I . . . I think it's dead.'

He shot me a glance, a highly disbelieving one. 'Uh?'

'I think it's dead . . . it hasn't moved.'

'Not at all?'

'Not a muscle.'

He relaxed – infinitesimally. Well, at least he let go of my arm. 'You . . . absolutely certain?'

'No . . .' He grabbed my arm again. '. . . But I've got the feeling.'

'Russ . . . make sure, there's a pal.'

'Eh?'

'Give it . . . a poke or something.'

'What with – me finger!'

He shuddered. 'God, no . . . get a pole or something.'

I was daft enough to look round the compartment for a pole!

'How about a newspaper?' he suggested.

'Bit on the short side, isn't it? It would climb up it.'

He shuddered again.

'Ever since I was a kid I've been terrified of those bastards . . .'

'Me, too.'

'We've got some beauts in Aussie – big as your fist – just like that swine.'

'What d'you reckon it is, Buzz – a tarantula?'

'Yeh, it's a tarantula all right – and a big one. Jezus, he must be eight . . . nine inches, toe to toe. Ugh, filthy bloody things . . . hey . . . Russ . . .'

'Mm?'

'He's not movin', is he?'

'No mate.'

'You reckon he *is* dead?'

'I reckon. Look – there aren't any air holes in the box.'

'Do they *need* air? Have they got lungs?'

'Christ knows. I know they've got eight great fat hairy bleedin' legs, though. Just look at the sod. It could snatch a baby out of a pram that thing.'

I left his side and took one extremely tentative step towards the bed, bending down as I did so to peer at the monster, prepared to leap back again if it so much as twitched an eyebrow.

But it didn't. It remained rock-still, or so it seemed from that distance! I took another step . . . and then another, my skin beginning to crawl as I got closer to it and began to see fine details of it . . . its hundreds of beady eyes . . . the hairs on its great fat body and finger-thick legs . . . the . . . THE HAIRS!

'Jesus Christ . . .!'

I fled, crashed into Buzz. 'Whaassaammaarraa?'

'Buzz . . . its hairs . . . they're *moving*!'

'Where . . . where?'

'There . . . there! On its bloody legs! They're waving about!'

Eyes staring like bottle-stoppers, he chanced a lean forward.

'I . . . I can't see them!'

'Go closer.'

'Are you kiddin'!'

'Buzz, that bloody thing is alive!'

'Oh, God. What we gonna do?'

'Do? Kill it – before it gets us! Hit it with something . . . drop my ca . . . your case on it from a great height! *Squash* the bugger!'

'Uh, do you *mind*?'

'Buzz, those things are deadly! If it takes a flying leap off that bed and makes a dash for you, you're a gonner! It'll sink its flamin' great teeth in your legs and in ten minutes it'll be all over.'

'Why *my* leg?'

'Because mine won't be here, mate. I'll be hanging upside down from the light, first move it makes.'

'It's my light, Russell – you take the luggage rack.'

'I don't care – just so long as we have a plan. Then I'll chuck the case at it from up there.'

'Russ . . .'

'Mm?'

'It ain't movin', mate.'

I shook my head. 'No.'

'I wonder . . .'

He bent a little closer, peering at it with a puzzled frown, then looked around the compartment. 'You know what I think . . .?'

'What?'

'Look – just reach over there and switch off the air-conditioning.

'Hm . . .?'

'Go on – switch it off.'

I did so – and heard him chuckle. 'That's it son – it was the draught . . . moving the hairs.'

I had another peer, went closer, and let out a sigh of relief. 'You're right . . . they've stopped. Thank God for that.'

'Well . . . what d'you think about it now?'

'It's certainly not moving.'

'Blow in its face.'

'Eh!'

'Give it a blow – right in the mush.'

I winced at the thought but gave a blow.

'Could you . . . get a bit closer?' he requested, from the safety of the far wall.

I blew again.

'You'll have to get even closer, mate.'

'I will, huh?'

'I reckon it's dead.'

'Then you come and blow closer.'

'Nah, it's dead alright.'

'Maybe it's drugged!'

'What for?'

'*I* don't know.'

'Go on, give it a big one, right up the hooter!'

'I'm fed up with this. Right . . . here we go.' Casting an eye towards the luggage rack, calculating leaping distance. I took a step forward and let the thing have it, then leapt back, awaiting results.

There weren't any.

'Dead!' pronounced Buzz. 'And if it wasn't before, it sure is now with those brandy fumes.'

I gave a nervous laugh and went closer, stomach squirming, until I was right up to it. 'Buzz . . . hand me that magazine.'

He did so, and, ultra-tentatively, I reached out and gave Herbert a shove.

Nothing.

'He's a goner, Buzz. Come and take a look at him.'

We stood over him, Buzz slightly to the rear, and inspected him in detail, appalled and yet fascinated by the terrible size and ugliness of the brute, now aware of a strange fish-shaped pattern on the back section of his chubby body and a wavy one on the front section, beginning to think that perhaps he wasn't so inately ugly after all, just despicable in what he represented – crawling death.

'Why?' Buzz asked suddenly, jerking me from my staring fascination.

'Hm?'

'Why a bleedin' spider? Why's everybody so anxious to get their hands on that flamin' thing? What's so important about it?'

I shrugged. 'Maybe he's very valuable . . . very rare.'

'I wish they all were.'

'I don't know, Buzz, it doesn't seem right somehow – all this fuss over a spider – rare or not.'

He shrugged. 'I don't know . . . people go potty over rare stamps . . . glassware . . . just about everything. I guess everything has a price, even spiders.'

'Mmm . . . well, what are we going to do with him?'

'Put him back in that box for a start.'

'Who is?'

'Mm . . .? Well, I thought . . .'

I laughed at him. 'You know, I never thought I'd see the day when I'd meet somebody who hated them even more than I do. OK – I'll do it. I reckon I owe you my life, anyway, this is the least I can do.'

I made a move towards the spider, lowering my hand from overhead as though I was going to pick it up in my fingers, and Buzz went through the roof.

'Russ . . .! Jeezus, man, you can't . . .!'

'No,' I laughed, 'I bloody can't.' Then I picked up the magazine.

Working it under Herbert. I got him onto the paper, swung him over the box and slid him in. He landed with a klonk.

'Stiff as a board,' I remarked. 'He's been dead some time.'

'Maybe he's stuffed. I suppose he is real – not a model or something?'

'No, I think he's real all right.'

'Wonder where he came from?'

I shrugged. 'Oh, Africa . . . South America . . . Italy. They have 'em all over the place.'

'Lucky old them. Here, get the lid on quick, cover the bugger up.'

I did so, both of us sighing with relief.

'Man, I need a drink,' Buzz announced emphatically. 'And a big sod.'

'Make that six, I'll join you.'

By the time he'd poured the drinks I had the package wrapped again in its brown paper, the ends stuck down with an Elastoplast from his shaving kit. Even now, fully wrapped, I had the greatest difficulty handling the thing, knowing what was inside.

'Cheers,' he said, handing me about nineteen fingers of courage. 'Boy, I need this.'

We both swallowed big gulps, lit cigarettes and sat on the bed, pondering the future, more mystified now than ever.

'Well,' he said nodding at the package, 'I reckon that is very rare and worth a fortune – to somebody.'

'Yes, but who? Obviously to Kokheimer, whoever he is, but who else? Who are those two guys in my compartment?'

He gave a wry laugh. 'I'd almost forgotten about them. Well, my guess is that that Bellamey fella pinched this spider from them to give it to Kokheimer who sent the coloured bird down to Miami to collect it.'

I nodded. 'Looks like it. But what do we do with it?'

'Christ knows. I'd like to flush it down the loo.'

'You . . . reckon it's worth a pile of money, then?'

He grinned. 'Thinking about a reward, Tobin?'

'Of course. I'm just broke.'

'We may get rewarded in currency we won't take to too happily – like a lump on the head.'

'I've covered that possibility. Bit of a quandary, really.'

'Well . . .' he said, swinging his feet onto the bed and settling back, 'I'm a firm believer in the old axiom "When in doubt – do nowt". I reckon we ought to just hold on to it and see what happens. If in a few days we're out of the woods, then we send the thing to the cops, anonymously, and . . .' he gave a vile chuckle, 'boy, I sure would love to see their faces when they open the box!'

'And then what?' I asked him.

He gave a shrug. 'Go on our merry ways. How long are you staying in New York?'

'Well, I'm scheduled for six days but the way things are going I feel inclined to cut my losses and head for home.'

'Six,' he was nodding. 'Well, I've got a four-day stopover, then I head for Canada. There's an indoor tournament in Victoria, on the west coast, starting the day after Boxing Day. Hey, that's great. Do you know New York?'

'Not at all, never been there.'

'Wonderful city. We could have some fun, Russ. I'm sure I could fix you up with a playmate.'

'You could?' I enthused, instantly forgetting our current problems.

'Sure. I've got a bird up there I've already arranged to see. I reckon she could fix you up with a pal without any trouble. We could have some great fun together.'

'Wonderful. But how come you're so sure about her being able to fix me up with a pal?'

He grinned. 'Because there are twenty-two of them working in the same place – and they're all terrific!'

'Yes? What sort of place is it?'

'A restaurant. They're waitresses, but, boy, you should see them!'

'I can't wait.'

'Well, mate . . . how about a bit of shuteye. I'm bushed.'

'Me, too.' I looked at my watch. It was almost three.

'We'll sleep head an' tail,' he said. 'Here, grab a pillow.'

We stretched out on the bed, Buzz put the light out and we began to settle down. I really was very tired. I allowed my thoughts to drift, disbelieving yet again what was happening to me and yet, remembering the crazy things that had happened to me in Nassau with Delphinia . . . and the ravishing Malinda . . . I reckoned this present predicament was not that much worse. I mean – how much worse can it get than being shot at?

Then a thought struck me. 'Buzz . . .'

'Mmmmm?'

'One thing we never discussed – how the heck I'm going to get off this train at New York.'

He gave a sleepy chuckle. 'Don' worry 'bout that, buddy . . . I've got an idea.'

'You have?'

'Sure.'

'What is it?'

'I don' think I'd better tell you . . . you'll find out.'

'Hey, Buzz . . .'

'Go to sleep . . . you're gonna need all your strength when we hit New York.'

'Eh? What for?'

He gave a swinish chuckle. 'For running.'

SIX

I *was* running – for my life! Chased by One-Ear and Stitch-Face down a long, dark, creepy alley festooned with cobwebs and alive with dirty great spiders. Suddenly – a voice called from a darkened doorway. 'Russ! Quick – in here!' I came to a halt and peered in. It was Evie! She was beckoning to me. I ran towards her, arms outstretched . . . 'Evie . . .!' but as I reached her she changed into a monster tarantula with eight-hundred glass green eyes and forty hairy legs. And I ran into the lot. Splodge!

I fought, yelled, kicked and punched and even spat in one of its eyes but all to no avail . . . then, as a final, desperate gesture I gave it a swift kick in the crutch. With a scream of agony the thing dropped me, and then I was falling . . . falling . . . hurtling through space . . . to land with a terrible . . .

THUMP!

I fell off the bed.

'Russ . . .! Whaassaammaattaa?'

I sat up and gaped at Buzz who was also sitting gaping at me, with the vacant, bemused expression of the rudely awakened.

'I fell out of bed,' I grinned.

'I'm glad you did,' he gasped. 'I was having the most horrible bloody nightmare . . .'

'About spiders?'

'How did you know?'

I glanced at the curtain, seeing daylight through the crack, and checked the time. 'Hey, it's lunch time, half-past twelve. Oh . . . that's a thought.'

'What is?'

'How do I eat?'

'Mmm . . . well, no sweat – I go to the diner for lunch and bring something back. I'll see what I can smuggle out.'

He got washed, shaved and dressed, then, looking very sharp in a navy blazer and grey slacks, ventured to the door for a listen.

'Seems all quiet.'

He opened it a crack and peered out.

'Their door's shut. OK – keep mum and don't answer the door until you hear three short knocks and one long. And keep it bolted in case the steward wants in to make up the bed or something.'

'Check. Three longs, one short.'

'Three shorts, one long, you nut. Jeezus . . .!'

With a grin he slipped through the door and I fastened the bolt.

While he was away I washed, shaved and spruced myself up with a clean shirt and a change of clothes and had just finished when I heard activity out in the corridor. Thinking it might be Buzz returning I went to the door in readiness for opening it, then realized it was not Buzz. It was them! Right outside the door!'

'Listen, Frank,' gravelled Charlie, 'you certain he's still on this train?'

'He's on it.'

'He coulda gotten off during the night.'

'Not a chance. Pop passed the word – every attendant on the train has got his eyes peeled. For the sorta money we're payin' he wouldn'ta got past them.'

'But we've checked the whole train, Frank.'

'So he's holed up somewhere's . . . maybe he is with a dame. Relax, Charlie, we'll get him.'

I heard their door slide open and them enter the compartment, but the door didn't close again. And as the conversation continued, more faintly but still audible since they were still only about six feet away from me, the picture of what was going on began to emerge a little clearer. Not much, but a little.

It was no good, though – I just had to take a look at these guys. It was maddening to hear them and not know what they looked like. Besides, if I was going to get bumped off, I wanted to know who was going to do the bumping, so's I could be elsewhere when the time came! So . . . very, very quietly I slid back the bolt, eased the door open a hair's breadth and stuck my eye to it.

Oh, God, I was sorry I did. They looked extremely tough and very nasty. As Buzz had already warned me, one guy had only one ear and the other had a flattened nose and a terrible scar down his left cheek. One-Ear, sitting on the left, on the seat, was dressed in a dark blue pin-stripe suit, white shirt and blue bow-tie, and Scar-Face, perched opposite him on the covered toilet, was wearing a grey lightweight suit and a red polo-necked sweater. One-Ear was a slim, dark-haired, rat-faced fink, and, in extreme contrast, Scar-Face was built like a bull, shoulders as wide as the compartment, and a jutting Desperate Dan jaw.

As I watched, mortified, One-Ear reached in his pocket for a pack of Luckies, shook one out and snapped a light to it with a gold lighter, then exhaled the smoke into Scar-Face's scar-face.

Scar-Face, leaning forward, gave a cough and said, 'Frank . . . you reckon Mistophoulus will be pleased I took out Bellamey?'

One-eared Frank gave a sneer that would've frozen mercury. 'Charlie . . . Mistophoulus is gonna be real delighted you took out Bellamey. What Mistophoulus is not gonna be delighted about is that you took out Bellamey after he got rid of the package . . .!'

Charlie stopped grinning. 'Oh.'

'And unless we find that punk Tobin who has *got* the package and relieve him of it, Mistophoulus is not only gonna be un-delighted with us, he is gonna be downright annoyed! So much so, Charlie, that we may as well start lookin' for a hole ta crawl into, because we will not be going back to Africa!'

'Oh. Yeah.'

Africa! Aye aye – bit of a clue there!

'But . . .' protested Charles, 'at least we stopped the leak, Frank.'

Frank sneered again, a very nasty man, this. 'Charlie, who're you tryin' to impress, hm? Mistophoulus stopped the leak himself in Cape Town when he took out Kresge! Bellamey was a cinch! It's the guy *after* Bellamey that Mistophoulus needs to know! An' it looks now like we're never going to find . . .'

Frank broke off and threw a hard look straight at me! I froze . . . died! How could he have known – he couldn't possibly see or hear me! I was immobile, a statue . . . actually what I was was a quivering wreck as I watched him get up from his seat and walk straight towards me.

Well, this was it. I was a goner . . . finished. Of course I'd hand over the spider but I could tell from his face it wouldn't make a bit of difference. He'd take me out like they took Bellamey out and laugh while he was doing it. I shut my eyes and waited. Any second now the door would fly out of my hand, there'd be a cry of discovery followed by a hard thump in the ear . . .

But no! The door wasn't flying out of my hand! I opened my eyes. There was One-Ear Frank, standing not three feet in front of me in his own doorway, so close I could see he had a cluster of hairs sprouting from the end of his nose, staring suspiciously at something down the corridor. And that something was . . . Buzz!

He hove-to from the right, caught sight of Frank and visibly faltered. I could detect his problem – how was he going to open the door with Frank standing there?

I'll give old Buzz one thing, by golly, he has terrific presence of mind in emergencies. Me – I'd have fumbled it, would have stood routed in my tracks, nonplussed, trying to decide what to do. But not Buzz. Maybe being a pro tennis player had sharpened him up for quick decisions, I don't know, but quick as a wink he found the answer, came quickly to his own doorway, got his hand on the door, paused, then turned on Frank with a big grin, fumbling for his fags.

'Excuse me . . . could you oblige me with a light? Oh . . . huh! . . . looks like I've forgotten me fags, too. I don't suppose you could . . .?'

Frank gave him a mean-lipped sneer, pushed himself off the door frame and slammed the door in his face.

Buzz was in like a shot, closing the door behind him. 'Phew! That was a close one!'

'Buzz . . . you were terrific! Jeez, I'd have turned to stone, seeing him standing there.'

'Didn't learn much from the old man,' he grinned, 'he was rarely home, but I learned one thing – when in doubt, brazen it out. You can get away with murder.'

'Well you were marvellous . . .'

'I saw those two in the diner, dissecting every bloke that came in. They really want you, son.'

'Don't I know it. I heard them come back, obviously from the diner, and couldn't resist a look at them. So I peered through the crack and heard some very interesting things.'

'What sort of things?'

'Well, for one – they've chased that damn spider all the way from Africa!'

'Africa! Hell . . . here, hang on, you'd better get tucked into this while you're talking, it's disintegrating fast.'

He stuck his hand in his pocket and with an expression of undiluted disenchantment drew out a soggy paper napkin.

'Oh, fuck, the gravy's come through.'

'Yerk! What is it?'

'It *was* quite a respectable hot beef sandwich half an hour ago. I ordered beef and made it down on my knee. I think I left too much gravy on it.'

'Yes, well . . . it's the thought that counts . . .'

'Yeh.' He hurled the soggy mess into the garbage can, wiped his hands on a towel, dived into his inside pocket and produced a banana. 'Any good?'

'Fantastic.'

'Eat hearty. Go on, what's all this about Africa?'

'Well, the one with a face like a burst clog – he's Charlie – and a proper one by the sound of things . . . not too much upstairs, Charlie, but a stink of a lot around the biceps . . .'

'I noticed. Looks a touch lethal, does Charlie.'

'Not only looks but *is*, Buzz. That bugger has done in Bellamey – the guy who slipped me the package!'

'What . . . you mean *killed* him?'

'Well, I don't know for sure. They kept using the expression "took out" and I've always thought that meant knocked off . . . killed.'

'They . . . they killed Bellamey . . . for that *spider*?'

'It certainly sounded like it.'

'Jeezus, mate, what have we got *into*!?'

'Buzz, I hate to think. Anyway, it's got something to do with Africa and a guy named Mis . . . hang on . . . Mistophoulus. Charlie asked Frank did he think Mistophoulus would be pleased that he'd "taken out" Bellamey and Frank told him he'd be bloody livid with him taking out Bellamey *before* they got their hands on the package – and that they daren't go back to Africa without it! Then Charlie said something like "well, at least we've stopped the leak" and Frank poo pooed that one, saying that Mistophoulus himself had stopped the leak back in Cape Town – by "taking out" a bloke named Kresge! And then he said that Bellamey was a cinch – it was the guy *after* Bellamey that Mistophoulus needed to know and that it looked now as if they were never going to find him! So what d'you think of that little lot?'

'Mmm.' Pulling his lip, Buzz sat on the bed and lit a fag. 'OK . . . so this guy Kresge was in cahoots with Bellamey – right?'

'Looks like it.'

'So what ever Kresge was up to, this Mistophoulus character discovered it in Cape Town and gave Kresge the chop . . . but . . . by that time this package was on its way to Bellamey, who was presumably based in Miami – check?'

'Check. So Mistophoulus sends these two bulls after the package, knowing from Kresge – whose arms he may have ripped off in order to get the information – that it was coming to Bellamey. Poor old Bellamey manages to deliver it to the train . . . then these two catch him . . .'

'And make him talk by ripping his arms off. But – what can he tell them – only that his instructions were to deliver the package to a character named "Miami" in compartment ten, car nine-oh-five-oh . . . right?'

'Right. So they do in old Bellamey . . . heck, Buzz, d'you really think they *did* knock him off . . .?'

He shrugged. 'People *do* knock people off, Russ – take a look in yesterday's paper, there.'

'Yeh . . . blimey . . . anyway . . . God, you just can't believe it when it happens so close to you, can you? I mean . . . it's a bit hard to believe that those two blokes over there actually murdered somebody a few hours ago . . .'

'And maybe planning to murder another one in a few more hours.'

'Eh? Hey, Buzz . . .'

'But let us ignore that gruesome possibility for a moment and go on with our deduction. So after Bellamey tells them that his pick-up contact is a "Miami" in compartment ten, they drive like hell and board the train, expecting to find . . .'

'But don't find – anything. So where does that leave them?'

'Stupendously up it. They haven't got the package and they haven't got Miami, the contact with the next guy up the line who we know is . . .'

'Kokheimer!'

'Kokheimer. Now they don't *know* it's Kokheimer – Frank said they lost the trail, but they *do* know about the bird, Miami Jo Dell, and they know she got off the train without the package. So therefore they know that dumb bloke named Tobin who accidentally intercepted the package not only *has* it but is unwittingly their link with the next bloke down the line . . .'

'How d'you figure that, Buzz?'

'Because of Jo Dell! They know she's not going to take this lying down and will have organized a little reception committee for you at Penn Station! All they've got to do is wait for you to be picked up there and they've picked up the next contact! So, all in all, son, it looks like you're a very important person right now . . . everybody just *dyin'* to make your acquaintance and relieve you of a certain little package – and anything they happen to find dangling, by the sound of things.'

'Oh, heck . . .' I gave a sigh. 'Buzz . . . one thing really puzzles me – why all this hooha over a flamin' spider? It must be very valuable.'

'Yeh,' he mused, fingering the packet, 'it must. Well, we've got to get a plan together – decide what to do with it. Where are you staying in New York?'

'The New Central Hotel – West 44th Street.'

'Times Square. It's a good central position. OK, I'll book in there, too. Let's get settled in, then we can think more clearly with these goons off our backs, whadya say?'

'I say fine – only one problem.'

'What's that?'

'How am I going to get from Penn Station to the hotel with two gangs after me?'

He grinned evilly. 'Have no fear – Malone is here. By the time I'm finished with you, you won't even recognize yourself. Do you play cards?'

'Hm . . .? Well, sure . . . why?'

'We've got nine hours yet. If we don't play something – by Penn Station we'll be stir crazy. How about rummy?'

'Yes, fine . . .'

He got the cards out of his grip, shuffled them and plonked the deck down in front of me. 'Cut for deal.'

We did . . . and as he looked at the card I'd cut he first frowned then gave a dirty grin.

'What's the matter?' I asked him.

'That . . .' he said, nodding at the card. 'I sure hope it's no omen, for your sake.'

'Mm . . .? Why . . . what . . .'

'It's the Queen of Spades.'

'Yes . . . well . . .?'

'Don't you know? It's the Card of Death, cock. Your deal.'

SEVEN

At nine o'clock, right on time, we drew into Washington DC, witnessing the dramatic spectacle of the White House illuminated by spotlights.

Half an hour later we slid into Baltimore . . . then on to Philadelphia, reaching it by ten forty-five. We were now getting very close.

'Just over an hour,' announced Buzz, checking his watch. 'We should be in New York right on midnight. Time we were getting ready.'

With this sudden realization my heart started thumping again, and little did I suspect then that it would not stop thumping (for one reason or another!) for the next two days!

'OK,' he said, packing away the cards we had long since

abandoned in favour of a snooze then more talk. He stood up and took his case down from the rack. 'They will all be lookin' for a young fella with light-brown hair, blue eyes, dressed in a suit and carrying a grey case and tartan grip – right? Pop will have supplied the information.'

'Unfortunately – yes, quite correct.'

'Right . . . for a start, get your shirt and trousers off.'

While I stripped, he opened his case and began pulling things out, pausing to ponder the appropriateness of certain articles before rejecting them or handing them to me.

'OK, that ought to do it. Get dressed in them and let's see how you look.'

'Buzz,' I laughed, 'you must be joking! It'll be midnight . . .!'

'Never mind – we'll cover it.'

'I shrugged. 'OK, if you say so . . .'

It took me fifteen minutes to climb into the clobber, Buzz inspecting the transformation every step of the way, shaking his head or grunting approval as the disguise was assembled. Finally he stood back, grinning happily.

'Terrific! Even your own mother wouldn't recognize you. How d'you feel?'

'Like a right cunt, I can tell you. Hell, Buzz, I'll never get away with it . . .!'

'Balls . . . of course you will. New York is a city of nutters. It'll be me who looks weird, dressed in a suit. Right . . . just a couple of extra touches and . . . voila! Well, what d'you think?'

He swung the cupboard open, presenting me with a full-length mirror and an image that doubled me over with laughter.

I looked a right one, I can tell you – dressed in white tennis shorts, two sweaters (one on and the other draped round my shoulders, both seven sizes too big!), ankle socks, tennis shoes (a mere three sizes too big), a white peaked sunshade, so huge it was almost resting on my shoulders, and sunglasses – oh, and three tennis racquets tucked under me arm.

'Bloody hell, Buzz . . . if the gangs don't get me, the cops are sure to.'

'Knickers,' he laughed, killing himself at my expense. 'They're used to fruitcakes walkin' around all dressed up. They'll think it's a publicity stunt.'

'What for – the nut house? Well, if you think so . . .'

'Look – all we need to do is fool them long enough to get out of the station and into a taxi, then we're home and dry.

When they realize they've lost you, and the package, Frank and Charlie will commit suicide in the station concourse . . . and the Jo Dell outfit will assume you got off the train somewhere down the line. Then, old son, we can settle down and have some fun.'

I nodded. 'Yes, you're right, Buzz. Once we're in the city . . .'

'Sure. Now your luggage. The grip they'll be looking for is already gone, courtesy of Jo Dell, and your case . . .'

'How in heck are we going to lose that?'

'Like this . . .'

He tipped everything out of his own case, then pulled my case off the rack and placed it inside his case, then he opened my case and stuffed all his gear into it, finishing off with my suit and all the clobber lying around, including the package.

'There', he grinned. 'Case solved.'

'Buzz, you're brilliant.'

'Oh ho, he's not just a big dick and an ace serve, you know.'

Another couple of minutes and there wasn't a trace of the old Tobin to be seen – no clothing, no luggage, not even a body.

'How about that?' he grinned triumphantly. 'And you've got somebody to carry your bags into the bargain.'

'Buzz, it's terrific. I'll never be able to pay you back.'

'I'll think of something,' he said, drawing back the curtain and peering out. 'Getting mighty close. Just another few minutes.'

He released the curtain and gave me a final inspection, chuckling with fresh laughter. 'Man, do you look something. I'd give anything to see their faces at Wimbledon if you walked out on Centre Court like that. I reckon you'd win, too. Your opponent wouldn't be able to serve for laughing.'

'Thanks a bundle.'

'OK – now, it's a dead cert that Frank and Charlie are going to make a run for the barrier as soon as we get in – so we ought to be in the thick of the crowd as we go through it. Just act naturally . . . ha! . . . be yacking to me about the Miami game, make like I'm your manager or something, then we make a bee line for a taxi, OK?'

'Yes,' I said, 'but . . .'

'NEW YORK . . . TEN MINUTES! PENN STATION . . . TEN MINUTES!' a steward bawled along the corridor, triggering off a terrible jangle of nerves all over me.

'Oh, Gawd . . .'

'Ssssh!' Buzz held up his hand and cocked an ear towards the door, then moved to it and listened.

I joined him, hearing a rumble of voices from compartment ten, now a movement in the corridor as they vacated the compartment and moved off the left.

'Like you said,' I said, 'they're wasting no time.'

'No. I reckon they'll walk right through the train to the front end so's to be close to the barrier when the train stops – in case you have the same idea.'

Soon – the clatter of wheels across a multitude of points and the train slowed to a crawl. Buzz crossed to the window and looked through the curtain. 'We're here, buddy . . . and guess what?'

'You can see sixteen blokes waiting for me with sub-machine guns?'

'No,' he laughed. 'It's snowing!'

'Ha!'

'Comin' down hard. Nice that – New York in the snow. Real Christmassie . . .'

'Christmas! Blimey, I'd forgotten all about it.'

'Great place at Christmas, New York. Wait till you see the shops on Fifth Avenue . . .'

'I should live so long.'

'Ah, you'll be all right . . . come on, we're in! Let's get lost in the crowd.'

'Looking like this?'

He picked up the now very heavy suitcase, put it down by the door, slid the door open an inch, peered out, turned for a final check on the compartment, had a last smirk at me, then fully opened the door.

'Come on, let's go.'

'Know any good prayers?'

'Ah well,' he said, heaving the case out into the corridor, 'we've all gotta go sometime, and what better place than in New York at Christmas? The blood'll look *so* colourful against the snow.'

'Fun-nee!'

* * *

I started getting strange looks, and smart-ass remarks even before we got off the train.

'Hey, Alice, did yuh *see* that guy?'

'The wingding in the fancy dress? Sure. If it wasn't for his ears, that sunshade would be round his waist! Yuh sure see some nuts around these days.'

Buzz turned and grinned, then paid for it immediately as the case caught a compartment doorway and shot back, cracking him on the shin.

'Ooo . . . fuck!'

'Serves you right,' I laughed. 'It's wicked to mock the afflicted.'

We reached the external door and went down the steps, at the bottom of which old Pop, the talkative steward stood in attendance.

He smiled benignly at Buzz. 'Hope yuh had a good journey, sah . . .' then almost swallowed his flashing teeth as he clapped eyes on me. He gaped, perplexed, wondering where in hell I'd got on. But I didn't give him time to think about it. I was past him with barely a nod and began addressing Buzz volubly in Spanish.

He did a double-take and gaped. 'Huh?'

'Just a thought,' I muttered. 'If I'm rattling away in Spanish as we go through the barrier . . .'

'Yeh! Great idea. Just so long as you don't expect an answer.'

'Just keep saying "si . . . si", I'll do the rest.'

'All right. Hey, where did you learn Spanish, anyway?'

'Majorca. I was a courier there, too.'

He grinned. 'No kiddin'. You've been around a bit yourself, son.'

'A bit. I never seem to get any smarter, though.'

'Hey . . .' he said, suddenly very serious. 'Up ahead . . . as we thought – right by the barrier.'

My stomach somersaulted. 'Oh, blimey . . .'

'Now, keep calm . . . and do what you said, start yacking at me in Spanish, like you were mad at a line-judge's decision or something . . .'

With my heart thumping holes in my ribs we drew close to the barrier, surrounded by a sizeable crowd, all, it seemed, looking straight at me. We'd overdone it, I was sure . . . I mean, the outfit really was ludicrous. It mightn't have been so bad if the clothes had fit me, but with the over-size shoes slapping the ground like a clown's, and the sweater hanging on me like a pup-tent, I was certain Frank and Charlie would see through the disguise immediately.

Well, by God, they deserved to because they were certainly staring at me hard enough, not only me but every male in the crowd, stripping them down, taking them apart, giving them a second go as they passed through the barrier.

Then, suddenly, old Pop was there, sidling up to them, asking them a question, getting an irritable shake of the head from Frank. And *then,* by God, Pop turned and faced the crowd, joining the search, and looked straight at me!

I lowered my face, muttered to Buzz, 'That bloody steward's on to me, Buzz, I'm sure! Did you see him talking to Frank?'

'Yeh,' he muttered back, side-mouthed. 'He's lookin' right at you, now.'

'Oh, Christ. Is he . . . saying anything to the others?'

'No – just staring at you like you were his long lost son.'

'Buzz . . . what are we going to do if they rumble me?'

'Run for the nearest cop . . . there are always some in the concourse upstairs.'

'Upstairs!'

'Well, up-escalator, to be precise. We have to ride up to the concourse to get out to the street.'

'Oh, hell . . .'

All this time we were shuffling forward, getting closer to Frank and Charlie.

'Aye aye,' Buzz murmured worriedly.

'What? No, don't tell me.'

'The steward's slipping a word to Frank – about you.'

'Oh, Jeezus . . .'

'He's shaking his head . . . probably telling Frank he can't remember you gettin' on the train . . . Russ . . .'

'Y . . . yes?'

'Right now is the time to give the performance of your life. Remember what I told you about my dad – when in doubt – brazen it out. You've got to create a scene, make a bloody great noise, put them off just long enough to get us upstairs and into a cab . . . all right?'

I gulped. 'I'll . . . try.'

'You'd better,' he said earnestly, 'because Frank and Charlie are beginning to take a very great interest in you . . . in fact, to the exclusion of all other men . . . aye, aye – they're separating! Charlie's going through the barrier . . .!'

'Oh . . .'

'Right . . . here's your start! You're not only a lousy tennis player, Tobin, you're also as blind as a bleedin' bat! That second serve was out by a foot and a half and if you had as much guts as you have gall, you'd admit it like a man and confess you lost to a much better player . . .!'

I rounded on him, gasping at the insult. '*Oh, no es verdad*?'

'*Si . . . si!*' he rapped back.

Then I let him have it – in Spanish – and began waving one of the racquets around as though I was going to clonk him one.

'Well, maybe *you're* as blind as that bloody old fool of a judge – except, that is, when you're collecting ten per cent of my earnings! *That* you can see clearly enough, you two-faced, back-biting bastard . . .! You're a leach, Malone! A parasite! You're a bloody awful manager and as far as I'm concerned the only useful thing you do is carry my luggage . . .!'

The crowd parted as though by magic. Those in front of us whirled, stared at this maniac with the flashing racquet and got the hell out of it. Buzz barged ahead, muttering ferociously, his face flushed and grim, and I charged right after him, still ranting, 'OK – you're finished, Malone! Go find yourself another player to screw! *Good* managers come ten a penny, your kind – fifty.'

With the cheek of the devil he made no attempt to avoid Charlie but made straight for him, forcing him to back out of the way. Charlie frowned, perplexed, and threw bemused, enquiring glances at Frank who was now behind us. And then, to my enormous relief, I saw Charlie shrug and start back towards the barrier, leaving our path clear all the way to the escalator.

Still keeping up my infuriated harassment, I followed Buzz onto the moving stairs, shouting up after him, 'If I were you, Malone, I'd make an appointment with an eye-specialist first thing tomorrow and get your eyes fixed . . .!'

And at that moment my sun-shield slipped down over my eyes and I fell sprawling up the escalator.

'Perhaps you should join him, senor,' laughed a voice in Spanish behind me.

I scrambled up and turned round, discovering a grinning priest.

At the top I flip-flopped off the escalator and hurried after

Buzz who was going like the clappers, playing his part to perfection, then I flapped up a flight of stairs to the street exit, aware of eight million amazed eyes following me all the way.

Out through the huge glass doors and over to a taxi rank, gasping as the icy blast whipped up me shorts and got to work on everything it touched.

'Jeezus . . .!'

Buzz plonked the case on the pavement and beckoned a cab. The driver got out, saw me, gave a popeyed start and looked as though he was going to climb back in again.

'The New Century Hotel,' demanded Buzz. 'It's on West 44th.'

'Er . . . both of you?' frowned the driver, a little ferret-faced bloke with a big nose.

'Yes,' answered Buzz.

'You're sure he don't want Forest Hills?'

'Nope,' grinned Buzz. 'He lost his luggage in Miami – he's got nothing to change into.'

The driver shrugged. 'Well, one thing . . . if this snow keeps up he can always strap them racquets to his feet! OK – in yuh get.'

We climbed into the cab, searching the station entrance for signs of pursuit, then, as the driver pulled away, we exchanged great sighs of relief and collapsed.

Buzz got out his fags and I took one with a shaking hand. 'God, that was close, Buzz. They were on to me, I'm sure. That steward gave them the tip, sure as eggs.'

'You were terrific,' he grinned. 'You should have seen yourself. You even frightened me! What in heck were you saying to me?'

'That you were a no-good, double-crossing, ten per cent thieving bastard.'

'Well, it certainly worked. Nobody followed us out of the station, I'm certain. You didn't see any sign of Miami Jo Dell, I gather?'

'Not a glimpse – though she could easily have been there in the crowd. Still, if Frank and Charlie didn't recognize me at that range, I'm sure she wouldn't.' I heaved a sigh. 'Boy, I was scared . . . still, I think we're in the clear, Buzz.'

He nodded. 'Should be OK from here on . . .'

'You fellas just come up from Miami, huh,' said the driver, having to shout a bit because of the bullet-proof perspex panel separating us from him, his voice entering the rear compartment through the pay hole. 'Kinda hot down there, huh? Me, I can't stand the heat, brings me out in a rash.'

A curious statement since the temperature in the cab must have been nudging four hundred Fahrenheit.

'Evil city, Miami,' he continued. 'Hear they pinch a lotta baggage down there. You guys are well out of such a criminal environment, up here in nice, clean, law-abidin' New York.' He chortled at the joke and shot through a red light, nearly taking out four pedestrians who had dared to cross on a green.

'Your foist visit to New York?' he enquired.

'It is for me,' I told him.

'Aw, you'll love it. Great little city at Christmas time. Take a bus along the avenues and feast yuh eyes on the lights. Terrific sight. Hey, maybe you'd like a little flip round now, huh?'

'Er, no, thanks,' said Buzz. 'We're anxious to get to the hotel.'

'OK wid me. Never let it be said that Honest Jake Lean ever conned a tourist into anythin'. That I don't believe in. A guy's gotta sleep wid his conscience, ain't he? An' I sure couldn't sleep wid mine knowing' I'd taken an innocent tourist for a ride . . . if yuh get my meanin'.'

Moments later, as we turned into West 44th Street, Honest Jake reached out and pulled down the meter flag, then continued slowly until we reached the hotel.

'There yuh go, fellas, safe an' sound. I'll get ya bag.'

He got out and went to the rear of the cab. As I opened my door, Buzz gave me a nudge. 'Watch this.'

'Mm?'

'Go on, out you get.'

Jake came forward and dumped the case at our feet. 'Well, have a nice vacation, fellas – make the most of your foist stay in our great city.'

'How much do we owe you, Jake?' asked Buzz.

'Well, heck, as this is your foist visit, I'd like ta start yuh off wid a good impression – so we'll make it just five dollars an' skip the tip, how's that suit yuh?'

'Well, that's very kind, Jake,' said Buzz, 'thanks very much.'

He slipped Jake a folded bill, picked up the case and turned to enter the hotel.

'Hey . . .!' It was Jake. 'Hey, mac, I'm afraid yuh made a mistake – this is only two dollars!'

Buzz stopped and turned. 'Not our mistake, Jake – yours.

I didn't say I hadn't been here before . . . an' I had that meter trick pulled on me by another crooked bastard, two years ago. We owed you one dollar ninety-five when you pulled the flag at the end of the street. I reckon two covers it.'

'You . . . goddam punk . . .'

Buzz let the case drop and Jake was off, hurling more abuse as he slammed the cab door and shredded the gears into first.

Laughing at the screech of tyres and the ignominy of Jake's departure, Buzz once more picked up the case and we entered the hotel.

'Honest Jake Lean,' he chuckled. 'Bloody crook.'

'Buzz, what would I do without you? I'd have paid him five and given him a tip.'

'We've all got to learn sometime, cock. Three days in this town and you can cheerfully face anythin' the rest of the world throws at you.'

We entered the foyer, a vast room dotted with couches and potted palms and once again I became the centre of popeyed attention for a hundred curious eyes. I was beginning to feel I'd got two heads or a trailing tail.

We crossed to the desk, encountering more amazed stares, including one from the receptionist who bit the end clean off his pencil.

'Yeah?'

'Er . . . my name is Tobin,' I told him. 'I'm booked in with Sun Time. I've just arrived from Miami.'

He covered me from head to toe, mouth open. 'You forget somethin', mister?'

'No, I always dress like this. You never know when a game crops up.'

Buzz gave a snort. 'My name's Malone,' he laughed. 'I'd like a room, too.'

The clerk shook his head. 'No chance. It's Christmas. Everybody makes New York at Christmas. You'll be lucky to get one this side of Westchester.'

'Oh, blimey . . .'

'Look,' I said, 'how about putting an extra bed in my room?'

'No need. There's one in there already, you've got a double. We don't do singles.'

'Well, fine . . .'

He nodded at Buzz. 'You got baggage?'

Buzz looked down at the case. 'This is mine.'

The clerk transferred to me. 'How 'bout you?'

'It's mine, too.'

'Cosy. Sign the register.'

He collected the key and threw it on the desk. '402 – real handy for the elevator.'

Buzz picked up the case and we headed across to the lift, every eye in the place following us. When we got there, he pressed the ascend button, and as we stood waiting for the car he said in a loud voice, for the benefit of the gawpers, 'Well, we made it, kid. By tomorrow every cop in the State will be lookin' for a goose-pimpled tennis player. Sure was a great idea of yours ta hit the Chase National dressed like that. Gee, this case is gettin' heavy. A million bucks sure weighs heavier than I thought it would . . .'

'Buzz, you nutter . . .!'

'Here's the car, now, kid. Let's go and divide the loot.'

The doors opened and we got in, Buzz killing himself laughing as we rose creakily to the fourth floor. 'You should've seen their faces! Yours was quite something, too!'

The elevator gave a cough and stopped. The doors opened and there was our room – right opposite.

'Like the man said,' said Buzz, 'real handy. We'll be lucky if we get a wink all night.'

'Oh, you plan on sleeping then?'

'No,' he grinned.

I opened the door of 402 and walked in – into a small vestibule, the bathroom door on the right, then through a second door and into the bedroom.

'Mmm,' went Buzz, looking round. 'Sun Time are hardly what you'd call the last of the big spenders. Still . . .' he thumped a bed and winced, pretending he'd sprained his wrist, then slung the case onto the bed and unlocked it.

'Right – a quick sluice, then down to the business at hand.'

'Which is?' I said, stifling a yawn.

He looked up, shocked. 'Why – the girls!'

'Now?' I looked at my watch. 'It's half-past midnight!'

He shrugged. 'So?'

'Well . . . it's too late to do anything tonight, surely mate? I mean . . . they're probably in bed by now.'

'Not these birds,' he grinned. 'They don't finish work until three.'

'Three!'

'Ho! This is a swingin' town, Russell. Everything goes on right around the clock.'

'Well, if you say so . . .'

'Don't you feel like a night out on the town?'

'Do I!' I grinned.

'Attaboy – OK, get the heck out of that ridiculous outfit and into a suit . . .'

'Aw . . . do I have to change?'

Fifteen minutes later, shaved, showered and smelling like a rose, I emerged from the bathroom to find him reaching a number.

'Hello . . . could I speak to Miss Fifi Labouche, please . . .?'

'Wey hey!' I laughed.

'. . . yes, I know it's against the rules, but this is a matter of life and death, miss. This is her doctor, reporting on the X-rays . . .'

'Ooh, what a whopper!'

Hand over the mouthpiece, he grinned at me. 'They're a mite touchy about personal calls, but . . . well, hell, this is a matter of life and death! Hello . . .? Hello, Fifi! Baby, it's me – Buzz the Ball Boy! Mm . . .? Yeh, I know I fibbed, but I just had to speak to you . . . mmm . . .? . . . yes! – right here in town, just got in. What you doin' tonight . . .? Great! Terrific. Now, listen, I've got a pal with me – English fella, you'll love him. Can you get him fixed up to make a foursome? How about Jennie? Oh, she is, huh? Well, who else? OK, you do that – we're at the New Century, room 402. 'Kay, lover, ring us back.'

He blew a big kiss down the phone and got one back, making him wince, then put the receiver down.

'Russell, she is a livin' doll . . .'

'French, I presume?'

'As mustard. Jennie can't make it, she's off with a cold – and no wonder, the way she runs around. But Fifi is going to find you a playmate and call us back.' He leapt off the bed, pulling off his tie. 'Right – a quick lick and we're off. I'm starved. We'll go over there and have a bite. It'll give you a chance to meet the girls while we're eating.'

'Great. Then what?'

He shrugged. 'Who knows! Take them for a drink . . . a dance. We'll play it by ear. You'll love that Fifi, she's a honey – spitting image of Bardot.'

'Really?'

'Legs up to her armpits. Gorgeous. Right, I'm going to have a quick scrape.' He entered the bathroom, singing, resembling a man who has an imminent date with a beautiful girl.

Five minutes later the phone rang and out he rushed, smothered in shaving cream.

'Hello . . . yes, angel, what's the news? Huh huh . . . huh huh . . . oh ho! Beautiful! OK, now we're coming round for a meal – be there in twenty minutes. Can you get us a table? Aw, you're a honey. OK, see you.'

He slammed down the shaving-creamed phone and did a little jig. 'Russell . . . you're in! Man, oh, man are you *in*!'

'Why . . . what . . .'

'You've got Slinky Linka – Fifi's table mate! Smashing bird . . . melts icebergs at two miles.'

'Really? Linka . . . what nationality is she?'

'Russian. Surname totally unpronounceable . . . Sobagobalov or something, but you should worry.'

'But she . . . does speak English?'

'Ha! You should worry about that, too. Wait till you see her. Conversation, I warrant, will not be uppermost in your acrid mind.'

'Great,' I laughed.

He made to return to the bathroom but checked in mid stride and turned, cocking an approving eye at my ensemble – midnight-blue mohair suit, blue silk shirt and dark blue tie.

'Slinky Linka is gonno *love* you – and it serves you right, you sensuous swine, you deserve all you get – which could well be plenty. Russ, pour us a drink to celebrate. You'll find Scotch in the case.'

Ten minutes later he was adjusting the knot of his brick-red tie and slipping the jacket of a charcoal-grey suit over his powerful shoulders.

'OK – how do I look?'

'Ready to overcome all opposition.'

'Opposition?' he frowned. 'What's that?'

'Hoo, get him! Well, cheers . . . here's to it, whatever it is.'

'Whatever, wherever, whenever.' He drained his glass. 'Come on – let's slay 'em.'

As we rode down in the elevator I asked him, 'Where is this restaurant, Buzz?'

'Not far – just over on Lexington.'

'You know your way around pretty well.'

He shrugged. 'New York is easy. All the streets run east to west, all the avenues north and south. We'll take a cruise round tomorrow and show you the sights – maybe take you up the Empire State Building. You can see the lot from up there – provided it isn't blowing a blizzard.'

We hit bottom, crossed the foyer and went out through the street door, stopping in our tracks. It was blowing a blizzard. 'Oh, my God, just look at it,' exclaimed Buzz. 'We'll be lucky to make Lexington, never mind the top of the Empire State.'

He waved to a waiting cab and it drew up at the curb. We climbed in, already freezing.

'The Peekaboo, Lexington and . . .'

'Got it,' grinned the driver.

He started off, shot across a brightly lit intersection and continued east.

'Times Square,' said Buzz.

'Mm . . .?'

'Times Square – back there.'

I couldn't see a thing, the windows were steamed up.

'Great,' I sighed. 'All my life I've wanted to see New York and when I finally get here, what do I see? The inside of a cab.' I rubbed the window and peered out . . . then up . . . and up . . . 'Ah, now I can see something?'

'What?'

'Bleedin' snow, mate.'

We reached the restaurant in a matter of minutes, paid the driver, then ran for the foyer, arriving wind blown and snow flecked.

'Good evening, gentlemen . . . you have a reservation?'

It was a dark-haired head waiter, a real tough character who looked like George Raft.

'Yes,' said Buzz. 'We're personal friends of Miss Labouche.'

'Your name, sir?'

'Malone.'

'One moment, please.'

He disappeared through a curtain that hid the restaurant from the foyer and while he was gone I had a look around the place. It was obviously no Wimpey bar. The colour scheme was red velvet and gold and, like all good restaurants, there was the distinct smell of money emanating from the kitchens.

George Raft reappeared, this time managing a smile.

'This way, gentlemen . . . second booth on the left.'

We waltzed through the curtain and immediately slid into a high-backed booth that hid the rest of the room from view.

'Would you care for a drink before you order?' asked George.

We ordered Scotch and from under his arm he produced two menus, each the size of the *New York Times.*

'Well, now . . .' said Buzz, rubbing his hands. 'what d'you fancy?'

'I'll let you know in about four days. This isn't a menu, it's "Gone With The Wind"!'

We began to peruse, and a few minutes later heard the chink of ice in glasses close at hand, then a voice smooth as warm cream coo-ed, ''ello, baby . . .'

I glanced up . . . and damn-near died. Blood rushed into my face and my heart gave a thump like a bass drum – partly because the girl standing there with the tray was one of the loveliest blonde pigeons I've ever seen . . . but mostly because she was stark, screaming naked from the waist up! A topless waitress! Totally unabashed by my popeyed gape. There she stood, her beautiful boobs standing pert and proud, their big rosebud nipples standing out like acorns because of the draught from the door.

I coughed, choked and lowered my face, suddenly finding an imaginary something in my right eye. Buzz, the bastard, was quietly killing himself laughing.

'Hello, angel,' he grinned, taking hold of her hand. 'You look terrific. I'd like you to meet a good pal of mine, Russ Tobin . . . Russell – say hello to Fifi.'

'Hello, Fifi,' I muttered, now rubbing my left eye.

'Buzz Malone . . .' Fifi chided him as she put down the drinks, 'I sink you are a stinker. You didn't tell Russell zis was a topless restaurant, no?'

'God's honour, it slipped my mind, Fifi . . .'

'Ha! Look at heem, he is embarrassed. Zat was a feelthy treek. Never mind, Russell, you will get used to eet in a little while, I promise . . .'

'Oh, no, it's . . . quite all right . . .' I stammered, risking a glance at her, and then, so help me, I was floored again! For walking up to her was a tall, slender, ravishingly dark-haired creature in fishnet tights with a pair of knockers Da Vinci would have chucked up painting for.

''ello,' she smiled, blinding me with a magnificent set of choppers. 'And 'ello, Buzz! Nice to see you again.'

'Not half as nice as it is to see you again, Linka,' he grinned.

Linka! Oh, my sainted aunt! This was mine!

Buzz, now on his feet, nodded at me. 'Linka, this is Russ Tobin, a very good mate of mine on his first trip to New York. And for tonight, he's all yours.'

'Da.' she nodded, eyes bright with gratifying enthusiasm. 'That's goot!' She stuck out her hand and shook mine. *Shook* mine? She bloody near wrenched me arm off! Strong as a Siberian steppe horse, this one. 'Das ver' goot – you arre a ver' nice-lookink fella.'

'Thank you,' I grinned. 'You're a nice-looking fella yourself.'

'Ha ha!' she laughed. 'Is goot joke. You make Linka laugh. Linka make you happy also, you see!'

Oh, boy.

'Vell, vat you boys vant to eat?'

'I . . . don't feel terribly hungry now,' I said, trying awfully hard to keep my eyes off her wonderful charlies.

'Ah, sid down, sid down,' she laughed,' and Linka vill bring you a plate of delicious rib beef. You tell heem, Buzz, aboud Linka's ribs.'

'Incredible,' chuckled Buzz, shaking with laughter.

'So I can see,' I said. 'All right, thank you, Linka, I'd love to try your ribs.'

'And forr you, Buzz?'

'Yes, please,' he nodded, wiping tears from his eyes.

The girls took the order and departed, swinging their gorgeous backsides down the aisle and out of sight.

'You . . . bastard!' I gasped.

'Oh, man, you should've seen your face when you looked up and saw Fifi standing there. I thought you were going to have one on the spot!'

'Very funny.'

'Your first time in a topless restaurant, I take it?'

'Obviously.'

'Ooh that was rich.' He wiped his eyes again and tucked his hanky away. 'Well . . .' he looked up, beaming devilishly, 'what d'you think of them?'

The grin severed my face. 'Fantastic! By God, Buzz, you really can pick 'em. I don't know what Fates put us in opposite compartments on that train, but here's to them. That Linka is really something . . . but, by heaven, she's a powerful bird, son. A real handful of woman.'

'Fancy a spot of dancing afterwards?'

'With her – anything.'

'Well, we'll see how it goes. If she's like Fifi she'll be game for anything. Fifi sort of . . . lives life to the full, you might say.' He expelled an exhausted breath.

I shook my head. 'A topless restaurant. You know, to be honest, I never really fancied the idea of going into one. I didn't thing they'd mix, somehow – sex and steak, boobs and beef . . .'

'And now?'

I grinned. 'Who needs food? I'm going to order seventeen courses – just to get them here seventeen times.'

'Tobin – one thing I've noticed about you – you're extremely adaptable. Not two minutes ago you were ready to dive under the table with embarrassment, and now look at you – biting on the bit like a rampant stallion.'

'Ah, Buzz, if one is to enjoy life to the full, one has to open oneself to the nectar of "difference", the enchantment of uniqueness, the essential wonder of the hitherto unexperienced. The giraffe sees all; the ostrich naught but the worms beneath its feet. As disagreeable as the sight of Linka's luscious lollipops is to me, I must prevail if this be the local custom. When in Rome and all that. Have no fear, I'll stick it out – right to the bitter end.'

'I'll bet you bloody will.'

'Oh, man . . . here they come now. *What* a couple of little darlin's.'

Linka hove-to, flashing her laser-beam smile, and placed a plate of something before me but who was looking?

'Therre you arre, Petrushka, beef for *strrength*! After zat meal yourr energy vill know no bounds.'

'Zis one needs no beef,' nodded Fifi, plonking a small mountain of ribs in front of Buzz. 'But a leetle extra never did any 'arm. Now – anysink else you fancy, cheri?'

She leaned towards him, her big blue eyes wide with mock innocence.

Buzz released a deep voracious growl. She laughed at him and wagged her finger. 'Naughty, naughty. You finish your beef before you get dessert. OK, we leave you to it. You want anysink – just press zat bell button.'

They were hardly out of sight before I pressed it, bringing Linka back immediately, her brow arched suspiciously.

'You forgot somesink, Petrushka?'

'Er, yes . . . do you have any salt, Linka?'

With a censorious smile she leaned right across the table, almost blinding me with her left boob, produced the salt from behind the napkin containers, and placed it in my hand. 'You know somesink, Rusell Tobin . . . I sink you arre perhaps just as naughty as yourr friend here.'

'Who . . . me?'

'Yes, Meester Innocent – you! I sink you arre a quiet tigerr – no?'

'Me? Nah . . .'

'Ha!' she laughed. 'OK – ve vill see. Now – anysink else you vish?'

'No, I appear to have everything now, thank you.'

'So polite,' she smiled, winked at Buzz. 'Butter would not melt in his mouse. Ha! Linka he does not fool forr a moment.'

Off she went, longlegging it down the aisle.

I watched her until she disappeared, then gave a languishing sigh. 'Buzz . . .'

'Eat your beef, quiet tiger.'

'That is one heck of a woman. You sure she didn't throw javelin in the last Olympics?'

'Come to think of it, I do believe she breaks horses in her spare time.'

'Only horses? How about backs? By gum, I'll bet she's crippled a few in her time. She's a blinkin' dynamo.'

'And I also seem to recall she's a karate black belt . . .'

'Eh?'

'Something like that.'

'Ah, come off it . . .'

He grinned. 'Eat your dinner, I was only joking . . .'

'Thank God for that!'

'No – she's only a brown belt. Good looking bird, though, hm?'

'Wonderful.'

'She obviously goes a bundle on you, son.'

'You think so?'

'Of course. You could be in for the night of your life, mate.'

'You . . . reckon?'

'Huh huh. Linka is a *very* fussy bird. But, by golly, when she likes, she really . . . well, you'll see. Russell . . .?'

'Mm?'

'You're not eating. Aren't you hungry?'

'Strange as it may seem, Buzz, I've . . . suddenly lost my appetite.'

'Force yourself. I reckon you're gonna need it.'

Huh! If Linka had served me whole *steer* it wouldn't have been enough nourishment to cope with what happened later!

She was unbelievable.

EIGHT

'Cripes, just look at it. If it keeps up like this it'll be knee-deep by morning.' This was Buzz, teeth chattering.

We were huddled in the 'stage door' of the restaurant, waiting for the girls. We'd only been there three minutes and were already frozen stiff. At that moment a taxi slewed round the corner and Buzz ran out, waving like a maniac.

'Hey . . . hey . . .!'

It slithered to a halt, making s's in the snow, then backed up, mounted the curb and almost ran over his foot.

The driver lowered the window. 'Where to, mac?'

'We don't know yet. Can you wait a couple of minutes – the girls are just coming.'

The driver shrugged. 'Sure – just so long as the tick of the meter don't offend yuh.'

Buzz nodded. 'Well, if we're paying for it we may as well use it. Hey, Russ . . .!'

I ran out, shivering feverishly in my Miami summer suit, the material so thin you could shoot peas through it, and climbed gratefully into the warm interior. Buzz got in after me, chattering and phewing.

'*Jee*zus, it's cold.'

'Funny thing,' observed the driver, a laconic sort of bloke, 'sometimes gets like that here in winter. I tink it's sumpn to do wid the temperature. You guys oughta bear it in mind for next year . . . get better equipped.'

'Thanks for the tip,' sneered Buzz, muttering side-mouthed to me, 'which is more than he'll be sayin' to us!'

We'd just about thawed out when the restaurant door opened and out came the girls, buried in delicious furs, Fifi in a blonde fur, probably musquash, and Slinka Linka in dark brown to match her hair.

Buzz opened his door and got out as they scurried across to the cab with exclamations of delight.

'Aw, Buzz, you are so clever, finding a cab,' said Fifi, pinching his blue cheek.

In they scrambled, burying me in perfumed fur, Linka grabbing my arm and snuggling up close.

Buzz got in and closed the door. 'Right – where to, girls?'

'Ah,' said Fifi, 'we have been tinking . . .'

'God help us,' grinned Buzz. 'All hell breaks loose when these two start "tinkin' ".'

'Well . . . as eet ees Russ's first visit to New York, we thought maybee he would like to experience a Greenwich party . . .'

Buzz's eyes lit up. 'Hey, what a great idea. We were going to take you dancing or something, but . . .'

'We can dance at ze party, no?'

'Sure. Well – head on girls. Where to . . .?'

Linka gave the driver an address and off we went, almost collecting a fire hydrant on the way.

'This party,' Buzz asked them, 'are the people friends of yours?'

They shrugged in unison. 'We know some of zem,' said Linka.

'What do they do?' I asked.

Linka laughed. 'Mostly each udder. Some paint . . . some play music . . . most of zem do nossink, you vill see. But don't vorry, Petrushka . . .' she gave my arm a squeeze,' you vill kom to know harm. If one of zose female predators so much as smiles at you, I vill decapitate herr.'

'Thanks very much.'

She smiled, leaning very close and pursing her luscious lips at me. 'Tonight you arre Linka's . . . zat is, of course, if you *vish* to be.'

'Oh . . . yes. I . . .'

'You like me?'

'V . . . very much.'

'Goot. Zen ve haf a *super* time. Ve haf some real fun.'

'Terrific.'

'Teerreefeek! I like ze vay you say zat. I like ze vay you say everysink. You arre a nice man. How long do you stay in New York?'

'About five more days.'

'Goot! Five days is nice – not too short, not too long. Maybe if ve like tonight, ve do it again, hm?'

'Well, certainly . . .'

Buzz gave a laugh. 'Hey, Linka, take it easy on the poor fella. After tonight he may be in bed for those five days – recovering!'

Linka flashed a smile. 'Not zis one. He's strong, I can tell. He may not haf yourr disgusting muscles but I detect grreat stayink power.' She rounded on me. 'It zat not so, Petrushka?'

'Well . . . I . . .'

'You arre right – don't tell. Keep it as a pleasant surprise forr Linka.'

We were there in minutes, and, loath to leave the cuddly warmth of Linka's fur, I got out and started freezing all over again. Linka joined me, wrapping an arm around me to protect me from the icy wind, and looked up at the house we'd arrived at.

It was a towering town house, a 'brownstone' as the Americans call them, with a basement, a bridge of steps leading up to the front door, and numerous storeys lost to sight in the swirling snow.

'Top floor, I'll bet,' I said. 'And no elevator.'

'No,' she laughed, 'just ze first floor.'

Buzz paid the cabbie and said, 'Lead on, girls, you've got the password.'

We climbed the treacherous steps. Linka pulled an ancient bell knob and almost immediately the door opened. A hundredweight of dark khaki hair and matching beard peered out and from somewhere within its matted depths an erudite voice proclaimed, 'If you come bearing the gift of anarchy to help swell the bubbling cauldron of sacro-dimentional-effortism – welcome. If not – fuck off.'

'We can do better zan zat, Frump Face,' replied Fifi, pleasantly, hauling a parcel from under her coat. 'We bring a litre of Seagrams V.O.'

'Then you are thrice welcome. Bon soir, Fifi, angel of the night . . . and Linka, my Cossack pussy cat . . . enter and welcome. Hi, fellas, how's tricks?' He gave us an open-handed wave, like he was cleaning a window.

Fifii made the introductions. He was Frump Face Findus, professional layabout and all-round social catastrophe, though he greeted us cordially enough.

'Tobin,' he said, clicking his fingers thoughtfully. 'Once knew a Tobin in Singapore. Ran a cat-house back of the market. No relation, I suppose? Come – the party's a-go-go. The king is in his counting house and the maids are in the parlour. Ascend – but watch out for the blackbirds, they're kinda thick on the ground up there.'

I threw a glance at Buzz but could see he didn't know what Frump Face was talking about either.

We climbed a dark, carpetless flight of stairs that emanated the odour of boiled cabbage and a few other things besides – a mystifying montage best, I thought, left undetected. Not the most salubrious stairs I have climbed, I mused – nor the most inviting house. Come to think of it, if it hadn't been for the girls obviously knowing their way around, I'd have been four miles down the street, running hard, and I had the feeling Buzz would've been right alongside me.

We arrived at a landing and turned left, coming face to face with a terrifying *papier-mâché* mask draped around the single bulb suspended from the high ceiling. But Linka, in the lead, didn't even flinch. On she went, finally arriving at a door at the end of the landing.

'Enter!' commanded Frump Face, but she already had it open.

As I crossed the threshold I knew we were in for a weird old time. The room, not large and extremely dark, lit only by a couple of dim wall lights encompassed again by evil-looking masks, was heaving with people, little more than vague shadows on the floor where they lay around on piles of cushions, the only furniture in the room. The atmosphere was so dense with incense and fag smoke you could have chopped it out in blocks and built an igloo.

'Huh huh,' went Linka. 'Somebody got herre before us.'

'Go on through!' invited Frump Face from the rear, and on we went, in single file, stepping over recumbent bodies and outstretched legs, me keeping very close to Linka in case I was suddenly snatched away, to disappear forever into the labyrinthine maze of the great unwashed, way down there in the bosom of Hell.

'Enjoyin' yourself?' chuckled Buzz, immediately behind me.

'Enormously. I just wish I'd brought me seeing-eye dog and me gas mask.'

'Cheer up, there's light ahead.'

And so there was. Linka finally led us out of the valley of the shadow of death and into a huge, more brilliantly lit (I mean this one had *four* such wall lights!) room, where much the same sort of thing, plus excruciatingly loud sitar music, was going on in the hellish antechamber, with the incredible addition of a vast water bed, possibly ten feet square, on whose transparent plastic bosom wallowed an enormously fat red-haired fink dressed in a blue and silver robe, granny glasses, and wearing a ridiculously tiny gold crown on his head. He was almost totally surrounded by an assortment of lovelies attired in various stages of nakedness, mostly total, and was having his toe nails painted bright green by a super little Chinese doll who hadn't a flamin' stitch on!

I pulled up so sharp Buzz ran into me.

'Bloody mother!' he gasped in my ear.

'Hail!' proclaimed the king, lifting a golden goblet in our direction. 'And welcome . . . to the palace of Sacro-Dimentional-Effortism!'

'Thank's very mu . . .' I started to say.

'Beware . . .! – the infidel in our midst!' he bellowed, taking a mammoth bite out of an apple and hurling it across the room, smiting a tall skinny bloke smack in the middle of his painted forehead. 'Sanctuary for the anti-Gods is nought but pillage of the indefensible!' insisted the king, spitting apple all down his robe. 'Hail the diabolical sacrifice and death to all transmutites!'

'Still talkin' ze same crap, Charlie?' laughed Linka, peeling off her coat and revealing a breathtaking gold mini dress and mind-boggling gold thigh boots.

No introductions were made, we were suddenly just in the thick of it, surrounded by a million and a quarter weird ones, the air thick with gunge and the drinks being handed out in small buckets.

Now the music had changed, the sitar rubbish giving way to good old ordinary mind-battering pop that was shaking plaster off the walls.

Linka, seemingly aloof and obviously enjoying herself, was writhing and churning in front of me, driving me blind with the squirming gyrations of her slender, butch-booted thighs and flashes of heaven as her tiny dress occasionally rode that inch too high.

I glanced in the direction of the bed where His Majesty Charlie was now discussing dialectics with a negro dressed like a Red Indian while simultaneously having his face painted in rainbow stripes by the Chinese chick and idly fondling the breasts of two girls, one tucked under each arm.

I grinned at Linka. 'What's he supposed to be?' I shouted, battling the thundering speakers.

She laughed. 'Charlie? He's ze leader of ze Sacro-Dimentional-Effortism Party. In fact he's their founder!'

'Oh, really. But what does he actually *do*?'

'Mostly what he's doing right now!'

'Oh. And what do the Sacro-Thingummies do?'

'Much ze same!'

'I see. Forgive my ignorance . . . but what precisely *is* Sacro-Dimentional . . . whatsit?'

She gave a humourous shrug. 'Take your pick! Zat's ze beauty of it – it can mean anysink you like – just so long as it doesn't entail any work!'

'That figures.'

'If you arre caught working – you're out! Actually . . . I sink zey are dedicated to bringing down American society – in general terms, you understand. Ze details zey leave to ze individual. As long as you arre anti-law, anti-order, anti-government, anti-family, anti-everysink zat is wholesome and sveet-smellink – *and* of course anti-work, you arre judged a fit member for Sacro-Dimentional-Effortism and velcome. If you arre a female you may even get to share ze water bed vith His Majesty – a *very* great honour.'

'Yes, I can see it would be. And . . . how many S-D-Es are there, Linka?'

'Fortunately for America – only about one hundred, in fact most of zem are herre – but their numbers are growing! It is becoming a very popular movement.'

'Yes, of course – and I can see why. What greater aspiration can a girl hold than to spend her life on the water bed being fondled by such an attractive fellow?'

She laughed aloud, opening her lovely mouth very wide. 'Such enchanting cynicism. I love you. You arre one heck of an attractive fellow, Tobin! I sink I must haf you!'

'Eh?'

'Does zat shock you?' she laughed.

'Well . . .' I grinned.

'I am glad it does – even a leetle bit. I find such naivety . . . heart-varming – yes, zat is ze vord. It varms my heart.'

'I'm . . . very glad.'

'Not half so glad as you vil be later, Petrushka,' she smiled, incinerating me with half-closed eyes. 'Zat I promise you!'

* * *

Time passed. God knows how much because I'd swallowed four or five buckets of booze by then and time appeared to be no longer of the essence.

Suddenly I found myself face to face with Buzz who was sprawled on the same pile of cushions having his hair plaited with ribbons by a kook bird in a soup-stained kaftan and flying glasses.

'Hello mate,' I said, 'how's it going?' and it took him all of four seconds to recognize me, he was so motherless.

'Russ, you old bastard! Where've you bin?'

'Right here, son – apart from one visit to the loo I rather regretted.'

'Yeah, I was there.'

'Rough.'

'Rugged.'

'What a bunch of gunks. Just look at them.'

'Huh – you think it's bad in here! You wanna see what's happenin' in a bedroom along the landing! There's more screwin' going on in there than in a nut-and-bolt factory. They're doin' it all over the place – on the floor, up the walls – there's even a couple at it in a grand piano!' He gave a chuckle. 'Talk about "Hairs On A G-String"! I was mighty tempted to strike an F-major chord and whip his bollocks off!'

I winced.

'Here . . .!' he gasped, 'just look at King Charlie goin' at it heavens hard! Aw, that's a bit much, mate, isn't it – I mean in public.' He gave an alcoholic titter. 'Hey . . . wouldn't it be a hoot if he missed the bird and drove it straight through the plastic! Zunk! Whhhhhoosshh! Hee hee . . . eight billion gallons all over the floor . . . rushin' down the stairs like Niagara!' His expression changed suddenly – to one of devilish contemplation. 'Hey . . . now *there's* a thought . . .'

'Buzz . . .! Now, Buzz, you wouldn't . . .'

'Who *me*? Nah, I wouldn't do a rotten thing like that, Russell . . . here, what's this bloody bird doin' to my hair? Gerroff, Nellie, go an' play with yourself.'

He gave her a shove and she disappeared backwards over the mound of cushions, legs spread, naked as day under her kaftan. I don't think Buzz even noticed.

'Hey, Buzz, what's the score with the girls. Are you going somewhere with Fifi later?'

'Too true, son. She's got a little pad four blocks away. What about you?'

I smiled. 'Well, Linka sort of led me to believe . . .'

He nodded. 'Yeh, I know. Fifi passed the word. The bird fancies you no end – so that's your lot! You'll be going to her place, no doubt. Well, you won't have far to go.'

'No? Why's that?'

He gave a chuckle. 'Because she lives right here – in this house.'

'Eh? Aw, come on . . .'

He was shaking his head. 'Hell, man, it's nothin' like this. It's right at the top . . . different world. I haven't seen it, but Fifi says it's a gas.'

'I see. I couldn't imagine Linka living . . .'

Suddenly we were not alone. A big, haggy blonde, encased in the flimsiest floral garment cut so low you could see her navel, was kneeling beside Buzz, gazing imploringly into his bloodshot eyes and muttering invitational obscenities.

'You wanna jump, big boy . . . you wanna make it with Alice? Come on, get to it . . .' her hand streaked towards his flies and he leapt back four feet. But she was after him, crawling up the cushions on her hands and knees, clawing at his zip. 'Come on, Sweet Dick, let's get old handsome out here an' make music. What you savin' it for – to stir your Martini? Get it in Alice an' let's live a little . . .'

'Ger . . . roff!' snapped Buzz, bashing her grasping hand away. 'Go and fuck Christopher Robin! Get lost through the looking glass.'

'Oh, you're a gay boy, huh?' she sneered. 'Got it hot for Sonny Jim here, hm?'

'Ha!' He laughed. 'That'll be the day! You hear that, Russell . . .?'

I gave a tut. 'Now, Buzz, no need to be ashamed,' I lisped,

bringing Alice round to face me. 'Makes you sick,' I said, tossing my head. 'Two years we've bin goin' out and he *still* denies it in public.'

'Shoot,' she seethed. 'Jeezus, ain't there an all-man cock in the room?'

'Try Charlie,' I said. 'He's having a breather.'

She fixed me with a *very* mean look and appeared to be about to land me one, when suddenly a presence loomed at my elbow, a hand shot past my face and grabbed a handful of Alice's greasy locks, yanked her to her feet and sent her hurtling across the room to plunge headfirst into the water bed.

Boooiiinnnggg!

Back she rebounded like she'd been shot from a cannon, straight into Linka's awaiting fists.

Thump! Thwack! Pow!

With a 'Get out of herre, you feelthy slut!' Alice once again flew through the air with the greatest of ill-ease, this time landing plumb on the back of King Charlie who was just about to put it in again.

'OOOOWWWW!' yelled Charlie.

'OOOOHHHHH!' screamed the bird underneath him.

'I'LLFUCKINGKILLYOUYOUCRAZYRUSSIANBITCH!!' bellowed Alice, thumping Charlie in the ear as she fought to extricate herself from the tangle of thrashing limbs. And then, by George, she was off the bed and coming hard at Linka, nails clawing, teeth bared, eyes blazing murderously.

'YAAA!' she yelled, and struck with her claws. But Linka's beautiful face was no longer there and neither, of course, was Linka.

Neat as ninepence she swayed away, pivoted, ducked, and . . . pow! A straight-arm in the teeth and Alice was sailing backwards, arse-over-elbow, homing in once more on Charlie boy who was sitting there like Canute, wide-eyed and disbelieving the waves that were about to engulf him, a huge erection about to bend at right angles under Alice's hurtling weight.

'YAAAAAAAHHHHHHH!' he bellowed, his eyes bulging with agony.

'AWWWW . . . SHURRUP!' screamed Alice, rocking and rolling on him, finally twisting herself out of his lap to reveal his limp and wilting lily going down like a burst tyre. 'YOUBLOODYRUSSIANBAG!' she raged, quite beside herself with anger, and in she came again, this time lashing out with her feet, scattering the crowd, determined this time to annihilate Linka.

Ice-cool and magnificent, the lovely Linka watched her come, and then . . . biff! . . . bam! . . . wallop! – a graceful, balletic side-step, a miraculous pirouette and a breathtaking boot in the arse and poor old Alice was at it again, hurtling unerringly into the nest of iniquity and landing with a sickening thud on top of three squirming females all having each other simultaneously and swapping recipes into the bargain.

Then the Cats of Hell broke loose. In the twitch of a whisker forty-seven screaming females hurled themselves onto the bed and began thumping, groping, biting, scratching and screwing each other like mayhem was the in thing, and while all this was going on I was staring at Buzz who was ogling the bulging water bed like a starving man eyes a hot meat pie.

'Buzz . . .!' I called.

His head shot round, teeth bared in a sadistic grin.

'You wouldn't dare!'

'Who wouldn't?'

'Buzz . . . you can't . . .!'

He roared with laughter. 'Who bloody can't?'

His hand flashed to his pocket. 'Stand by the lifeboats!'

'Buzz . . .!'

'Come on!' yelled Linka, grabbing my arm and pulling me to my feet as though I was filled with hydrogen. 'The crazy dope is going to . . .'

Too late! The crazy dope already had! Ziiiippp! went the penknife. 'Ha . . . haaaa!' he cried exhultantly.

Whhoooffff! A wall of white water, solid as perspex, leapt out of its plastic tomb and struck him in the chest, hurling him backwards towards us, bowling us over, throwing us into the mound of cushions, arms and legs whirling, coughing, choking, taking in gallons of the stuff. Sppllootť! The tidal wave slammed into the wall and thundered back, seeking escape, finding it through the door into the outer room. Screams and yells from there, bodies splashing about on the floor like stranded walruses, everyone wondering what in hell had happened. Everything floating, floundering, screaming, shouting . . .

'Come on!' cried Linka, laughing unroariously, and once again dragged me to my feet. Buzz was right behind me and somehow or other Fifi was in there now, helpless with laughter, falling down every time she got up, belabouring Buzz with affectionate thumps on the shoulder and gasping, 'You crazy . . . crazy eediot . . .!'

On through the outer room, laughing and sloshing, knee-deep in water, suddenly feeling the surge of current as the door to the landing was forced open and with another whhhoosshh! the bloody lot surged out into the hall and shot through the banisters just like Niagara as Buzz had envisaged.

'Come on . . . !' urged Linka. 'Oh . . . ohhhh!' she groaned, weak with laughter, holding her stomach with one hand while pulling me along with the other, out onto the landing then a right turn to a flight of ascending stairs.

I glanced behind me, discovering Buzz and Fifi no longer there. Then Linka collapsed on the stairs, tears streaming down her cheeks. 'Oh, *Russ*, how many times I haf vanted to do zat . . . to vipe the stupid, self-satisfied smirk off Charlie's useless face . . . to drown the Sacro-Dimentional-Effortists in their own stinkink vater bed . . . Petrouchka, you are soaked to ze skin, your lovely suit; Nefer mind, ve vill dry it on ze radiators . . . come, quickly, ve haf a long vay to go – up to ze very stairs! My God, zat vas too vonderful for vords. I *vish* ve'd had a camera, but no matter. Come! I'll race you to ze top!'

* * *

Up and up and up . . . Linka bounding ahead, switching on lights, pausing to look back and encourage me with laughter. 'Come, baby . . .'

'Linka!' I gasped, 'I'm carrying four hundred pounds of water!'

Slosh . . . slosh . . . slosh . . . round the bend and up yet another bloody flight of stairs. No wonder she was in such terrific shape with all this training.

Finally the very last flight. Leading up to a single door.

'You made it!' she laughed, plucking a small purse from the top of her thigh boot and extracting a key.

'Oxygen!' I gasped, crawling up the stairs on my hands and knees. Dammit, she wasn't even breathing hard!

'There's some inside,' she laughed, pulling open the door. Oh, my God! Inside was *another* flight of stairs! I released a horrified groan, playing the fool, and collapsed at her feet. 'No . . . no! I can't . . . I can't . . . !'

'Zen I shall carry you . . .'

I shot to my feet. 'Oh, no you won't.'

'Come,' she laughed, 'zis is ze very last, I promise you.'

Through the door and up the stairs, becoming aware of a fabulous studio apartment as I climbed into the open room.

'Wow!' I gasped.

'You like it?'

'Wonderful. Heaven after hell.'

'Come . . . let's get you out of zose vet things.'

We sloshed across the polished wood floor and entered a bedroom that could well have been a Hollywood set and a luxury hunting lodge, not butch but strong, fur and leather like the lounge. Through this room into a large bathroom, half of which contained a mini gym, complete with a cycling machine, a rowing machine and wall-bars.

'This is terrific!' I laughed.

'An inheritance from my father – he vas an athletics champion. I like to keep fit, it makes me feel . . . vell – goot.'

'It certainly makes you look "goot".'

She opened a cupboard door and threw me a yellow towelling robe. 'Here – put zis on. I vill go and make some special Russian coffee to varm us up.'

'But what about your wet clothes?'

She looked down at herself, unconcerned that the little dress was plastered so tightly to her body she might as well have been naked.

She shrugged. 'No matter. Another few minutes vill make no difference.' Then she was off, striding back through the bedroom, zinging with energy, humming to herself.

Gingerly I peeled off my jacket, shedding four gallons of water, then removed my shirt which came away from my skin with a sucking noise. I wrung it out in the bath and hung it over a rail. My boots delivered a pint each, my socks just a few ounces, but my trousers made up for them. My pockets must have been full to the brim.

A quick rub-down with a towel and as I slipped on the robe, back she came, carrying two steaming mugs.

'Ah, you changed – goot. Here, zis vill revive you.'

'What is it?'

'An old Russian recipe used to revive victims of frostbite.'

'Sounds lethal.'

I took the mug in both hands and ventured a sip. Wow! It was neat rum!

'Goot, hey?' she grinned. 'Vith zat inside you no cold germ has a chance. Now – I vill get changed.'

'Oh . . . well, I'll go into the bedroom.'

A taunting smile. 'You . . . prefer to?'

'Well, I . . .'

'I thought you may want to stay and dry my back?'

'Well . . .'

She exploded with laughter. 'Go on, Petrushka, I only tease you. I von't be a moment.'

With a grin I wandered through and sat on the bed, noticing she hadn't closed the door and further noticing, with thumping heart, that from where I was sitting I could see fleeting glimpses of her in a full-length mirror. Then, as she began undressing, I realized from her smile that she knew darn well I could see her.

'How is ze drink?' she called, unzipping the dress.

'Terrific! Beats English tea hands down.'

God, there went the dress, over her head, and only the flimsiest, tiniest pair of pants underneath. Daft, isn't it – I'd been ogling her naked breasts all night in the restaurant but now, because I wasn't supposed to see them, they were suddenly twice as exciting. Or maybe it was because she was now attired only in a pair of devastating thigh boots that . . . oh, wickedness thy name is foul imagination . . .'

'OW!'

'What's ze matter?' she called.

'I . . . spilled the scalding drink on my knee.'

And no wonder – my hands were trembling like a couple of tuning forks.

She gave a laugh and disappeared from view, and the next time she appeared the boots were gone . . . in fact everything had gone. There she stood, fixing her hair, naked as marble.

I had to put the cup down.

Once again she disappeared, moving to the cupboard, then a moment later in she came, fastening a blue satin gown which fell open as she walked, exposing her long, slender legs.

'Ah, that feels better.'

'Linka . . . you look fabulous.'

'And you, Petrushka, look pretty fabulous yourself. Come . . .'

She took my hand and pulled me on to the huge bed, on to acres of silky, fawn-coloured fur, urging me over her, murmuring eagerly, 'Now . . . ve make love.'

'Hm mm,' I grinned.

'I haf a surprise for you.'

'Oh?'

She raised her arm and pressed a button set in the wall above the headboard, and, so help me, the entire bed began to vibrate, gently, barely more than a hum.

'Come,' she said, 'lie down beside me and let it tickle your spine.'

I stretched out alongside her, touching all the way down, and took hold of her hand.

'Now close your eyes,' she said softly, 'and let the vibration seep into you . . . relax . . . and let it pass through your flesh and into your bones . . . let it go deep . . . deep into your loins.'

'Oh, boy.'

'It's goot?' she chuckled.

'It's fantastic. I'm tingling in places I never tingled before.'

'And zis is only ze beginning . . .'

She raised her hand again and adjusted the control and the vibrations increased, sending a fizz up my spine and raising the hairs on my neck and scalp.

'Wow!'

'Ha ha! Zat got you.'

'Linka, this is terrific! Where did you find a bed like this?'

'I had it made, Petrushka. I'm a great believer in massage to relax . . . and titillate.' She raised herself up and gave a little chuckle. 'Ah ha, I see it has found anudder victim! You obviously find it . . . exciting.'

I opened one eye and found her gazing at Herc who was making a tent . . . well, more a marquee, out of my bathrobe.

'Linka,' I laughed, 'this may come as a surprise to you, but *you* would have produced that result – without vibration.'

'So?' she smiled. 'Keep your eyes closed . . . and just lie quite still.' She moved away from me, slipped off the bed, and was back immediately, kneeling over me. 'No peeping now . . .'

'All right.'

Gentle as butterflies, her fingers flicked over me, untying the sash of the gown and slowly opening the two halves. Then . . . a gasp. 'Ah, Petrushka . . . a monument! Just lie quite still and let me play.'

'Be my guest.'

Then a touch so very gentle, feather-light . . . round and

round . . . up and down . . . making me jump and twitch and chuckle, finding all the areas of sensitivity.

'Is it goot?' she whispered.

'It's blinkin' marvellous.'

'He is a fine-looking boy. You must be very proud of him.'

'We're . . . very good mates. We do what we can for each other . . . wow!'

A deep, throaty chuckle. 'You like zat?'

'Well, *he's* crazy about it . . .'

'Then . . . how about zis?'

Yaaaarrrroooopp! The sizzling envelopment of her oven-hot mouth curled up my toes and braced every muscle in my body. At least I presumed it was her mouth – it could have been the mug of rum!

On she went, taking her time, relishing every nuance of my reaction, now and then repeated a particular piece of mischief that gave me special pleasure, and then, unexpectedly . . . she straddled me.

I opened my eyes, discovered her lip caught fast between her teeth and her eyes wide with excited anticipation.

'I . . . must have him,' she gasped, almost as though she was expecting an objection, and then, breathlessly, she lowered herself . . . down . . . down . . . down until, with a final groan of ecstacy, she hit bottom. 'Oh . . .! Oh, zat is vonderful . . .! I can feel him right up here . . . right inside me.'

She clasped her stomach, close to her ribs, and I laughed. 'Well, thanks for the compliment, but I feel that might be just a touch high.'

'You sink so?' she grimaced. 'You're not sitting vhere *I'm* sitting.'

'You look wonderful up there, Linka.'

'I feel vonderful . . .' She took her hair in both hands and piled it upon her head, stretching sensuously like a great cat, arching her splendid body and driving down onto me, reaching for every vestige of me, taking it all and yearning for even more.

'He feels so varm,' she sighed plaintively, '. . . and so hard . . . and throbby – no, don't move!' She smiled at me. 'You don't have to do a thing, Petrushka, ze bed is doing it for you.'

'It is?'

'Hm mm . . . I can feel the vibration through you . . . right up through him and into me. It's . . . glorious.' She shivered. Her body flushed with goose-bumps and a haze of fine hair rose on her arms, then an anguished mewing sound broke from her trembling lips. 'Oh . . . oh, God . . .' She began to squirm, her lips caught again between her teeth. 'Oh . . . oh, Russ . . .'

'Yes, honey?'

'It's . . . beginning. I can feel it coming . . . the whole incredible . . . thing . . . it's there . . . right down in the root of you . . . of us . . . oh! . . .'

As though in torment, as though the thumb-screws were being tightened and the rack had begun to stretch her limbs, she rolled her head from side to side with a snarl of erupting agony, her breathing chaotic. And as the torment mounted so her movements grew . . . at first a pelvic jerking, an involuntary spasm, fingers distended into grasping claws . . . next – a great shudder that doubled her over, evoking from her a muted cry of delicious anguish, her fingers reaching for mine, not solely for support but to help transmit the sharing of her pleasure. And now the thing erupted and she was away, riding me hard towards heaven, rocking and pounding, eyes and mouth wide with delirious expectancy, gasping, 'Oh . . .! Oh . . .! Oh . . .!' with each impact of flesh against flesh. And then . . .

'RUUSSS! I'M COMMMIIINNGG!'

And with one great stentorian gasp she most certainly came. Oh, boy, she blew! And I reckon if I hadn't got my fingers out of there fast she'd have snapped them off like matchsticks.

'Aaaa . . . AAAWW! she bellowed, then threw herself forward and smashed both fists in my pillow, then up again, raising clenched fists in jubilant salute to the ceiling, then down again, staying there this time to pulverize the pillow with repeated, ecstatic blows, murmuring away to herself in Russian which somehow made the whole thing sound so much more violent.

'Oh, *baby* . . . baby . . . baby . . .' she wailed, reverting to English. 'Thank you . . . thank you . . . thank you . . .'

'But I didn't *do* anything,' I laughed.

'You did . . . you did . . .'

Then . . . flump. She collapsed on me, groaning and giggling, racked by oversensitivity, gradually recovering and snuggling her nose into my neck and finally coming to rest.

'How d'you feel?' I murmured, stroking her soft, silky hair.

'Feel . . .? Like I'm impaled by the Leaning Tower of Pisa . . . but vonderful.'

She raised her head and smiled at me, then suddenly sat erect, wincing at the renewed penetration, and turned off the vibrator mechanism.

'Enough of zat. Zat vas forr *my* pleasure. Now . . . ve do somesink forr you.'

'Oh? And what have you got in mind?'

She smiled diabolically. 'Have you . . . ever done it on a rowing machine?'

'Ha!' I laughed. 'No, can't say I have.'

'It is unbelievable! Come – you shall be Oxford and I Cambridge. But ze beauty of zis race is – zat everybody vins!'

* * *

Heaven knows what time we finally fell asleep – I mean collapsed in each other's arms in a state of utter and total catatonia, but I reckon it was close on seven because daylight was beginning to creep through the venetian blinds. Too blasted even to speak we dropped like felled pines onto the snug fur, our arm around each other, pulled the trailing edges of the bedspread over us and died instantly.

A while later I veered towards the surface, took her lovely breast in my hand and wriggled close behind her, relishing her exciting warmth, then dropped over the edge again, finally waking hours later with a start, finding her gone.

At first I wasn't too concerned. I just lay there, smiling at memories of the night and wondering whether she had yet recovered. But after a while, hearing no sound from kitchen or bathroom, I opened my senses to the condition of the apartment and knew instinctively it was empty.

'Linka . . .' I called, knowing I'd get no reply.

I got off the bed and went into the bathroom, finding it deserted, though warm and damp from recent use, the perfume of her soap lingering on the moist air.

Troubled now, but telling myself she'd just popped out for milk, bread, fruit juice, I toured the flat and finally found the note, on the floor where it must have fallen from the bed.

'It said: 'You were sleeping so peacefully I didn't have the heart to wake you – and I *know* you need the rest, you beautiful brute. Work calls – my daytime job – otherwise you would have found me very close. Come in tonight for dinner, if you wish. If not . . . phone. And if not that . . . adieu, my Cossack. Memories are made of nights like this. Go with love . . . Linka.'

Well . . . a daytime job, would you believe. Didn't she *ever* sleep?

Dispiritedly I showered, then went in search of my clothes, finding them, unbelievably, hanging in the kitchen beautifully pressed, the discovery bringing a lump to my throat. What a girl.

I got dressed, made the bed, tidied the place and had a last look round. Still a beautiful nest but nothing without its bird. Never mind, there was still tonight, and maybe four more nights after that!

Feeling more cheerful I went down her stairs and closed the door firmly behind me.

Down on the first floor I encountered a very sad sight – King Charlie, dressed in swim trunks, his crown askew, was mopping out his pad.

'Good morning,' I bade him.

'Yeah,' he grunted.

'How's the flood?'

He heaved a sigh. 'Yuh know what them bastards did – they punctured my water bed. Four thousand gallons ran through this door an' down the stairs. But what the heck – maybe they needed a wash at that.' He gave me a close second look. 'Say . . . ain't I seen you before somewheres?'

'Who – me? No, not me.'

'Weren't you here last night?'

'Well, *en passant*, you might say, Charlie – on my way upstairs to visit an old friend. Tell me, Miss Linka . . .'

His eyes lit up. 'She was in here first thing, picking up her fur coat. What a dame.'

'Charlie, do you happen to know where she works during the day?'

He gave a snarl and nodded. 'Hu huh . . . through the hours of nine to five she is shackled to the lords of the capitalist pigs who defile the very essence of equi-distribulistic-structurism and debase the very life-blood of socio-estabulatory-dissentialism.'

'Mm?'

'Man, she works in a bank.'

'A . . . *bank*!'

'Like I said. She's a teller . . . a dispenser of vile artifice . . . a distributor of anti-social-fruitifaction . . . a . . .'

'I got the message, Charlie. A teller! Good God . . .'

I made to move off.

'Er . . . sir!'

'Yes, Charlie?'

'Would you conceivably have a dollar on yuh – I'm outta coffee.'

NINE

By a stroke of great good fortune I managed to flag down a cab the moment I hit the pavement, otherwise I'd have frozen to death within the minute. The snow was not as thick on the ground as I'd expected – perhaps it had abated during the wee small hours – but there was still a good six inches of it lying around and a whole lot more overhead threatening to drop any minute.

I was grateful I'd picked a sullen driver because I didn't feel like talking, and with scarcely a note from him for the tip he was off in a stream of slush.

I shivered into the hotel and elevated to the room, entering quietly in case Buzz was asleep, but as I opened the inner door I heard him in the bathroom, singing his heart out and thoroughly enjoying his little self.

Right, I thought, I'll soon put a stop to that! So I thumped on the door and in a gruff American accent yelled, 'Hey, mister dis is da management! Will yuh can dat goddam racket. Eight people have just booked out!'

'Up yours, Tobin!' he shouted, then roared with laughter and yanked the door open. 'That is the worst American accent I've ever heard!'

'Oh, is dat so?' I said, twisting my lip like Bogart. 'Well, now, lissen here, Blue Eyes, this is where you get yours, see . . .'

'Ah! Now, don't tell me! That's Jimmy Stewart! Very good, too.'

'Piss off, Malone – it was Edward G. and you know it. Well – how did you get on, son?'

'Sort of . . . like this, actually. She was lying there . . . and I . . .' He broke off, laughing. 'By God, Tobin, what a night. Blimey, that kid makes the Kama Sutra read like the flippin'

Beano. She knows more ways to . . .' he gave a cough and grinned. 'Well, anyway, how about *you*? You look sufficiently shagmogrified to banish all doubts as to what happened.'

'Buzz, man, you would not believe it . . .'

'Sure I would.'

'No, I mean . . . about Linka . . .'

'Sure, I would.'

'Will you shut up a minute. I mean what she does during the day . . . her *job*! She's a blinkin' bank teller!'

'Eh?' he gaped, his mouth forming a big black hole in the wall of shaving soap. 'A *what*?' he laughed.

'A bank teller! King Charlie told me – I met him on the landing as I was coming out.'

'Nah, I don't believe it. *Linka* . . .!'

'Well, that's what Charlie said.'

'Huh!' He gave a shrug. 'Well, maybe he's right. I gave up being surprised about people years ago. Hey, had any breakfast?'

'Not a bite. My belly thinks its throat's cut.'

'Right – how about gettin' on the blower and rustlin' up a couple of steaks?'

'You know, I've always wanted to do that, ever since I saw it on the pictures. "Send up two steaks and a fifth of rye".'

'Well, now's your chance. Get the scotch, too, we're running low.'

'Right!'

Half an hour later we were sitting at a table by the window, overlooking a stupendous view of forty-seven filthy back yards and a multi-storey car park. Where *has* all the glamour in life gone?

'Buzz,' I said, taking a bite of very indifferent steak and dissipating the taste with a slug of Scotch, 'I don't wish to sound complaining, but I have a complaint. I am thoroughly, heartily, completely and comprehensively fed up to the tits with being broke, you know what I mean?'

'Broke?' he gulped, forcing a lump of his own steak down. 'You mean you're skint . . . flat . . . busted?'

I shook my head. 'No – thanks all the same for the offer.'

'What offer? I wasn't going to offer anything, I was going to call the management and tell 'em you couldn't pay for the steak.'

I grinned. 'No, I'm not exactly flat busted yet, though things *are* getting a touch tight round the artichokes . . . and if I don't get back to London soon I *will* be in schtuck. But I didn't mean that kind of broke. I mean I'm fed up having to settle for second best, like this hotel for instance. Just look at it; the central heating thumps and rattles like there are rats in the pipes, this bloody steak's awful, and the view is diabolical unless you happen to be a garbage connoisseur. Just think of all the fabulous views we could be enjoying at this moment – Central Park . . . the rivers . . .' I put down my knife and fork, defeated by tasteless mediocrity. 'Buzz, old son, I want *money*. Real money! Millions and millions of it.'

'Yeah,' he agreed, also surrendering to the steak. 'I know what you mean. I earn pretty good money, but by the time I've paid expenses, taxes and sent some home to me mum there isn't a heck of a lot left.'

'Buzz . . . I wonder . . .'

'Mm?'

My eyes went to his case on top of the wardrobe. 'That spider . . .'

'Yeah, I've been thinking about it.'

'I wonder just how valuable it is?'

He shrugged. 'Hard to see it's worth anything, bloody horrible splodge.'

Deep in thought, I shook out my cigarettes and gave him one. 'Buzz . . . maybe we did ourselves a big disfavour – getting away from Frank and Charlie and Miami Jo Dell. If nobody knows where to find us – *and* the spider – we can't possibly cash in if there should happen to be a reward.'

'Yeah,' he said uncertainly. 'I still don't like the idea of doin' business with that lot, though.'

'No more do I, but it's not doing either us or them any good sitting up there in its little cardboard box, is it? It's what they call . . . a Mexican stand-off, kid,' I said, switching to Bogart.

'Your lip's gonna stick like that one day – doin' impersonation of Cary Grant.'

'So – whadda we do, Blue Eyes?'

He stood up, fag in the corner of his mouth, hands hitching up his trousers. 'Why you doity rat . . . we get da phone book out, see . . . an' we look up dis guy Kokheimer, see . . . an' we tell him "Kokheimer . . . we got your stinkin' spider, see – an' if you ever wanna see dis baby again, you drop one million used and unmarked bills in the ladies' lavatory, corner of Broadway and Fulton midnight sharp." '

'Buzz, that's *very* good. Gregory Peck is not the easiest guy to do . . .'

But Buzz was not listening. He was crossing the room and pulling out a forty pound telephone directory from beneath a small table which I swear gave a sigh of relief.

'Here,' he said, throwing the book at me and almost breaking both arms.

Hey, wouldn't it be a giggle if there was a Kokheimer? Now, let's see . . . Kakhandler . . . Kikstart . . . Kisspiddler . . . Kuntstruck . . . oops, gone too far . . .'

'*Kuntstruck*? You're joking?'

'Yes,' I laughed, but the laughter quickly died. 'Hey . . . oh, my God . . .'

'What? *Is* there a Kokheimer?'

'No.'

'Oh.'

'There are three!'

'Eh?'

'A.W. . . . D.Z. . . . and P.G. Prof.'

'Well, whaddya know.'

I looked at him. 'Well . . . what do we do now?'

Pause.

'Phone 'em. All of them.'

'And say what?'

Another pause.

'Play it cool. Ask them . . . if they've mislaid anything . . . I don't know! You'll have to play it by ear.'

'*I* will?'

'Certainly – it's your flamin' spider.'

'Mmm. Well, one thing – they can't kill me down the phone. Can they? Let's see what turns up.'

I got up, humped the directory over to the bed and picked up the phone. The hotel operator came on. Nice chap.

'Yeah?'

'Er . . . could you get me a New York number, please?'

'That's what I'm here for. Lemme have it.'

With pleasure – right up the crutch.

I gave him the number and heard him muttering to himself as he dialled it, then he cut out as it began to ring . . . and ring . . . and ring . . .

'Any luck?' asked Buzz, sitting opposite me on his bed and smoking my fags.

'It's ringing but I don't think there's anyone home . . . eight . . . nine . . .'

'What you doin'?'

'Counting. You're supposed to give them fifteen in case they're in the loo . . . thirteen . . . fourteen . . . nah, that's it . . .'

'HELLO!'

'YIPE!' I snatched the receiver away, my ear blasted by the raucous bellow.

'HELLO!' she demanded again.

'Er . . . hello, is that Mrs Kokheimer . . .?'

'Is that Dumberry's? Now, lissen here, you dumb bastards, you promised to be round here at eight *sharp* to clear this sink! How come it's noon already and yuh still ain't here! Mister, I'll tell yuh, there's a stink in this kitchen that'd make a *skunk* throw up, and if you . . .'

'Mrs Kokheimer . . .! This is not Dumb . . .'

'. . . get round here by one . . .'

'Mrs Kokheimer, I'm sorry to disappoint you but this is not Dumbuggers . . . berry's . . .'

'Huh?'

'This is *not* Dumberry's . . .'

'Then how'd you know about my sink?'

'Er . . .'

'Lissen, are you guys tappin' my phone or sumpn? How come you know what's goin' on in my . . . say, lissen, who the hell *are* yuh, anyway?'

I sighed at Buzz and shook my head as he whispered, 'Who are *Dumberry's*?'

'Mrs Kokheimer,' I continued, 'you don't know me, but . . . well, have you by any chance mislaid anything recently?'

'Mis . . . mis*laid* anythin'? Sure, I have, I've mislaid a god-dam *plumber*, that's what I've . . .'

'No, it wasn't a plumber I had in mind, Mrs Kokheimer . . .'

'A *plumber*?' frowned Buzz.

'Sssh! No, this was considerably smaller than a plumber, Mrs Kokheimer . . .'

'Oh, smaller, huh? Was it . . . bigger than a breadbox?'

'Er, no . . .' Hand on phone, to Buzz. 'This is ridiculous – she's lost a bleeding plumber, not a spider. It's a waste of time.'

'Well, ask her outright if she's lost a spider.'

'Eh, Mrs Kokheimer . . . have you by any chance lost a spider . . .?'

A strangled silence, then . . .' WILLIE SHARK . . . IF YOU DON'T GET OFFA THIS GODDAM PHONE AND STOP PESTERIN' PEOPLE WITH YOUR STUPID TRICKS . . .'

I slammed down the phone and massaged my ear. 'Christ, what a voice.'

'Wrong party, I presume?'

'Can you believe there are people in this world who have *not lost* a spider recently? Ridiculous . . .'

'Right – who's next?'

'Malone, I do believe you're enjoying this.'

He laughed. 'It's the way your eyes cross whenever somebody screams down the phone. Who's next?'

'Kokheimer . . . D.Z.'

I picked up the receiver and once again Laughing Larry answered with his customary good humour.

'Yeah?'

'I have another New York number, if you'd be so kind.'

I gave it to him . . . and waited, this time not so long.

'Yeah?' said a voice.

'Er . . . Mr Kokheimer.'

'Yeah, speakin'.'

'Mr Kokheimer, you don't know me, but a "certain article" has come into my possession that might conceivably be of interest to you . . .'

'SSSSSSShhhhh ! !' he went, not unlike an empty aerosol can. 'Lissen – how many times I told you guys never ta call me on this number! An' who the hell gave it to yuh anyways – Grapefruit Garson?'

'Er . . . no . . .'

'Den it musta been that meat-head Ice-Pick Paloni!'

'Mr Kokheimer . . .'

'Shut up! OK – now you're on – what yuh got? Ice?'

'Er . . . no . . .'

I was making faces at Buzz and waving him over to listen into the earpiece, and with my hand over the mouthpiece I whispered, 'This guy's a fence! He thinks I've got something hot to sell!'

'Well, what, then!' rapped Kokheimer. 'Come on, I ain't got all day.'

'Sounds like this could be the one!' gasped Buzz. 'Ask him if he knows Bellamey.'

'Mr Kokheimer . . . does the name . . . Bellamey . . . mean anything to you?'

Silence. Then ... 'Bellamey? Yuh mean "Burpgun" Bellamey?'

'Could be,' I answered laconically, slipping into Bogart.

'Go on.'

'Well, what we've got came from him.'

'Oh, yeah?'

'Yeah.'

'Huh huh . . . now that's mighty interestin'. An' just *when* did Burpgun pass this "commodity" to yuh?'

'Yesterday.'

'Yesterday,' huh. Now, that's *real* interestin' – an' also kinda miraculous – considerin' Burpgun was cut in half by Piano Petrocola up in Chi two years last Easter!'

'Oh.'

'Now, lissen here, punk, say what yuh gotta say an' get outta my hair! What the hell have yuh *got*?'

'We've got a . . . spider, Mr Kokheimer.'

An appalled pause, followed by a gasp. 'Look, wh . . . who is this? Who the hell *are* yuh? N . . . now, lissen ta me, I had nuthin' ta do with that heist, yuh hear! An' Spider knows damn well I didn't! He knows I wouldn't touch that stuff – it was Sweatpea Swartz, common knowledge!'

'No, I'm afraid you misunderstood, Mr Kokheimer . . .'

'You tell Spider ta lay off, yuh hear! An' get the hell off my phone – an' *stay* off!'

Crash!

This time Buzz shared the wince.

'Well, what d'you know,' he exclaimed. 'A real live fence! By heck, Russell, it's amazing what an innocent phone call turns up. We may have stumbled onto a revolutionary method of crime detection. All the cops have to do is wade through the phone book telling people they've found a spider and . . . well, maybe not. Right – who's last?'

'Kokheimer . . . P.G., Prof.'

'Sounds distinctly unhopeful. OK, buddy, get to it.'

Once again I picked up the receiver, catching Happy Harry in mid-guffaw.

'Yeah?'

'I realize it's a frightful bore, old chum, but I have yet a *third* New York number.'

'Some days are like that. OK, what'll it be?'

I passed the information and he dialled.

It rang eight times before the voice answered – well, not so much a voice as a boom from the tomb.

'Professor Kokheimer's residence.'

I covered the mouthpiece. 'Buzz – I've got through to *God*!' And into the phone I said, 'Good afternoon, would I be addressing Professor Kokheimer?'

'No, sir, you would not. This is his manservant. Who is calling?'

'Er . . . Professor Kokheimer doesn't know me, but . . .'

'Your name, sir . . . and, if you'd be so kind, your business.'

'My name is . . . Malone . . .'

Buzz gasped, 'You bastard!'

'. . . and my business . . . well, let's say I may very well have something that belongs to the professor.'

'Oh, really', he boomed. 'It being, sir?'

'Look . . . if you don't mind, I'd prefer to discuss this with the professor. It's . . . rather personal.'

Pause – during which time I just knew he was going to put down the phone. But then . . . 'One moment, please.'

Several ticked by.

'What's happening?' asked Buzz, lighting yet another of my cigarettes.

'Lurch has gone for his master.'

'Who?'

'Frankenstein's monster – the prof's manservant. You've never heard a voice like it. Makes Lon Chaney sound like Shirley Temple. "Your name, sir . . . and if you'd be so kind – your business." I'll bet he's got rivets in his neck. Hey up, someone's coming . . .'

There were sounds of activity the other end, a sort of scuffling, then someone picked up the phone and immediately dropped it again, accidentally on a table, blasting my ear again.

'Cor!' I winced.

Then, like balm on my throbbing organ, a voice of genteel musicality. 'Yes, Mr Malone, this is Professor Kokheimer. What can I do for you?'

He sounded such a nice bloke I was sorry I'd lied about my name.

'Professor, this is not Malone . . . my name is Tobin. Mr Malone is my . . . associate. Professor, this may sound rather confusing to you and the chances are you won't know what I'm talking about, but it's possible we have something in our possession that you are expecting.'

Nice mannered chap, too – willing to listen patiently. 'Go on, Mr Tobin.'

'Professor, may I ask you a question? Does the name "Bellamey" mean anything to you?'

'Bellamey . . .' he said thoughtfully, then gave a short laugh. 'I knew a Bellamey at University, but that was many years ago . . .'

'No, I don't think this could be the same fellow. This one didn't seem the university type somehow.'

'May I ask you what it *is* you have that you think I may be expecting, Mr Tobin?'

'It's . . . a package, professor,' I said guardedly. 'I've just come up from Miami . . .' I paused, hoping that "package" and "Miami" would get some reaction. They didn't.

'How unfortunate,' he laughed. 'Journeys in the reverse direction are infinitely preferable this time of the year.'

'Er, yes. Professor, just outside Miami, at the next station up the line in fact, I was handed the package by a man named Bellamey who insisted I get it to "Kokheimer".

'Yes,' he said, waiting for me to go on.

I gave Buzz a shrug and continued dispiritedly, knowing I'd struck out for the third time. 'Well, it was obviously a case of mistaken identity on Bellamey's part, professor, because I don't *know* anybody by the name of Kokheimer, not personally, that is. And so we've been through the New York telephone directory and . . .'

'Discovered me,' he said cheerfully. 'Well, I'm sorry to disappoint you, Mr Tobin, but I know nothing of a Bellamey or a package – and to my knowledge I'm not expecting delivery of anything . . . certainly nothing from Miami.'

'Oh, I see. Well, I'm sorry to trouble you, professor . . .'

'That's quite all right. It was kind of you to take the trouble to telephone. I hope you find the right Kokheimer, it's a fairly unusual name to be sure.'

'Yes, well, goodby, pro . . .'

Buzz was tapping me on the boot and mouthing, 'Ask him if he knows a Mis . . . Miscrop . . . you know – whosit . . . in Africa!'

'Goodbye, Mr Tob . . .'

'Oh professor . . .! Just . . . one more question if you wouldn't mind. Do you happen to know a man by the name of Mistophoulus . . . he lives in Africa . . .'

'Mistophoulus!' A chuckle, tempered by mystification. 'Why, yes, I know a Mistophoulus . . .'

I slapped my hand over the mouthpiece. 'Bingo! He knows him!' Back to the prof., very excited. 'Well, professor in that case, this package will certainly be for you!'

'But . . . Mr Tobin . . . I . . .' The poor guy was obviously flummoxed. 'Er, do you know what is *in* the package? Did this man Bellamey tell you what it contained?'

'Professor, we *do* know what it contains . . . I'm afraid we opened it – hoping to find an address.'

'Of course,' he said understandingly. 'In the circumstances I'd have done the same thing myself. And what *does* it contain, Mr Tobin?'

Well, here goes, I thought – in for a penny, in for a few thousand dollars, maybe. I winked at Buzz who was nodding vigorously, full of hope. 'It's . . . a spider, professor.'

If I expected any extravagant form of reaction – a gasp, a pregnant pause – I was disappointed. All he said, calm as you please, was, 'Indeed. Not the most pleasant revelation for you, I imagine. Most people detest our little arachnid friends. Is it a *large* spider, Mr Tobin?'

'It's a bloomin' monster, professor,' I said, and he chuckled. 'I think it's a tarantula.'

'Ah, you know something of spiders, then?'

'Only that I can't stand them.'

He gave a laugh. 'Perhaps that's because you don't know them. Well well, so Mistophoulus has sent me a tarantula . . . but how on earth did the package get into the hands of this Bellamey . . . in Miami! You say there's no address on the package?'

'No, nothing.'

'How very strange. I must admit to complete bewilderment. But . . . how did you know about Mistophoulus, may I ask?'

I sighed. 'Well, it's a long story, professor, and quite involved . . .'

'But one I'm most anxious to hear,' he insisted pleasantly. 'Tell me, Mr Tobin, where are you now?'

'I, er . . .' Caution, Tobin, play it cool. He sounds a nice, innocent old guy, but don't forget Frank and Charlie and

Miami Jo Dell. You don't want them bursting into the room ten minutes from now. 'Er, Mr Malone and I are just passing through, professor . . . on our way to Canada.'

Buzz was nodding, approving my caution.

'Just passing through?' said the prof. 'Then . . . I take it you are currently in New York city?'

'Yes, that's right.'

A pause. 'Mr Tobin . . . I hesitate to impose further on your kindness, having gone to all this trouble to locate me, but I wonder whether you could spare the time to visit me here at the house . . .?' My heart boinged. 'I am, naturally, interested to discover what species of spider Mistophoulus has sent me, but . . .' he chuckled again, 'I must confess to an even greater curiosity concerning your story. I really would be obliged if you and Mr Malone could find time to visit me here on Riverside Drive . . . and rest-assured you would most certainly not be out of pocket as far as expenses are concerned . . .'

'Er, one moment professor . . .'

Again I covered the mouthpiece. 'He's invited us up to his house – on Riverside Drive! And has just intimated that "we most certainly would not be out of pocket as far as expenses are concerned" . . .!'

'A reward!'

'Could be his subtle way of putting it – yes.'

'Wow! Well, what d'you think?'

I shrugged. 'He certainly sounds a nice old chap . . . and unless he's a damn good actor I'm certain he doesn't know anything about all this.'

Buzz curled his lips. 'So – he's a murderer with acting talent.'

'Er . . . are you there, Mr Tobin?'

'Yes, sorry, professor, I was just conferring with Mr Malone.'

'I should explain that, of course, I would be most willing – if I were able – to come to *you* for the package, but unfortunately I'm confined to a wheelchair . . . and with only Krantz, my butler, and I in the house, I really . . .'

'I quite understand, professor – and I'm sorry to hear . . .'

'Oh, no matter. Look . . . if, as you say, you are just passing through New York, may I suggest you come to the house for dinner tonight? Forgive my forthrightness, but I feel some suggestion is necessary as a starting point, I mean, this evening may not be suitable for you . . . in that case, how . . .'

'Oh, no, this evening would be fine professor, but . . . well, look, may I just confer with Mr Malone again and we'll try to work something out.'

'Well, indeed you may. Good heavens, I am in *your* debt. You must suit yourselves precisely. Confer by all means . . . call me back if you wish . . .'

'No, no, I . . . don't think that will be necessary, professor, but . . . well, there's one question I'd like to ask you before I talk to Mr Malone . . .'

'And what is that, Mr Tobin? My goodness, you sound . . .' he gave a laugh, '. . . positively suspicious over the telephone. Is there some aspect of this business that gives you *cause* for suspicion? Mystification I can fully understand, but I assure you there is no cause for alarm of any kind.'

'No . . . I'm sure,' I said, unconvincingly. 'But I would just like to ask you . . . under what circumstances you know this Mr Mistophoulus?'

'Mistophoulus!' This time he gave a hearty laugh. 'Is it Mistophoulus that's worrying you? Good heavens, he is simply a supplier of entomological samples. Forgive me, Mr Tobin – perhaps long before this I should have explained that I am an entomologist – in lay terms, a bug hunter, a collector and student of all insects. And dotted around the world I have various agencies working on my behalf, in Europe, the Far East, South America – and, of course, in Africa. Pietro Mistophoulus is my accredited and highly respected agent in Cape Town, who sends me any particularly interesting specimen he comes across, sometimes cabling me beforehand and sometimes not, depending on its value. Hence I can only assume that the spider you have in your possession is of minor value, unworthy of the expense of a cable, though how on earth it found its way unaddressed to Miami is quite baffling. However, I hope this explanation has eased your mind?'

'Indeed it has, professor,' I said grimly, pulling a face at Buzz. 'And if you'll just give me a moment to speak with Mr Malone . . .'

'Of course, of course.'

I covered the phone and heaved a dejected sigh.

'Boy, oh boy, did *we* guess wrong. Mistophoulus is merely his agent in Cape Town – sends out samples of bugs now and again. If the bug is valuable, Mistophoulus cables the prof. that it's on its way – if not, he doesn't bother. And so – since in this case no cable was sent . . .'

'That mess up there is not worth the box it comes in.'

'Probably less. Well, son, what are we going to do? Do we go out and have dinner with him tonight . . . or simply bung the spider in the post?'

'Dinner? He's invited us to dinner?'

'Sure. He's one of the old school – terribly polite. Actually he sounds a lot of fun.'

Buzz shrugged. 'Well . . . why not? We could go early and meet the girls later. Riverside Drive isn't far – about fifteen, twenty minutes in a cab. Sure – let's go. I've just got to see what that Lurch looks like.'

'OK,' I grinned. 'Hello, professor . . . yes, we'd like very much to come to dinner, thank you. We're at Times Square – only about fifteen minutes away. We'll get a cab. What time would you like us?'

'How would eight o'clock suit you?'

'Perfectly.'

'Well, I look forward to meeting you both. Until eight then.'

I rang off and turned to Buzz. 'Well, son . . . hey, what's the matter?'

'I'm thinking.'

'What about?'

'Russ . . . there's something bloody wrong somewhere, mate. The professor might sound a nice old bloke – and maybe he *is* a nice old bloke – but let us not forget those Frank and Charlie characters and the conversation you overheard about them "taking out Bellamey" and about Mistophoulus "taking out Kresge" . . . *and* don't forget Miami Jo Dell tried to smother you *and* pinched your grip . . .'

I heaved a sigh and shook my head. 'Ee, I don't know, Buzz. I wish I knew what the hell was going on. One minute it looks as though the spider is worth millions and the next minute it's not worth the price of those phone calls. Looks to me as though *some*one's lyin' through their little spiked teeth and I sure would like to know *who*!'

'Well,' he said, stretching out on the bed, arms behind his head, 'there's only one way to find out – and that's to have dinner with the prof. And we have exactly . . .' he looked at his watch, 'five hours and twenty-two minutes to decide whether we do or we don't. Personally speaking, I have already made up my mind what I think we should do – and will now take a short nap to restore my batteries for the festive occasion.'

'You obviously think we should go.'

He grinned. 'Come what may, it sure beats playin' tennis.'

'OK,' I said, also stretching out, 'we go. And if I die before my time I shall return and haunt the nuts off you. There's one thing that bothers me a bit, though . . .'

'Oh?' he said, eyelids already drooping. 'What's that?'

My eyes travelled significantly to his case on top of the wardrobe. 'I wonder what an entomologist is likely to serve for dinner? I mean, if Herbert isn't valuable . . .'

'Yerk,' he grimaced. 'You rotten devil, Tobin.'

'Oh, I don't know . . . a few chips . . . peas . . . pleasant dreams, Buzz.'

TEN

We awoke at seven, ordered tea, got dog-piddle (one tea bag passed very smartly over a gallon of lukewarm water), got changed, prepared ourselves for the storm by wearing three T-shirts each under our dress shirts, and did a final recap on our preparations for come what may.

'I'm taking my passport and traveller's cheques,' I said. 'I don't trust Jovial George on the switchboard downstairs, he's far too happy. The minute we're out of the front door he could be up here rifling me undies.'

Buzz nodded. 'I always carry mine, anyway.'

'I must say you look pretty devastato, son. Very chic.' Which he did in a mid-grey striped suit, pale blue shirt and dark blue tie. I had on a black jersey job with a black and white paisley-patterned shirt and matching tie. A pretty sexy pair, come to think of it.

'I feel like Garth,' I said, flexing me biceps that were currently sweltering under the three T-shirts. 'But we'll be warmer than last night. Right – you ready?'

He tipped a puddle of 'Saracen Blade' after-shave into his hand and slapped his cheeks, oohing and aahing.

'You want to watch that stuff, mate,' I told him. 'You'll cut your bleedin' throat.'

'Ready,' he said, picking up the package. 'And fit for anything.'

We descended to the lobby, stinking up the elevator with a fierce combination of 'Saracen Blade' and 'Tiger Bite', waved a cheery bonsoir to Laughing Len on the switchboard and plunged through the street door.

Whhoosshh! The bitter north wind sliced through our clothing and into the bones before you could say knife. Three T-shirts? We needed thirteen.

One thing about living on Times Square, there are always plenty of taxis and we flagged one down before we'd staggered fifty yards.

'Riverside Drive and 159th?' I asked the driver, a funny little guy wearing ear muffs and a striped muffler.

'Eh?' He removed one of the ear muffs.

'Riverside Drive and 158th?'

'Sure, why not,' he said jovially. 'Step in before yuh freeze ta death.'

We scrambled in, teeth chattering like machine guns.

'Blimey, it's cold,' gasped Buzz.

With trembling hands we got the fags out and soon had a good comforting fug going.

'You know,' I said, rubbing a hole in the steamed-up window, 'one of these days I must come back and see New York. All I've seen so far is the inside of five cabs and three million tons of snow flakes.'

'Aw, it's the greatest little town on oith,' commented the driver, completely removing his ear muffs as though preparing for protracted oratory. 'You're foist trip here?'

'Mine, yes, but my fr . . .'

'Lissen – did you know that over *fourteen million* people visit New Yoik every single year?'

'Is that a fact?' I said. 'No, I didn't know that. Did you know that, Buzz?'

'No, I didn't know that, Russell.'

'My friend didn't know that either,' I told the driver, whose name, according to his I/D card, was Hermann Schitz.

'Uh huh,' he nodded, patronisingly. 'An' did you also not know that on any single *day* we have over *one quarter of a million* visitors to New Yoik?'

I shook my head. 'No, Mr Schitz, I didn't know that either.'

'Me, neither,' said Buzz.

'Well, now, maybe you did not *also* know that these visitors may arrive here over one of our thoirteen major bridges – which do not, incidentally, include our *forty-five* smaller commoicial bridges. Or they may arrive by boat at any one of our three hun'erd and fifty waterfront piers. An' what, you may ask yourself, do these visitors *do* when they get to New Yoik? Why, they visit our *thoity-three* museums, our *thoity-two* colleges an' univoisities, our *nine hun'erd and fifty* public schools, our *four thousand* choiches, *eighty-seven* parks, *seven hun'erd an' twenty-five* playgrounds, *four hun'erd and fifty* tennis courts, *thoity* swimmin' pools, *twenty* picnic areas, *four hun'erd and . . .*'

Buzz gave me a nudge in the ribs. 'You getting all this down?'

I tapped my head. 'Right in here. You just never know when it'll come in useful. What street are we on now?'

'This is Broadway and . . .' he rubbed the window and peered out. '. . . and 59th Street. That's the beginning of Central Park over there.'

That did it. Radar Ronnie picked up the words 'Central Park' and was off.

'Yes, siree, that's Central Park all right – an *eight hun'erd and forty* acre oasis amidst Manhattan's concrete canyons. Bein' *two and one half miles* long and *half a mile* wide, the park consists of beautifully laid lawns, flower beds, lakes and bridal paths. It also contains a *zoo* . . . and during the summer months people congregate on the Mall to enjoy free band concerts and dancing.'

'Get away,' said Buzz, stifling a yawn.

'Fancy that,' said I.

'Yes, siree. The value of the park in toims of real estate is, of course, almost im*poss*ible to estimate . . .'

'Of course,' droned Buzz, pretending to fall off his seat, fast asleep.

'. . . but assumin' that an acre of land in Manhattan is woith upwards of *half a million* bucks, right there you got yourself a piece of land worth anythin between *a half billion* and *one billion* dollars . . .'

'Fancy.' Buzz grimaced at me and murmured, '*Eighteen thousand* taxis in New York and *we* had to get James A. Fitzpatrick!'

On we went, cutting west from Broadway onto Riverside Drive, then holding the snow-swept Hudson River close on our left all the way to 158th Street – a good five miles drive. Finally Hermann pulled off Riverside at Trinity Cemetery and began curb-cruising down a long, dark, deserted crescent, trying to find the house.

'What was the name again?' he asked, his face screwed up at the window as he attempted to peer through the blizzard.

'Haven Grange,' I told him.

'Huh! Not much around here deservin' of *that* name,' he chuckled. 'Werewolf Haunt would be more like it. Real creepy neighbourhood you picked yourselves.'

He had a point. Not that we could see many houses through the driving snow, but it wasn't necessary – the *gates* were morbid enough. Heavy, black iron jobs set in towering stone pillars, real Wuthering Heights stuff, looking as though they hadn't been opened in centuries.

'Haven Grange . . .' he muttered, directing an externally mounted spotlight from inside the cab, trying to pick up a name on a pair of crumbling pillars. 'Nope . . . that one looks like . . . Edgecombe Manor. Wrong house, thanks be – I sure wouldn't fancy drivin' up there!'

'I don't fancy driving up *any* of 'em,' murmured Buzz, expressing my feeling precisely, for without exaggeration the grounds of all these houses, looming dark and very overgrown, were forbidding in the extreme. And although we couldn't see the houses it was a foregone conclusion they were all gloomy mausoleums, eighty-roomed Victorian sepulchres shrouded in mist and mystery and what the heck were we *doing* here!

'Buzz . . .' I said.

'I know.'

'What d'you think?'

'I think we're bloody balmy.'

'We . . . could go back and phone him – tell him we couldn't find the place in the snow.'

'Now you're talking.'

'Hmm . . .' I said thoughtfully.

'What?'

'Well, it's just . . .' I shrugged. 'He sounded such a nice old guy.'

'So does Dracula before the moon comes up.'

'And he's made dinner for us . . .'

'Son, from the looks of these places, we could *be* dinner.'

'Yeah, I know . . . well, we've only got two choices: either we go on or turn round now.'

'The hairs on the back of my neck say we've only got one choice: the second one.'

'Well . . . if you think so . . .'

'Hey!' It was Hermann, his face covered in snow. 'There she is! Haven Grange!'

'He bloody would,' said Buzz.

We peered through the snow, making out a pair of ten-foot iron gates surmounted by spikes, and beyond them – a solid mass of totally uninviting darkness.

'There's a bell and a talk-piece over on the pillar,' said Hermann, coming to a halt.

I looked at Buzz. He looked at me.

'Well . . .?' he said.

'Mm . . .?'

'You did all the talking. He doesn't know me.'

'Wouldn't this be a good time to get acquainted?'

'No.'

'Oh.' I heaved a sigh. 'Well, looks like Hermann has made the decision for us.'

I got out, clumped through a foot of snow to the bell button and gave it a poke, praying that no one would answer. For a while nobody did. I stood there shivering, peering through the gates at the snow-covered jungle beyond, unable to see more than twenty yards of driveway before it turned sharp left and was lost behind a clump of towering rhododendrons.

Well, that was it – nobody at home. Was it *our* fault the bell wasn't working? At least we'd tried. Gleefully I made to turn back to the cab when a grille, set above the bell button, gave a couple of crackles and Kranz's sombre boom came through.

'Yes, who is it, please?'

Defeated, I turned back and spoke into the grille. 'This is Russ Tobin, Mr Krantz. The professor is expecting us.'

'Indeed he is, sir. I will open the gates for you.'

Immediately, from a small wooden box-like structure just inside the gates to the right, came a whirring and clacking of ancient machinery, and the gates began to open inwards.

'Please drive straight up to the house, Mr Tobin, I shall await you there.'

'Thank you.'

I climbed back into the cab, shivering uncontrollably.

'OK – in you go, Mr Schitz.'

'Er . . . I won't be hangin' around, you un'erstand, gents. I gotta get back to town. Hope you weren't expectin' me ta wait around or anythin'.'

'No,' I said, 'We'll be staying for dinner.'

'Ya kiddin',' he muttered.

He drove through the gates and slowly followed the winding drive which took three or four decisive bends around more huge clumps of rhododendrons before finally straightening out for its approach to the house.

House?

It was a flamin' castle!

As it came into sight around the last forest of rhododendrons, Buzz and I shot forward in our seats, mouths open. It was enormous! I've seen a few Gothic monstrosities in my time – we've got some beauties back home in Liverpool – but this was the granddaddy of them all. A solid, stolid, squalid, towering, looming monster of a place, black with age, forbidding in the absolute from its iron-studded, porch-protected, siege-withstanding front door to the top of its castellated, granite-faced, Norman church-like tower.

'You're . . . eatin' dinner *here*?' gulped Hermann.

'They sure don't build 'em like this anymore,' whispered Buzz, aghast. 'Except on film sets for "Blood Of The Ghoul" and "The Beast Who Drank Brains" . . . oh, Christ . . .'

'What's the matter?'

'Look – the front door just opened . . . and that's *got* to be Lurch.'

I had a peer. 'Oh, blimey . . .'

He stood there in the gloom . . . a tall, cadaverous creature with a gaunt, white face, immaculate in crumpled tails, his hands dangling almost to his knees.

Hermann cleared his throat and gunned the accelerator nervously, impatient to be off. 'Well, here y'are fellas . . .'

I put the money in the tray and turned to Buzz. 'Well . . . after you, son.'

'Yeah,' he grunted, and opened his door.

We'd hardly set foot on the ground before Hermann was off, executing a skidding U-turn in the snow and into the first bend, out of sight.

Bracing ourselves we approached Krantz who appeared to grow alarmingly the nearer we got, finally reaching six foot six as we drew close to him.

'Please come in, gentlemen,' he bade us, his voice, deep and lugubrious like a slowed-down recording, booming around the porch.

I passed close to him, smelling moth balls and feeling suddenly puny in his shadow, and entered the house, regretting we'd come the instant I stepped over the threshold.

The baronial hall was a vast, stone-flagged barn of a place, empty but for a couple of heavy oak tables against the walls and a man o' war staircase that climbed the far wall to a galleried landing, it's prodigious weight threatening to pull the entire house down.

Suspended from the ceiling, which was so high it was out of sight, hung a huge black wrought-iron chandelier from which half a dozen miserable light bulbs offered just enough illumination to a score of gruesome mounted animal heads to frighten the living daylights out of you but scarcely enough to light the far reaches of the hall itself.

It was, to boot, an icy, draughty, totally cheerless place, and if Hermann Schitz had still been parked outside I'd have about-turned on some pretext or other and been off so fast my shoes would've smoked.

'If you would kindly wait in the drawing room, gentlemen, the professor will be with you in a moment,' announced Krantz, closing the door with a resounding clang. 'This way, please.'

We followed in his moth ball wake, noting how bad he was on his feet, poor soul, and as we crossed the draught-swept floor, Buzz touched my elbow and made an agonized face.

'I wanna go home!' he whispered. 'I want me Mum!'

I compressed a laugh, straightened my face just in time as Krantz pushed open a pair of tall oak doors and turned to gesture us in.

'Please make yourselves comfortable – the professor won't be a moment.'

'Thank you,' I said.

We entered the room and the doors closed behind us.

Comfortable!

The room was a bug house – its walls choc-a-bloc with glass cases containing insects, butterflies, moths, spiders and a billion other unmentionables, all so obnoxious to us that at first we hugged the table in the centre of the room, finding comfort in distance. But eventually, human inquisitiveness overcoming repulsion, we gradually ventured nearer and nearer the cases, open-mouthed with horror.

'Just look at *this* bugger!' gasped Buzz, indicating a dark-brown centipede, over a foot long and as thick as a sausage. 'Man, just imagine finding that inside your vest!'

'How about your underpants?'

'Yerk!' he shuddered. 'If he didn't bite it off, he'd bloody kick it to death.'

We moved slowly on, discovering in time a case of dragonflies, some so huge you'd swear they'd been manufactured.

'South American,' I read. 'Huh . . . and to think I fancied exploring the Amazon by canoe as a kid. By heck, Buzz, you'd have seen some fast paddling if I'd clapped eyes on one of those sods. The tidal wave would've swamped Peru!'

'Then how about these babies,' he said, indicating a caseful of hairy, hellish-looking scorpions. 'How'd you like a couple of those in your knickers?'

We moved on, ughing and yucking at some terrible spiders, so immersed in their horrific fascination that we didn't hear the door open, heard only a cheery, chuckling voice behind us saying. 'How accurately your reactions epitomize man's relationship with spiders: fear and fascination.' We turned. 'Good evening, gentlemen, I am Kokheimer. I'm delighted to meet you.'

He came across to us in a battery driven wheelchair, a slim, jovial man with bright blue eyes and a marvellous head of white wavy hair, dressed in a tweed suit and woollen shirt.

'Russ Tobin,' I said, taking his firm though somewhat rheumy hand. 'And this is an Australian friend, Buzz Malone.'

'A great pleasure, Mr Malone . . . and I can't thank you both enough for venturing out on such a terrible night. It's more than kind of you . . . ah, Krantz . . . a glass of sherry, gentlemen?'

Krantz had entered with a decanter and glasses on a silver tray. He set it on the table and while he poured, Kokheimer was saying, 'I trust you weren't too dismayed by first sight of the house. It's a gloomy old barn, I'm afraid, but we've been here for donkey's years and its size suits me. Heaven knows where I could find a more modern home with sufficient space for my menagerie.' He gave a chortle. 'Besides – Krantz wouldn't permit me to leave. It's as much his home as mine, eh, Krantz?'

Krantz affected an expression as close to a smile as he probably ever got – more a pained twisting of the upper lip – and rumbled, 'Indeed it is, sir.'

With gracious formality he proferred the tray all round and then departed, closing the doors behind him.

'Your health, gentlemen,' said Kokheimer. 'Dinner will be served in about half an hour. I'm sure you two young fellows are starved, so I told Krantz to lay on a couple of good thick steaks, hope that meets with your approval.'

We told him it was very kind.

'Not at all. I appreciate what you've done for me. You know, Mr Tobin, since you telephoned me I've given your story a great deal of thought and for the life of me I still can't make head nor tail of it, nor will I until I, or rather my son, Alex, contacts Mistophoulus in Cape Town. Alex, who incidentally you will meet at dinner, does all the travelling on my behalf these days and knows Mistophoulus better than I. After you called, I telephoned Alex about this strange package, and he, of course, is just as mystified by the whole business as I am – so he and his wife Ariadne are coming to dinner to help sort things out. Alex, of course, works with me here but they now have their own apartment in Lower Manhattan.' He chuckled. 'Adriadne refused point blank to live in this house – and I can't say I blame her. Not exactly the snuggest nest for a couple of newly weds, hm?'

He sipped his sherry and put the glass back on the table. 'But now, if I may, I'd like to take a look at this spider Mistophoulus has sent. Perhaps it may shed some light on the mystery.'

'Of course,' said Buzz, taking the package from his pocket and damned glad to get rid of it.

Kokheimer took it, placed it in his lap, about-turned the chair and started towards a single door at the far end of the room. 'Come – we shall take it to the laboratory and have a good look at it. Please bring your drinks.'

We followed him through the door into a room that could have been the post-mortem parlour of the local morgue. It smelled of chemicals and antiseptic and its white walls, like those in the drawing room, were filled with glass cases of insects, but in addition this room had numerous shelves and counter tops which held dozens of bottles containing the most gruesome things floating in formaldehyde.

In the centre of the red-tiled floor stood a Formica-topped table where, undoubtedly, the dastardly dissections were performed. No wonder Ariadne hadn't cared for the thought of living here. I wouldn't have been so flaming keen myself!

'Now . . .' With obvious gusto Kokheimer drew his chair to the table and began unwrapping the package, got the lid off, searched in his breast pocket for a pair of steel-rimmed glasses and settled them on his nose. Then he peered inside.

Moments passed, the silence broken only by occasional grunts, 'Uh huh . . . hmmm . . .' from Kokheimer. Then, putting the box down, he opened a drawer, took out a pair of wide forceps, and very gently lifted Herbert out and set him on the table.

Even now, knowing what he looked like, Buzz and I shuddered at the sight of the huge, stiff, hairy brute.

For a while longer Kokheimer prodded, poked and perused Herbert, muttering, 'Very interesting . . . yes, indeed, very, very interesting . . .'

I swapped a hopeful glance with Buzz, then asked Kokheimer, 'Does it . . . give you any clues, professor?'

'Hm mm . . . huh huh,' he went, having another poke, then, with a sigh he turned to us, smiling regretfully. 'Nothing unusual, I'm afraid, gentlemen – except perhaps for its size which is large without being rare. It's a good specimen of a biting but non-venomous solpugid generally though erroneously referred to as a "tarantula", though it is not of the *Lycosa* family – which is mainly found in Southern Europe. The spider itself, however, does in no way detract from the mystery surrounding its arrival here . . . and I look forward keenly to your explanation, Mr Tobin, which – if I may suggest – you keep for the dinner table so that Alex may also hear it, and to save you repeating it.'

'Yes, of course,' I said, engulfed by disappointment that Herbert was just a plain old overgrown spider and not some exciting – and valuable – rarity.

'In the meantime,' smiled Kokheimer, 'it would be my pleasure to show you around my collection – show you, if you wish, some real tarantulas. Would it be of interest to you?'

We said it would, not having the heart to disappoint the old boy who was obviously keen to do it.

'Right, then . . . let us start with some big, juicy spiders.'

'How many different kinds of spiders are there?' I asked, as we accompanied him across the room.

'Oh thousands, Mr Tobin. I detect you are British . . . did you know that there are more than six hundred British species alone?'

'Good lord, no, I didn't. I might have guessed, though – I seem to have had most of them in my bath at one time or another.'

He gave a chuckle. 'Our old friend *Tegeneria*, the cause of many a female shriek.'

'And quite a few male ones, too,' I grinned. 'I wonder why we are so frightened of them?'

He shrugged. 'Who indeed knows? Perhaps the reason lies hidden beneath many centuries of odd superstition regarding spiders. Do you know – according to the ancient Greeks, that is – how this spider business all began?'

We said we didn't.

'Well, their explanation goes like this: Arachne, the daughter of Idmon of Colophon, was renowned for her skill at weaving. So good was she that it was said that the goddess Pallas herself must have taught her. But this Arachne hotly denied and flung out the challenge: "*Certet mecum, nihil est quod victa recusem*" – "Contend with me, for there is nothing that if defeated I could refuse".

'Pallas, disguised as an old woman, begged her to take back her boastful words and when she wouldn't, Pallas revealed her true identity and challenged Arachne to a weaving contest.

'In her tapestry, Arachne depicted women cheated and seduced by the deceits of the gods – and so outraged was Pallas by this record of godly crime that she beat Arachne over the head with her boxwood shuttle until, tortured beyond endurance, Arachne put a noose around her own neck. Then Pallas, out of pity, lifted her up and saved her life, but sprinkled her with a few drops of Hecate's herb, and, touched by the venom, poor old Arachne's hair, nose and ears fell off, her head and breasts grew smaller, her slender fingers clung as legs to her sides, and her lovely body changed to that of a spider, doomed to spin forever.'

'What a terrible shame,' said Buzz. 'Nice bird like that.'

'And there, Mr Tobin . . .' said the professor, pointing to a case behind me, 'are your tarantulas – some real ones. *Lycosa tarantula* – also known as wolf-spiders.'

'They'd certainly make me howl,' muttered Buzz.

'It's a species widely distributed in southern Europe with its headquarters centred around the town of Taranto on the shores of Apulia in southern Italy, and perhaps the best-known of all species. You have no doubt heard of the dance called the "tarantella" . . .?'

We told him we had.

'Perhaps, then, you have also heard of the malaise, the sickness called "tarantism", the first case of which was reported in Italy in 1370. It was the name given to the extraordinary effects which were alleged to follow the bite of this spider and which, incredibly, could only be cured by music and dancing! The symptoms of tarantism were apparently quite alarming; pain and swelling, paralysis, nausea, delirium . . .' he smiled, 'continued priapism and . . .' now he laughed, 'shameless sexual exhibitionism against which the drugs of those days had no effect whatsoever. The only cure was, apparently, prolonged and extremely strenuous dancing which resulted in copious sweating. There has been, however, a lot of cold water poured on the theory that the tarantula was responsible for all these carryings on and a much more likely theory substituted, it being that the introduction of Christianity abolished all public exhibitions of Bacchanalian excess, and, unwilling to give up such fun, the people very cleverly devised other pretences! I personally go along with the substitute theory.'

'Just shows you,' said Buzz, 'the length people will go to for a good orgy.'

We moved slowly down the room towards the drawing room door, the professor in turn enthralling, amusing and horrifying us with information about his little pets, at one point stopping to feed a dead fly into a spider's web and treating us to a gruesome close-up of the ensuing banquet.

'There are, of course, many varied ways in which spiders capture their food,' he explained, relishing the spectacle before us, '*and* many different kinds of web. There are the *Atypidae* or Purse-web spiders . . . the *Cribellate* or Lace-web spiders . . . and there are Crab spiders, Jumping spiders, Lynx spiders, Comb-footed spiders, Pirate spiders, Orb-web spiders . . . and, of course, Money spiders.'

'Ah!' I said, 'at last one I can actually tolerate – provided it's no bigger than the head of a pin! I don't care if it doesn't bring me any money, just so long as it doesn't get any bigger than that.'

Kokheimer laughed. 'I can see you're a confirmed anti-arachnid, Mr Tobin, so I won't discomfort you any longer. Let's go into the drawing room and have another sherry before dinner.'

He led the way into the other room and had just reached the table when the double doors opened and into the room came a striking looking woman in her early thirties. She was very beautiful in a pallid sort of way, but too severe for my taste, almost frighteningly so. Dressed in a black trouser suit, its funereality relieved only by a gold spider brooch in the lapel, and her raven black hair drawn back in a tight chignon to emphasize the sharp regularity of her features, the effect was chic, expensive and terribly cold. Seeing her, my thoughts went immediately to the story of Arachne and I figured that *she* must have looked something like this woman just before Pallas turned her into a spider, and didn't have all that far to go!

Immediately behind her came a tall, tanned, handsome man, probably in his early forties and bearing a distinct resemblance to the professor. He was dressed rather formally, too, in a charcoal-grey pinstripe and light-grey tie, the pair of them looking as though they'd just come from the cemetery.

'Father . . .' this guy smiled, taking in Buzz and me as he crossed the room.

'What's the weather doing out there, Alex?' asked the professor.

'Blowing a blizzard.'

'Ariadne,' nodded the prof.

'Hello, father-in-law,' she answered, her tone as cool as her demeanour.

I'd just seen more passion in those jars of formaldehyde.

'Alex . . . Ariadne . . .' said the professor, 'may I introduce Mr Russ Tobin . . . and Mr Buzz Malone, the gentlemen I was telling you about.'

We shook hands and said hello, then Alex said to me, 'An incredible story, Mr Tobin. We're very grateful for the trouble you've gone to, but we're completely baffled as to who this chap Bellamey could be. Have you had a look at the spider, father . . .?'

The professor nodded. 'Yes . . . but it only adds to the mystery. It's nothing special, Alex – take a look for yourself – it's in there.'

The two of them went into the laboratory. While they were gone, the professor poured us more sherry and talked some more about spiders, a subject I was beginning to get heartily sick of. Nice as he was, I couldn't help feeling I'd had enough of this house and began to think of Linka, wondering what she was doing and how long it would be before I could get to her. And one glance at Buzz told me he was thinking the same about Fifi.

So it was with some relief that Krantz arrived at that moment and announced dinner was ready and Kokheimer called his son and daughter-in-law to join us. Jeez, she was a creepy bird, cold and aloof, closely resembling a *Tegeneria* herself – though I admit that if she'd appeared in my bath I'd have felt very disinclined to swish her down the plughole. Belting figure . . . wonderful breasts.

Chatting away about Herbert to Alex, Kokheimer led us out of the drawing room, across the draught-swept hall and into a dismal dining room, its walls heavily oak panelled, the lighting appalling.

Kokheimer took the head of the table in his wheelchair, Ariadne sat on his right with Alex next to her. I was placed on the professor's left with Buzz next to me, and as soon as we were settled the soup was served.

Etiquette preventing Kokheimer Senior from leaping in with a barrage of questions, we talked generally about New York and London and Sydney until the steaks were in front of us, then Alex got down to basics.

He was a man of some presence, obviously well educated and bulging with self confidence and certainly not without charm, and yet somehow I didn't like him. Maybe it was Ariadne that did it – her aloofness reflecting on him. I don't know what it was, but I couldn't altogether take to him.

As soon as the vegetables had been distributed he began, 'Well, Mr Tobin, if you can bear to go over it all a second time, I'd be most grateful. I realize it must be a bore, but I really am most interested in what happened.'

'Oh, he hasn't told it yet,' said the professor. 'I cut him short to save repetition. I showed him some spiders instead . . . and do hope they haven't put him off his steak.'

'Not at all,' I grinned, 'it's beautiful. Well . . . it began in Miami two nights ago, Mr Kokheimer. I caught the midnight train virtually as it was pulling out and in the confusion was put into the wrong compartment – correction, right compartment, wrong car – a very important point, and being tired I fell asleep almost immediately . . .'

I went through the story minutely, trying to remember all the details of action and conversation (playing down the sex scene with Miami Jo Dell to an absolute minimum, naturally), but telling them what Bellamey, Miami, Frank and Charlie had said . . . about them 'taking out' Bellamey . . . about Mistophoulus 'taking out' Kresge, the whole lot. The story, prolonged by a multitude of questions from the professor and Alex (Ariadne hardly said a blind word) lasted right through the meal, and when I finally finished and they'd had a good chuckle about my escape from the train dressed in Buzz's tennis gear the professor sat shaking his head in bewilderment and the other two seemed just as mystified.

'Well . . .' said the professor, stirring his coffee, 'you told me that most lucidly, Mr Tobin, but I'm afraid *I'm* none the wiser for knowing the facts. What about you, Alex?'

Alex gave a cynical snort. 'Father . . . if the story hadn't come from such an obviously reliable source as Mr Tobin, I would be inclined to call the whole thing a preposterous fabrication. Our dealings with Pietro Mistophoulus have always been inordinately straightforward. He finds the specimens he feels will interest us and sends them direct to us here. There has never been a middle man, either in Miami or anywhere else. As for this fellow Kresge . . . I vaguely remember meeting him in Cape Town, though why he should send our sample to this Bellamey character in Miami is a complete mystery. And this "Miami Jo Dell" woman – what an incredible name – is equally mystifying. As for the two strong-arm characters, Frank and Charlie . . . he let out a laugh, 'I mean, really! Frank and Charlie! They're straight out of Damon Runyan!'

'They were real enough to us, Mr Kokheimer,' Buzz insisted quietly – and did I detect from his tone that *he* didn't much care for Alex either?

'My dear fellow, I'm not for a moment implying that I think they weren't real,' smiled Alex. 'I'm merely saying that from our point of view the entire incident is totally preposterous.' He turned to the professor. 'I'm afraid, father, that this business won't be cleared up until I've had a word with Mistophoulus, but I'm sure it can wait until I get over there in a few weeks' time.' He snorted a laugh and shook his head, 'How utterly . . .'

'Well, anyway,' said the professor, smiling at Buzz and me, 'we appreciate that you've had rather a nasty time from one source or another – not the least from Mr "Tarantula" out there, and although we can offer you no explanation in way of recompense, we do hope that at least you've enjoyed your dinner. And now, if you'll forgive me, I'll say goodnight – doctor's orders I'm afraid. There's no need to rush away, of course – Krantz is bringing more coffee. Please stay as long as you wish, then I'm sure my son would be delighted to run you back to your hotel . . .'

'Of course,' said Alex.

Buzz and I stood up as the professor wheeled round and shook hands with us. 'Once again . . . thank you very much indeed for all your trouble. It was most kind. And as I said on the telephone, we won't hear of you being out of pocket on our behalf. Alex will make restitution, I know.'

'Gladly,' said Alex.

He wheeled away across the room and with a final goodnight disappeared through the door.

'A wonderful man,' I remarked as we sat down again.

'Indeed,' replied Alex.

Suddenly all the fun had gone out of the occasion and I began to feel distinctly twitchy under the cool gaze of Ariadne who now, for only the third or fourth time, addressed us.

'Mr Tobin . . . these two men, Frank and Charlie . . . you're certain they couldn't have followed you to the hotel?'

'Absolutely certain. They weren't in sight as we left Penn Station and after that there was no way they *could* follow us.'

'But . . . I thought you said you overheard them commenting on the fact that you were travelling by Sun Time?'

I frowned, missing the connection. 'Well . . . yes, they got that information from the train steward.'

She smiled smugly. 'Then surely they could trace your hotel through Sun Time?'

'I . . .'

A flush of sudden horror rushed my cheeks. I gaped at her . . . at Buzz, finding him doing the same to me.

'Oh . . .' I stammered. 'But . . . they couldn't . . . I mean, they haven't . . .'

'You mean they "hadn't",' she corrected, 'up to the time you left this evening? Perhaps not. It would take time to extract this information from Sun Time. But I would suggest that it's a distinct probability – and one that I, were I in the position, would most certainly follow.'

I gulped, the meal now lying like a cannon ball in my tum. 'Yes . . . I suppose . . . Buzz, we'd better get back and move out.'

He gave a swallow, also having trouble with his digestion. 'Yes . . . I think we better had.'

Alex nodded. 'All right, I'll run you back. But before you

leave I want to give you something. It's only right you should be rewarded for all your trouble.'

'Oh, no, really . . .' I half-heartedly protested, receiving a kick on the shin from Buzz.

'Nonsense,' smiled Alex, getting up. 'Come with me.'

We followed him out into the hall, expecting him, perhaps, to head for the drawing room, but instead he turned towards the staircase, saying with an apologetic smile, 'It's a bit of a climb, I'm afraid, but I'm sure you'll consider it worthwhile when you get there.'

'Oh, that's . . . quite all right,' I said, winking at Buzz.

Up the main staircase we went, our footsteps clattering on the wood and echoing through the cheerless hall. Up . . . and up . . . to the dismal galleried landing, then along it, passing more stuffed animal heads, to another staircase, then up and up again, urged on by pokes in the back from a jubilant Buzz who kept whispering, 'We're in, son . . . we're in!'

'Sorry about this,' panted Alex with a laugh. 'So many times I've tried to persuade father to install an elevator. Still . . . keeps you fit, I suppose . . .'

By the third staircase I was beginning to have grave doubts about that supposition . . . and by the fourth staircase I knew that something was definitely, positively wrong! The whole thing was wrong, Alex . . . Ariadne . . . this ridiculous climb after a heavy meal.

'Mr Kokheimer . . .' I gasped, collapsing against the wall, 'really, I . . .'

He stopped and turned, smiling disarmingly. 'I'm sorry about this, I really am, but I assure you that what you are about to receive you will consider worth every puff and pant. Come on, it's not far now . . . just a dozen more stairs or so.'

'Go on!' whispered Buzz, thumping me in the bum.

Kokheimer went on again, switching on dreary little lights here and there to light our gloomy way. Now the landing ended in a door which Kokheimer opened, revealing yet another flight of stairs, steep, narrow and walled on both sides.

'Last flight,' he announced cheerfully.

We clattered up them, discovering yet another door, a good solid job, at the top.

'Here we are . . .' panted Kokheimer. 'This is what . . . we call . . . our "treasure room".'

'Wow!' This was Buzz, his avaricious eyes glowing like fireflies in the dark. And I must admit mine were glowing a bit, too, at the word 'treasure'.

Kokheimer turned the key in the heavy lock and pulled open the door, entered the room, worked the light switch and gave a curse. 'Oh, damn, the bulb's gone. Either of you fellows got a light?'

'Yes,' we chorused, pressing forward anxious to please, flicking our lighters into life.

'Good . . . you go . . . phew, I'm bushed . . . you go in and light the way . . .'

We pushed past him, me in the lead, Buzz close behind me, holding our lighters high and peering around the room.

'That's it,' said Kokheimer, 'go right in, there's nothing to bite you.'

He was right – there *was* nothing to bite us. At first glance there appeared to be nothing period! So I had a second glance, swinging my lighter from side to side, when suddenly . . .

Bang! Click!

Silence.

The silence continued . . . nobody was saying anything. I turned and peered at Buzz . . . peered past him. 'Mr Kok . . . heimer . . .' My voice trailed away. He wasn't in the room! 'Hey . . .!'

Buzz gave a start, swung round. 'What the f . . .?'

'Hey!' I ran to the door, pushed on it. 'HEY . . . MISTER KOKHEIMER . . .!'

In the ensuing silence we heard the clatter of his feet on the stairs.

'BUZZ . . .!' I gasped.

He was at my side, rattling the door latch, choking with disbelief. 'He's . . . fuckin' hell, Russ, he's locked us in!'

'Wh . . . oh, Jeezuschrist.'

ELEVEN

As most of you know, there are certain times in your life when you just can't believe the things that are happening to you. I've felt it on quite a few occasions (while in that fabulous bath with the even more fabulous Malinda on Paradise, for instance, when her husband returned home unexpectedly and I had to hide under their bed, and later on had to listen to the big fat pig rogering her up top!) Awful.

So many times I've said to myself – this is a dream, it just can't be happening to *me*. And here I was saying it again.

I mean, really – just think about it. Not forty-eight hours ago I was climbing onto the New York train, minding me own business and looking forward to a few innocent days holiday in the great metropolis, and look at me now! Locked in a creepy room at the top of a creepy tower in a dreadful Victorian abomination in up-town Manhattan! And up to me armpits in some nefarious business concerning tropical spiders! It was all too blinking unbelievable. And yet – here we were, Buzz and I staring at one another in the flickering light of two upheld lighters, wreathed in clouds of our own frozen breath and wondering what in hell had hit us.

'Russ . . .' he said, wonderingly.

'Yes, Buzz . . .?'

'The bastard's . . . locked us in! HE'S BLOODY LOCKED US IN!'

'But . . . he can't! I mean . . . I've got a date with Fifi!'

'I know.'

'I mean . . . is this . . .' he laughed, bewildered, '. . . *real*? Are we . . . really locked in a bleedin' *tower*?'

'Yes, we are, Buzz.'

'But . . . *why*? I mean . . . one minute we were sitting having dinner and . . .' a thought struck him. 'Russ . . . it had something to do with Ariadne knowing Frank and Charlie could trace us through Sun Time, didn't it?'

I nodded, 'I think it did.'

'But *why*? Don't tell me – it's sticking out like a sore cock! *They* don't want us falling into Frank and Charlie's hands . . . because *they* are in this business up to their sneaky eyeballs! Think about it! Bellamey throws the spider at you and says "get this to Kokheimer" – right?'

'Right.'

'And we've been assuming he meant the professor – because the professor was in the phone book and because he's an entomologist, OK? But there's *another* bloody Kokheimer floating around here, son – and that's bloody Alex . . .!'

'Of course!'

'And who is it that goes over to Africa and knows Mistophoulus?'

'Alex!'

'Right. Now, supposing Alex gets into mischief with this Kresge bloke . . . starts doing a private deal behind Mistophoulus's back. And Kresge sends stuff over to Alex via Bellamey in Miami, follow me?'

'Right down the line.'

'And Alex sends Miami Jo Dell down to Miami to pick the stuff up from Bellamey . . .'

'Yes, go on. You're a blinking marvel at this detecting business. Me, I can't find me own socks.'

'OK – so Miami Jo Dell goes down there, makes a hash of the pick-up and reports back to Alex that a guy named Tobin has the spider . . .'

'And we, thinking it's safe to approach a nice old professor, walk right into Alex's web! But, Buzz, the professor . . .'

'Probably innocent of what's going on. You saw his reaction to the spider. He couldn't understand why Mistophoulus had sent it, it was so ordinary. Which probably means . . .'

'Yes,' I nodded. 'That the spider *itself* is not important.'

'Right. Alex isn't just importing spiders, son, there's something else going on here – and *we* are not about to find out what it is. Alex and Ariadne do *not* want us around on two counts – one – they don't want us leading Frank and Charlie to them!'

'Of course – Alex Kokheimer being the "next party down the line" that Frank was talking about.'

'Correct.'

'Boy, I wonder what Kresge did send over from Cape Town?'

He shrugged. 'That, at the moment, is the least of our worries. The biggest is getting out of this bloody tower!'

He held his guttering lighter flame aloft and peered around the room. It was a dismal hole – bare boards, bare plaster, devoid of any fixture, furnishings or features, except for a small diamond-paned window in the far wall. We crossed to it, tried the rusted handle but it was set like concrete. We rubbed at the grimy glass in an attempt to see out, but outside dirt and snow obliterated every millimetre of it.

Buzz snapped out his lighter and felt in his pocket, producing the penknife that had caused so much grief to King Charlie's water bed, then he got to work on the handle, chipping away rust and ancient paint where the handle met the iron frame.

He worked for three or four minutes, then took off his boot and smote the handle an upwards blow . . . and it shifted. Now he worked on the frame, tapping it all round with the heel of his boot. It clicked and cracked as metal parted from ancient metal and suddenly it sprang open half an inch.

Whhoofff! A force thirty-seven gale swept through the gap bringing with it snow, withering cold and the promise of early pneumonia.

Push . . . push . . . push. Buzz got his weight behind it and shoved the window fully open, both of us gasping in the sub-zero hurricane.

'F . . . fat lot of g . . . good that did us!' he gasped, eyes watering and screwed up against the driving snow. 'C . . . can't see a flaming thing!'

Out he went, elbows on the sill, head and shoulders well clear.

'See anything!' I called.

His voice returned on the gale, raggedly, through already frozen lips. 'Yeah! A ninety-foot drop – straight down!'

'Move over!'

I joined him, the wind and cold tearing at my cheeks, ripping through my clothing as though I was naked. I looked down . . . and instantly regretted it. Nothing – but a faint smudge of white waaayyy down there. I peered left . . . right.

'Buzz . . . the drainpipe!'

'Not a chance, cock. It's covered in ice . . and it looks pretty crook to me.'

Leaning further out still, he reached for it, got his finger tips to it and gave it a shove. A six-foot length wobbled, tilted, then went hurtling down to land with a terrific crash half an hour later.

'Possibly not,' I grinned, turning on my back and peering aloft, picking out the vague outline of the turrets a good ten feet above us, with nothing but solid wall between them and us.

'Buzz . . .'

'Yes, mate?'

'There's nothing out here for us but frostbite!'

'Right!'

In we came, slamming the window closed, shivering like two dogs in a cold bath.

'Jeezus!' he gasped, beating himself and rubbing life back into his face. 'Could they have picked a better night or place for their dirty deed?'

'Nope,' I said, running on the spot while checking my cheeks for gangrene. 'B . . . Buzz, this is r . . . ridiculous . . . th . . . they just can't do this to us!'

'Correction. There are laws to say they *shouldn't* do this to us. They've flamin' well *done* it!' He stopped beating himself and I stopped running. 'You realize, of course,' he said, lighting his lighter and cupping his hands round its pitiful warmth, 'that not a soul outside this house knows we're here?'

I nodded and scratched my lighter into life, finding succour from it's modest glow. 'Yes, but I'm trying very hard not to think of it. I . . . don't suppose there's any use shouting for help . . . maybe from Krantz or the professor?'

He shook his head. 'I'm sure that crafty bastard wouldn't have locked us up here if we could be heard.'

'No. Well . . . as a matter of routine, shall we take a look at the door?'

We did . . . and three minutes later the snapped-off portions of both pen-knife blades were lying at our feet. In disgust Buzz hurled the body of the knife across the room and sank into sitting position, his back against the wall, and I joined him.

'I wonder how long they intend keeping us here?' I said, giving him a fag and lighting one myself. 'And what do they intend *doing* with us? Hey, they're in a bit of a predicament now, aren't they?'

'*They're* in a predicament!'

'Well, you know what I mean . . . I mean they've tipped their hand! There's no going back for them. If they let us go this minute, they must know we'd call the cops and lay charges of abduction against them. So . . . what are they going to *do* with us?'

He gave me a very funny look. 'Try as I might I cannot help but think of what has happened to Kresge and Bellamey.'

I gulped. 'Aw, come on . . .'

He shook his head. 'Russ, we've got to face facts, man. We have inadvertently stumbled on to something mighty serious! It might even be a mafia operation, who knows?'

'Oh, blimey . . .'

'Well, it could be. Just remember Bellamey's state of mind when he passed you the package – he was terrified! And you don't get like that playing "tick". Russ, he was running for his life . . . and by the sound of things lost it! I tell you, I am of the opinion that Alex locked us in here with the express intention of . . .'

I shut my eyes. 'Buzz . . . don't say it. I know what you're thinking but don't say the words. Let's *think*! How are we going to get out of this . . . what are we going to do when they come for us?'

'Who says they're *going* to come for us – not for a few days anyway. By that time we'll probably have frozen to death – or at least be so weak they can do what they like with us . . . dump us in the Hudson . . .'

I shivered.

'Well,' he said, 'problem solved – crime unsolved. Just two tourists who got a skinful and fell in the river . . . just two more statistics in the precinct file. And they've got a lot of days to play with, don't forget. Nobody is expecting *you* anywhere . . . and they're not expecting me in Victoria for four or five days . . .'

'Buzz, please . . .'

'Well, those are the grizzly facts, son.'

'I bloody *know*!'

I drew up my knees and hugged them, already suffering from the misery of the insidious cold. The room was literally freezing and the prospect of another two or three hours, never mind days, in this temperature, without food and water, was unthinkable.

'Thank God we put these extra T-shirts on,' said Buzz, teeth chattering, also hugging his knees. 'Here . . . turn round, back to back.' He gave a brave grin. 'Tobin, as much as I enjoy your company, right now I wish like hell you were Fifi.'

'Funny you should say that . . . I was just thinking about Linka. Oh, man, the thought of her soft, warm bed . . . and being snuggled up close to her . . . warm . . . and naked . . .'

'Shut up, Tobin. Well, it serves us right – this is where greed gets you – right up it every time.'

'Buzz, I can't tell you how sorry I am – getting you into this. Boy, how fate controls our lives. There you were – settling down for the night on that train, blissfully ignorant of Tobin's existence . . . and the next minute, because you did me a good turn . . .'

'Ah, bollocks, I'm as much to blame as you. It's time I chucked up tennis anyway.'

'Well, maybe – but I'm sure you didn't have dying in mind as an alternative.'

'Well . . . no.'

I sighed and gave a shivering yawn, then heard Buzz do the same. We lapsed into silence then, both of us shocked by what had happened, and now for the first time, taking time out to think about it, allowing our minds to adjust to the awful reality of being locked in a freezing tower, prisoners of a couple of crooks who had total control over our freedom, our very lives! But lucid thought in that temperature did not come easy, nor did the ability to stay awake. Several times I felt myself drifting off but jerked awake again, conscious that Buzz was doing the same, and though I tried hard to keep my mind alive the freezing misery of the room finally overtook me and I must have slept.

The dream this time was a real shocker. Ariadne became Arachne, the spider woman, shrieking curses at me from the centre of a room-sized web and ordering me to be thrown to my death from the top of the tower. Up I went, carried bodily by Frank and Charlie and taunted all the way by a laughing Alex. 'You wanted a reward, Tobin . . . well, you shall have it! Just a few more steps . . . a few more!' Then – out onto the gale-swept roof, dragged pitilessly to the edge and bent over the battlements. 'There is your reward, Tobin, that tombstone ninety feet below!' Then a push and I was falling . . . hands outstretched in horror as the ground rushed up to meet me . . . down . . . down . . . down . . . plummeting towards the razor edge of the tombstone . . . a terrifying death only moments away, and then . . . crash!

I shot awake with a terrible fright, heart hammering, brain whirling wondering where the hell I was. Darkness everywhere . . . frightening, enveloping darkness . . . and out of it – a hand on my arm!

'Russ . . .!' hissed a voice.

'Wh . . .'

'Are you awake?'

'Christ . . . Buzz!'

'Of course it's me! Listen . . . did you hear it?'

'Mm . . .? Wha . . .'

'The click! Didn't you hear it? Someone was at the door! Just a second ago! Ssssh . . . listen!'

We listened . . . but all I could hear was the terrific thumping of my heart.

'They've gone!' he whispered, and worked his lighter, blinding me. 'Are you awake yet, son?'

'I . . .'

'I dropped off, too – but the click woke me. Russ, I think it was the lock! I think someone unlocked the door!'

I was on my feet, mind clearing fast, and over to the door, ear pressed against the panelling, hearing nothing.

Buzz took hold of the heavy latch, pausing for a quick pray, then began to lift it. At full lift he paused, threw me a glance of dire hope, and pushed.

The door opened!

Buzz sucked in his breath, gaped popeyed at me, and then, with infinite caution, began to open it further. An inch . . . two . . . some more. Now his entire head was through.

Back he came, eyes bright. 'No one on the stairs! Come on!'

Shivering with cold and nerves I followed him out, almost colliding with him before we'd even started down. He turned to me, whispering very close, 'Take your shoes off!'

We sat on the stairs, slipped them off and stuffed them in our pockets, then we began. Down . . . down . . . down, one stair at a time, treading the extreme edge, our hearts quaking with every creak and groan that sounded like thunder claps in the silence of the house.

Walking in absolute darkness we reached the bottom – and encountered the second door. Again, with ultra caution, Buzz opened it and very, very gradually peered out. Then . . . we were through.

Along the top landing we crept, hugging the banister, using it as blind men use their sticks, totally cocooned in darkness. A dozen steps and he stopped, felt his way with his stockinged foot, and located the first stair of the descending flight, but paused again to listen. No sound to be heard but the mournful howl of the wind around and through the house and the creak of twisted timbers, a dreadful, haunted sound in the dead of night.

God, what a terrible place. I reckoned the professor was off his chump living in a house like this. I wouldn't have had it as a gift. I'd have burned the bugger to the ground and built something light, modern and . . . yipe!

Buzz's hand touched mine, telling me he was starting down. By God, the way things were going I reckon it'd be a miracle if I ever saw thirty. I reckon I'd aged fifty years since yesterday.

Down again . . . very slowly and with painful caution, our

ears bristling for the slightest human sound and every nerve jangling like a fire bell.

We reached the next landing, paused yet again to listen, and then started along it, the minutes dragging by like days, the darkness a solid, terrible thing, oppressive and suffocating, so nerve-racking that you wanted to cry out, to strike at it and race down the stairs for the front door.

But race we could not; and inch we did. We turned the corner at the next flight of stairs and once again began our silent descent, one . . . two . . . one . . . two, a stair at a time, our senses always questing, probing the darkness for sounds, smells, voices, presence, threats!

Safely we negotiated that staircase and turned onto yet another landing. Dear God, how many floors had we climbed? Four . . . five? I tried to recall but couldn't, remembering only one *hell* of a lot of stairs.

It seemed unbelievable that we could make it all the way down without hearing a human sound – but we did. Suddenly Buzz stopped and caught my arm. Now, in the past few moments, the absolute darkness had abated and I could vaguely see that he was pointing down, over the banister rail. I peered over . . . and my spirits soared. There, on the floor below, was the galleried landing! Dimly now we could see the main staircase and at the bottom of it, the hall!

A squeeze on the arm from Buzz and we were off, now moving a little faster. Down the penultimate flight we went, no longer creeping but taking one stair per stride. Seven . . . eight . . . nine . . . ten, and onto the galleried landing. Now the hall was plainly in sight, lit by a sliver of light shining from the partly opened doors of the drawing room. And there, by heaven, was the front door. The door! Out through it and into the world! We only had to cross the hall, open the door and we were free!

So help me, if it hadn't been for Buzz I'd have bolted right then and there, would have thrown caution to hell and made a run for it. As it was he turned to me, finger to his lips, then started off down the long main staircase, now hugging the wall instead of the banister, and safely reached the bottom.

And that was when we heard the voices.

They came to us distinctly, not from the drawing room itself but beyond it, from the laboratory. Buzz made a face at me then began edging along the wall, shuffling sideways, until he reached the drawing room doors, and then . . . he stopped.

And stopped!

The silly bugger was actually taking time out to listen at the doors! I touched his arm but he waved me off. Crouched forward, his ear to the crack, one hand on his knee and the other holding me off, he looked like a discus thrower warming up for the chuck.

Ten seconds crawled by . . . fifteen . . . me heart in me throat and a mouth as dry as a ball of chalk, to say nothing of ice-cold off the stone flags striking up through my stockinged feet.

'Buzz . . .!' I whispered, but again he shut me up with a gesture, but then, by God, in the next second he was rounding on me, eyes wide and full of horror. 'They're coming!'

We were off, haring across the hall to the front door, hearts a-clamour, caution by no means yet abandoned but all fumbly and terrified. He grabbed the big iron ring, twisted it . . . and pulled, cursed vehemently, turned the huge key, pulled, and cursed again, now reached up and yanked down a bolt, pulled a third time . . . and the door flew open.

WWHHHOOOSSHH! The full blast of the storm hit us. Buzz fell back, letting the door go, and with a terrific crash it slammed into the wall.

That, of course, did it. Ariadne's cry echoed from the drawing room and Alex shouted. 'What the hell was that?'

We didn't wait to tell him. One, two, buckle my shoe – our boots were on and we were out of the front door like twin rockets from a bazooka, spurred on our way by the crash of the drawing room doors and the demented wail of a downhearted female – Ariadne. 'Alex . . . they've got away!'

Splut! Straight into a foot of snow and hell for leather down the drive, legs pumping and lungs shuddering from the shock intake of freezing air . . . around the first giant clump of rhododendrons and out of sight of the house.

'They saw us!' I gasped.

'They bloody did!'

'Well, now they've got to catch us! I doubt if Alex is faster through this than we are – he hasn't got the same incentive!'

'By God, it pays to be fit!' he laughed.

'You're right, mate. Now I'm glad I don't smoke . . . and drink . . . and associate with wom . . .!' the rest was lost in a fit of coughing.

Pump . . . pump . . . pump . . . knees high, feet clear of the snow, around the bend and into another, enough light from the brightness of the snow to see a few precious yards ahead, going well, the fear of pursuit diminishing by the stride.

'Never . . . again . . .!' I gasped, chasing my own frozen breath, 'will I . . . accept gifts on a train . . . from a stranger. Finished . . .! Done . . . I will hie me to a monastery and . . . tread grapes.' I jerked a look behind, delighted at the complete absence of everybody. 'This . . . investigating life business is for the birds. I can . . . tell you what's out there in the big, wide world . . . trouble! No matter what form it comes in . . . it always adds up to . . . trouble? T for tarantulas . . . R for railway compartments . . . O for a sit down! . . . U for undressed ladies . . . B for Buzz Malone . . .' I laughed as he pulled a hurt expression. 'OK – B for Bellamey . . . L for . . .'

I stopped dead. Buzz skidded to a halt and peered at me. 'L for . . .?'

'I nodded through the snow. 'L for ladder, mate, to climb those bloody gates!'

He shot round. 'Christ . . . I'd forgotten them!'

We jogged on, our new-found lightheartedness once more plummeting as we drew close to the towering, spike-topped barrier that barred our road to freedom.

Panicky now, we quickly searched the wall on both sides of the gates but found only dense, impenetrable bushes. The walls were impossible to climb. Then suddenly – fresh nightmare! The sound of an approaching car!

Headlights showed as a brief glimmer beyond the forest of rhododendrons, then appeared again, brighter, as the car swept into the first bend. We whirled in fear towards the gate and made a clumsy, scrambling start up the first cross-member, but above this rose eight feet of unobstructed verticals, each bar a rod of ice, impossible to scale. A backwards glance and we could see the car was almost on us, its headlights flaring on the snow-covered bushes that lined the last bend.

'Buzz . . . they've got us!'

He jumped down, grim faced, fists clenched. 'Not yet they haven't! They . . .'

His words were lost in the sudden rumble and clank of machinery from the little shed that stood a few feet from me. And then . . . I was moving! The gates were opening!

'Buzz . . .!'

I jumped backwards from the gate and fell on my arse in the snow, but a hand from Buzz and I was up and running through the gates that were already beginning to close!

We were barely through when the car came into the final bend, headlights blinding us, its tyres zizzing on the turn, and with a roar of acceleration it hurtled down the straight. On it came – straight for us! We stood rooted, hypnotized by the slowly closing gates and the advancing car. They were going to make it! Close . . . close, you bastards! Faster . . . faster! They were on us! They were through Then suddenly the world disintegrated into the most God-awful scrunch and crash of metal and shattering of glass as both wings were ripped off that beautiful limousine and it came to a dead and ignominious halt, caught in the ruthless jaws of those powerful gates that kept on squeezing and squeezing and then I was flying through the air, jerked from my stunned gape by Buzz's mighty arm and we were off, heads down and knees up, around that crescent like greyhounds down from the slips, heedless of snow and ice and blizzard and every flaming thing else except that freedom lay ahead and that taxis ran on Riverside Drive just a couple of blocks away.

As we broke out onto the Drive we fell about each other, laughing and whooping and bashing each other and throwing snow and then suddenly Buzz was off, shouting and waving like a lunatic but bringing the cab to a slushy halt.

As I ran across, the driver's window came down and Buzz's head ducked in, then reappeared, grinning and giving me a wink. 'Son . . . I think our luck is changing.'

'Oh?' I panted, also looking in.

She was a cute, pert little blonde, armed with a cynical smile, tough as they come. With a wry grimace she took in our dishevelled appearance and slipped the cab into first gear, ready for an emergency getaway.

'Well,' she said, deciding to stay, 'you want to risk it, fellas?'

Buzz grinned. 'Do you?'

She nodded confidently. 'I reckon I can handle you two, but don't get any similar ideas, hm?'

'Ma'm . . .' sighed Buzz, spiritually collapsing. 'If only you knew.'

TWELVE

According to the I/D card mounted above the windscreen her name was Nicola Laffachaski, and the set, starey passport-type photograph did her no justice whatever, failing completely to capture her laconic confidence and endearing toughness.

She wasn't beautiful. Come to think of it, she was really quite plain, her short blonde/brown hair a trifle unkempt and her nose a touch too snub, but she radiated the tomboy pertness that men go for if the rest of the chemistry's right, and as it was right, we struck up a warm-hearted rapport immediately.

'Nicola Laffachaski . . .' Buzz read, settling back with a sigh, 'an angel out of the night. Nicola, you don't *know* how spot-on your timing was then.'

She threw a glance into the rearview mirror and asked, sympathetically, 'You guys in trouble?'

' "Were" in trouble. Don't get worried.'

She gave a light-hearted shrug. 'I'm not worried.'

'Pardon me asking,' I said, 'but isn't it a bit dangerous for a young lady to be driving a cab in New York, especially at night?'

She clicked her teeth and grinned. ' "Young lady" . . . I *like* that. The question, of course, is not entirely original, I get it about twenty times a day, but they always ask "Ain't it unusual for a *dame* ta be driving cab in New York . . . or a *broad* . . . or a *girl* . . . or a *bird* . . . or a *frail* – *never* a young lady. Mister, you can ride my cab whenever you like, just so long as you keep callin' me "young lady". Anyway to answer your question – yes and no.'

I laughed. 'Thank you. But what would you do if someone, particularly a man, refused to pay his fare?'

'I'd weigh the relative value of three bucks against my continued good health, dump him, then drive like heck without the money. Question answered?'

'Most succinctly. Thank you.'

'You're welcome. Now perhaps you'll answer mine – what kind of trouble were you fellas in?'

Buzz heaved a sigh. 'Nicola . . .'

'Nicky.'

'Nicky . . . we could tell you a story you simply would not believe . . .'

'Huh!' she laughed. 'I'm a cabbie, remember, an' I've heard some mighty tall ones. If you don't mind, I'd like to hear it.'

'Oh?' Buzz frowned. 'Any particular reason?'

'Yes,' she nodded. 'I collect 'em. I don't intend driving all my life – I want to write, you know, stories . . . novels. I drive this thing at night to keep eating and I write novels during the day. Also I pick up a lotta good plots doin' this job.'

'Good for you,' said Buzz. 'Well . . . this is more Russ's story than mine . . .'

'Are you Russ?' she asked, through the mirror.

'Yes, Russ Tobin. This is Buzz Malone – and he's wrong, it's every bit as much his story as mine.'

'OK, OK,' she grinned, 'don't come to blows about it. I don't care whose story it is so long as it becomes mine. Look – are you fellas in a tearing hurry to get back to the hotel?'

'Well . . .' Buzz looked at me. 'We've got a couple of dates later on but not until two or three o'clock.'

'That sounds like a story in itself,' she smiled. 'Well, lissen – how d'you feel about dropping of somewheres for a coffee? I've gotta break due anytime now. There's a diner down on 86th West I usually stop at – serves the best coffee and apple pie in town. What d'you say?'

I nodded at Buzz. 'If there's one thing I could use more than a cup of steaming coffee right now it's two cups.'

'Right,' he said. 'Nicky, you're on.'

'There yuh go,' she grinned and hit the gas.

Ten minutes later we were hunched over pie and coffee in a secluded booth, Nicky all eyes and ears.

'OK, who's gonna start?'

Buzz nodded at me. 'You take it.'

'All right.' I sipped my coffee, scalded my lip, lit a fag and began.

She was a marvellous listener. She sat riveted, blue eyes wide with amazement, coffee and pie forgotten, interrupting only to clear a point, 'wow-ing' and 'my *Gard*-ing!' as I told her everything and shuddering as I described Herbert, the tarantula. Finally, as I reached the point where she'd picked us up, she leapt in with a barrage of questions, almost breathless with excitement.

'But . . . for goshakes, why didn't you call the cops!?'

I shrugged. 'And tell them what? Think about it, Nicky – Frank and Charlie really haven't *done* anything to us, have they? And as for Alex and Ariadne . . . well, he *is* the son of Professor Kokheimer and we're only a couple of transient tourists. It'd be his word against ours . . . and, beside, this thing could get *very* involved and neither of us could afford to hang around New York for weeks . . .'

'Yeah, yeah, I can see your point. Anyway, gettin' mixed up with the cops is bad business – especially for a couple of foreigners. But . . . what in heck is the scene all about! Is there anything special about that spider?'

I gave a shrug, but Buzz, to my amazement, nipped in with, 'No, there's nothing special about the *spider*, Nicky . . . but there's something very special about what's *inside* the spider.'

I glanced at him and he gave a superior smirk. 'I got the answer through the crack in the door, buddy – while you were punching me in the arm. Alex and Ariadne were discussing . . . carats.'

I frowned. 'Carrots? You mean . . . vegetables?'

He laughed. 'No, you nut –car*ats* – as in . . .'

'Diamonds!' gasped Nicky.

Buzz nodded.

'Wow!' she exclaimed, eyes like saucers. 'What a genius way of smuggling them in! I mean, what customs man is going to open a tarantula! Diamonds . . . from South Africa! But, Buzz . . . how does this guy Kresge come into it?'

'Well, it can only be a guess – but I'd say this Mistophoulus character isn't so much in the insect business as the diamond smuggling business – slipping them out inside snakes and spiders and things. This chap Kresge who worked for him could have struck up a private deal with Kokheimer and every now and then pinched a stone or two from Mistophoulus, got them out inside a spider to Bellamey in Miami, who notified Kokheimer, who sent down a different courier each time to pick them up.'

'Yes, yes,' Nicky was nodding. 'Then Mistophoulus catches Kresge at it . . . finds out about Bellamey . . . and sends these two hoods Frank and Charlie to get back the stones *and* find out who Bellamey is forwarding them to. But ham-fisted Charlie knocks him off before they get the information and . . .'

'You got it,' said Buzz.

'And you two walked right into Kokheimer's hands. My *Gard*, you were lucky to get away. But . . . who d'you think unlocked the door in the tower – and unlocked the gates in the nick of time?'

I looked at Buzz. 'I think it was Krantz.'

He nodded. 'Me, too. I reckon he knows what's going on between Alex and Ariadne but wouldn't expose them because of the professor. They're very devoted to each other.'

'Yeah, could be,' Nicky said thoughtfully. 'But, heck, now where does this leave you two?'

'On our way back to the hotel,' said Buzz, 'to pick up our luggage and move into another hotel fast. Even if Frank and Charlie haven't thought of tracing Russ through Sun Time holiday, Ariadne certainly has – and by tomorrow *they'll* be after us. New York has suddenly become decidedly unhealthy.'

'Jeepers, what a *story*!' exclaimed Nicky. 'D'you fellas mind if I use it?'

'Be our guest,' I smiled. 'Better change the names of the characters, though – otherwise you'll find Frank, Charlie and the Kokheimers on your doorstep.'

'Sure . . . sure,' she rubbed her hands together. 'Hey, I can't wait to start it. Thanks a lot, fellas, I really appreciate it. And forget the cab fare – it's on the house. Well, come on, let's get you out of that hotel.'

'We might have trouble finding another,' said Buzz. 'We were told New York is bulging.'

She gave us a wink. 'Leave it to me, I know a place. One thing about bein' a New York cabbie – you get to know an awful lotta people. Let's go – I can feel Ariadne breathin' down my neck.'

* * *

In seven minutes we were drawing up outside the hotel.

'Keep your motor running, Nicky,' said Buzz. 'We'll be down in five.'

'Roger,' she said, saluting. 'I daren't cut it anyway – I'd freeze to death. Take it easy now.'

We piled out of the cab and ran across the pavement which, although it had obviously been repeatedly swept, still wore a coverlet of snow an inch deep. It was still coming down hard, driven by a howling wind which ripped through us like a scythe and chilled us even in the few second between cab and foyer.

We pushed through the door and crossed to the desk, blowing and shivering, and informed the desk clerk we were checking out. Reluctantly, he put down the book he was reading.

'This time of night?' he frowned. 'Well, OK by me. We've bin paid for another four nights for you, Mr Tobin, so we'll call it quits for both of you. Hope you make it to wherever you're goin'.'

He resumed chuckling over *The Virgin Soldiers* and we headed for the elevator.

'Isn't she a honey?' smiled Buzz.

'Nicky? She's terrific. I'd certainly like to read the story when she's written it. I wonder how she'll portray *us*?'

He shrugged. 'Factually – tall, handsome, brave, charming, amusing, intelligent, sexy . . .'

'How else?'

The doors opened, we got in, pressed the button, started up.

'When we get to the room we'll give the girls a quick call, hm?' said Buzz. 'How d'you fancy another night with Linka?'

'Nah, not much. She really is a nothing bird – ugly, skinny, passionless . . .'

'You know, you could be talking about Fifi?'

The doors opened. We walked across the hall and Buzz unlocked our door, joking, 'What I ever saw in that bird, I'll never know . . .' he led the way into the small hallway. 'Of all the beautiful girls in New . . .'

He stopped so suddenly I ran into him. 'Oops!'

He turned, face white as a sheet, and hissed. 'Get out!'

'Mm?'

'Get *out*! Our light just went out!' he whispered. 'There's someone in the ro . . .'

Crash!

At that moment the bathroom door flew open and there stood bloody enormous Charlie!

He gaped at us, as surprised as we were, but before he could make a move I was flying backwards, pushed in the chest by Buzz. I hurtled across the corridor and fetched up with a thud against the elevator panelling. Bang! Our door slammed closed, pulled by Buzz. I turned to run into the elevator but Buzz was there again, pushing me out of the way with a hoarse, 'NO!' In he nipped, thumped a button, then leapt out, grabbed my arm and we hared ten yards down the corridor to the emergency stairs.

Round the corner we shot then stopped, hugging the wall. Our bedroom door flew open a split second later.

'They're in the elevator!' yelled Frank. 'Get down the goddam stairs!'

Clatter . . . clatter . . . clatter . . . down the regular stairs they ran.

'Come on!' gasped Buzz, starting down the emergency flight.

'Buzz . . . our luggage!'

'Fuck the luggage! We'll get the girls to send it on! Come on . . . these will lead out the back way!'

Clatter . . . clump . . . clump . . . down the four flights on winged boots, hitting every fourth stair. We reached the ground floor and immediately in front of us was a door, undoubtedly leading to a rear alley. We went through it hard, straight into the reception foyer!

We stopped, scanned the room, spotted them over by the elevator, watching the indicator descend, their hands in their pockets as though they had something very nasty waiting for us in there.

'Go!' gasped Buzz and we went.

We were halfway across the foyer when Frank spotted us. He gave Charlie a push, moving him into action, but in the second or two it took Charlie to respond we were out through the front door and racing across to the cab.

Buzz yanked open the rear door and we fell in.

'Frank and Charlie . . . they were in our room!' he panted. 'Get going. Fast!'

'Oh, my *Gard* . . .!'

As she stamped on the accelerator, Frank and Charlie came hurtling out of the doors, slithered to a stop, then changed direction and pelted down the street, stopping at a yellow Buick convertible parked at the curb.

'Oh, Christ, they've got a car!' I cried. 'Nicky, they've got us!'

'First they've gotta catch us!' she said determindly, gritting her teeth and leaping the lights at Times Square. 'My dad taught me to drive and he was the most lethal cabbie in New York!'

'They're coming!' gasped Buzz. 'Right through the red light!'

'Obviously *very* anxious to talk to you fellas,' muttered Nicky, squeezing through the next intersection. 'Well, we'll just have to disappoint them.'

Buzz turned to her. 'Listen, Nicky . . . we don't want you caught up in this. Find a place and drop us.'

'What – and miss the finish of the story! Are you crazy? How will I know how to end it?'

'Just make it two dead bodies in the river,' I told her. 'Riddled with bullets. Buzz, I'm sure they've got guns.'

'So am I. How in heck did they get into our room? That receptionist didn't say anything . . .'

'Probably a finn to the floor maid,' answered Nicky. 'Those women would sell their mothers for five bucks. What are they doin' back there, Russ?'

'Just sitting there, Nicky – and, you know, I swear they're laughing.'

'OK . . . now, let's just calm down and do some thinking. It's obvious that moving into another hotel is out – right?'

Buzz nodded. 'Right. The moment we stop they've got us.'

'Right – so we just keep moving. Appealing to the cops is out because the two behind would simply deny everything and catch up with you later. So – what's the alternative?'

'The . . . airport?' I suggested.

Buzz shot me a look. 'And do what?'

I shrugged. 'Catch a couple of planes – you to Canada, me to London. We've got our passports and travellers' cheques – and I've got my return ticket. Maybe I can switch flights . . .'

Buzz was shaking his head. 'Russ, do you know what time it is?'

'Mm . . .? It's half-past midnight.'

'Correct – and the last flight out of Kennedy leaves around eleven. There'll be nothing until six tomorrow morning.'

'Oh.'

'Nicky . . .?'

'Yes, Buzz?'

'Do you think you can lose these two blokes long enough for us to nip out into an alley somewhere?'

'Aw, come on . . .'

'No, I mean it. These two are *very* rough characters . . . and they're in a very tight spot. They daren't go back to Cape Town without the spider *and* the name of the man Bellamey passed it on to. Nicky, they're going to sit on our tails until they catch us, I promise you. This is no game, love.'

She thought about it and finally gave a sigh. 'Well . . . if you say so. OK, hold onto your hats, fellas, here we go.'

Slloosshh. She hit a beautifully controlled skid around a corner and flattened the accelerator, throwing Buzz and me into a tangle of arms and legs.

'Whhhhoooopppeeee!' he yelled.

We struggled upright only to be upended again as she threw the cab into another bend and then another, going like the clappers. We shot across Park Avenue . . . then Lexington . . . Third . . . Second, heading east. Now she turned north and raced the lights across the numbered streets . . . 59th . . . 60th . . . 61st . . . cursing as we hit a red light and encountered a fire truck that swept in from our right and belted up the avenue, sirens wailing.

She skidded to a stop, fingers drumming desperately on the wheel and foot gunning the motor. And then – a cry from Buzz. 'Jeezus, they're right behind us!'

Nicky's head shot round. 'Hell, that guy can drive. OK – we'll just see *how* good he is!'

Baaarrrooommm! She was off again, spitting slush, the back end swerving like a hula dancer. On across 62nd . . . 63rd . . . 64th . . . then a right jiggle over to First Avenue, playing the lights all the way, slowing on a green then hitting it as it changed, leaving it for Frank and Charlie who steadfastly ignored every red and came straight through.

'Hell!' Nicky cried in despair. 'Is there ever a damn cop car around when you need one! All we need is *one* stinking cop to catch them coming through a red!'

On up the Avenue . . . then left . . . right . . . reaching the 100's . . . 116th . . . 117th . . . 118th . . . now heading west again, recrossing Second . . . Third . . . Lexington . . . and still they clung to us, sometimes dropping back a little then racing to catch up, Frank's insolent leer telling us 'why bother, we've got you! Sooner or later you'll have to stop and then we've got you.'

'Nicky . . .' I said, the thought striking me. 'How's your petrol?'

She glanced at the gauge. 'Almost a full tank. I've been thinking about that. I wonder how their's is? That could be the break we need. If they've got less than a tankful, they're gonna need gas before us. That Buick's a heavy car, drinks gas like a lush. This Ford isn't too bad. I reckon we could have a few miles on them.

'Just a couple of hundred yards would do,' Buzz observed wryly. 'Just enough to get out of their sight.'

'OK,' she nodded. 'That's it – we just keep goin' and pray they use up their gas before we do, what d'you say? As long as we keep moving they can't touch you. They're not going to shoot at you because they want that information from you. So we'll just run 'em out of gas, slip quietly into the darkness and tomorrow you boys can fly away.'

'And . . . if *we* run out of gas before they do?' asked Buzz.

'Then you're in a whole heap of *schtuck*,' she sighed. 'OK, so it's not such a bright idea but what else have we got?'

There was no answer to that.

In increasingly worried silence she rocketed across a dozen intersections, skidded around a score of corners, diced with a plethora of traffic lights and didn't gain a yard. That flaming Frank must have trained at Brands Hatch! And all the time the swine was laughing at us.

'Nicky, it's no use,' I told her, 'he's sticking like glue. Buzz we'll have to make a run for it. We can't let Nicky risk her neck like this . . .'

'Shut up,' she told me, 'I'm thinking. Listen . . . Buzz – you were going to Canada, right?'

'Yes, I've got a tournament in Victoria.'

'OK Russ . . . how do *you* feel about going to Canada?'

'Er . . . hm?'

'How do you feel about it?' she grinned.

'*Can*ada?'

'Sure.'

'Well . . .' I looked at Buzz who merely shrugged. 'But . . . when . . . how . . . ?'

'Right now . . . and by road,' she answered. 'You've both got your passports?'

'Well, yes . . .'

'Then how about me driving you there right now?'

'I . . .'

I gaped at Buzz who was grinning at her. 'Go on, Nicky . . . what's the plan?'

She gave a shrug. 'Simple – we head for Niagara Falls. I reckon I've just got enough gas to get there – it's about two hundred miles.'

'Two h . . .' I gaped. 'You'd drive us two h . . .'

'Sure, why not? It's nothin' on the turnpike. I do it a couple of times a week. And on a flat run at speed I reckon we can out-gas these two punks behind. Once we hit seventy that Buick starts gulping gas like there's no tomorrow. What d'you say?'

I gave a laugh and looked at Buzz, still stunned by the suggestion. 'But . . . will I be allowed in Canada?'

'On a British passport? Sure you will. But . . . Nicky, there's one thing that puzzles me – how is going to Canada going to help if Frank and Charlie *don't* run out of gas before we do? All they have to do is follow us over the border.'

She gave us a sneaky grin and tapped her nose. 'Don't worry about that – Nicola has an ace up her sleeve. All that matters is that we can make that border before our gas runs out. The rest will take care of itself, believe me.'

'Well . . .' he shrugged. 'It's up to Russ. How do you feel about nipping to Canada?'

'Me? Lovely, mate. I shall very likely have to take a begging bowl to the streets when I get there, but apart from that . . .'

'Don't worry about money, we'll manage somehow. I've got friends in Toronto. Well, that's settled then. We go to Canada . . . *but* – on one condition, Nicky.'

'What's that?' she asked.

'That we pay full fare for the round trip.'

'Aw, come on . . .'

'No!' we protested.

'You've been a terrific sport and a fantastic help,' Buzz continued earnestly. 'You're not going to be out of pocket into the bargain and unless you agree to take the money, and we'll know if you're lying about the price, we refuse to go.'

'Fellas . . . look . . .'

'No.'

'But you gave me the *story* . . .'

'No!'

She sighed. 'Well, if that's the way you want it – hold on to your toupees. Canada – here we come!'

She swung the car in one heck of a curve, pointing us north, then smashed us back into the upholstery as she trod the gas pedal to the floor.

THIRTEEN

Swish . . . click . . . swish . . . click . . . swish . . . click . . . swish . . . click.

The wipers were doing a splendid job. One thing about American cars, they're designed by people who actually *expect* snow to fall in winter. The snow tyres were thrumming away beneath us, their heavy treads smashing into the watery slush that covered the salted highways and ejecting it with utter disdain straight into the faces of the two goons still very close behind us.

Sitting erect, chin high, her tomboy profile lit dramatically by the dash lights, Nicola was driving superbly. After this, let no one utter a derisive word about women drivers. Nicky was as good as they come.

'How're we doing?' Buzz asked her.

She gave a nod. 'We're doing OK. We've done a hundred and thirty miles . . . seventy to go and I've got about a third of a tank left.' She laughed. 'I reckon we'll make it through the Immigration barrier with fifty yards to spare.'

'Mm,' went Buzz. 'I'd give my serving arm for a five-gallon dixie can in the boot.'

'Don't worry – I know what this baby can do right down to the last cupful. How're the punks doin' back there?'

'I can't see anything for their headlights,' I answered. 'But I shouldn't think they're too happy about your slush. They're getting the lot.'

'Well, they're in for a drop more. Hold tight!'

We had run up behind an enormous trailer-truck whose 1014 wheels were throwing back a veritable Niagara of filth. With a flick of the wheel, Nicky cut left, suddenly losing the battering spray, and gunned the cab down the side of the truck, overtaking it fast, then nipped in quickly in front and stayed close to it.

'Here they come!' I reported.

'They won't come far,' she laughed, 'because there's gonna be no room.'

Frank came on, reached the front end of the truck, tried to squeeze into the narrow gap behind us but got a deafening blast of horns from the truck and had to drop back.

'Ha!' laughed Nicky. 'Boy, he'll be getting some filth now.'

'Hell hath no fury . . .' quoted Buzz. 'Nicky, I'm so glad you're on our side.'

Five miles clicked by . . . ten . . . We passed a service complex, its petrol pumps agonizingly tempting, its cheerful lights welcoming, but on we went into the darkness again, committed to speed.

And then . . .

'Hey!' I gave a quick start. 'Nicky . . . I think they've turned off! Buzz, quick . . . behind the truck!'

Buzz whirled round, wincing at the truck's blinding lights. 'I can't see anything. What did you see?'

'A flash of yellow. I swear they peeled off at that petrol station.'

'Well, it's a fair bet,' said Nicky optimistically. 'That Buick must be using a lot of gas at this speed. Keep looking for it. If it has disappeared I'm gonna stop at the next gas station, just to make *sure* we reach the border. Even a couple of gallons will do it.'

On we went, Buzz and I now kneeling at the rear window, searching the truck's rear for a glimpse of yellow but unable to see anything beyond its headlights.

'No sign?' asked Nicky.

'Not a thing,' answered Buzz.

'Well, there's a service station coming up in five hundred yards. What d'you think?'

'I don't think they're there,' I answered. 'I'm almost certain I saw them turn off.'

'OK, we'll take a chance. Here we go!'

She slowed, signalled for the turn, then swept off right into the service area and as the truck thundered past Buzz let out a yell, 'We lost 'em! Baby, you out-gassed them!'

'Thank God,' grinned Nicky, sighing with relief. 'Look, fellas, I . . . I've got a confession – that coffee has kinda caught up with me and I need to pay a lightning visit to the girls' room. If I stop at a pump close to the can, will you two shoot in a couple of gallons while I nip into the rest room?'

'Of course,' said Buzz.

'I'll be as quick as is humanly possible.'

She drove between the ranks of petrol pumps and came to a halt fifty yards from the 'Ladies'.

'Right – she's all yours.'

We all got out. Nicky skipped off and disappeared into the loo, and while I opened the petrol flap, Buzz unhooked the nozzle and got busy with the pump.

'Well, son,' he grinned, 'our troubles are nearly over. About fifty more miles and we'll be over the border.' He turned away to check the meter, saying, 'Too bad about the girls, we'll have to call them from Toronto. They're gonna be mighty . . .' Suddenly he stopped, gaped across the area towards the entrance, gasping, 'RUSS – IT'S *THEM*.'

Yanking the nozzle from the car he hurled it at the pump, petrol still spurting from the pipe, slammed down the flap, pulled open the front door and threw himself into the driver's seat. Me – I was still standing there – stunned by the sight of the Buick bearing down on us at a hell of a lick.

'GET IN . . . GET IN!' Buzz was yelling at me, fumbling with keys, tramping on pedals and rattling the gear lever in desperate panic to get the thing started.

I yanked open the rear door, fell in and with a roar we were away, the door slamming hard and me taking a header into the floor, legs in the air and nose buried in the wet carpet.

'Godalbleedingmighty, where did they come from!' gasped Buzz. 'Hold tight . . .!'

Sssiiiiizzzzzz . . . round we went in a wild skid, the wheels fizzing up the slush, then getting a bite and away we went. I scrambled to my knees, head spinning, the world outside a mad kalaidoscope of whirling lights.

'Wh . . . where are we . . . they . . . Nicky . . . Christ, Buzz, we've got to get Nicky!'

Sssssswwwiiiissshhh! A magnificent slalom between two stands of pumps, missing them by an oil slick.

'They're right behind us!' gasped Buzz. 'Where in hell did they come from! They tricked us! They must've pulled off at that gas station but run right through it and back onto the highway . . . hold tiiiigghhtt!'

Whhhooossshhh! Around another island of pumps at an unbelievable angle, tilting hideously, slithering sideways then thumping down on all fours and off again.

I jumped forward. 'There . . . Nicky! Outside the ladies' loo! She's waving!'

'Can't . . . get her this time . . . got to shake these sods somehow!'

We flashed past Nicky, her face a mask of horror, then out into the parking lot, shot down an aisle between two broken ranks of cars, swerving round a car threatening to back out in front of us, braked hard for the turn, the rear end sliding appallingly, then on round the end of the building, the Buick still clinging to our tails with unbelievable tenacity. Back we went towards the petrol stands, Buzz jinking this way and that, trying to lay dummies for the blokes behind, suddenly hauling on the wheel and squeezing the Ford between two islands with nothing to spare, the tyres screaming down the parapet, zzzzzzzz . . . now finding purchase and up over the parapet, demolishing a stock of oil cans and a watering can.

'You did it!' I shouted, thumping him on the back. 'They're too wide to come through! They've had to go round! Look . . .!'

But Buzz had no time to look. He was gunning it towards Nicky who was jumping up and down like she was at Ascot and her horse was about to win.

A slithering half halt and she was in, into the front with Buzz, slamming the door and urging him on. 'Beautiful . . . beautiful . . .! Now, go . . . go!'

Thhhaaarrrooommmm!! Out of the parking lot, a quick jig left and we were back on the highway, the Buick a hundred yards and two cars behind us.

'Ohhh!' gasped Nicky, collapsing against the seat. 'I nearly died! I came out of the can and you were gone . . . I couldn't think what had happened – and then I saw you . . . playing tag round the pumps! Buzz, you were marvellous . . . marvellous!'

Buzz grinned self-consciously. 'Huh – we didn't even pay for the petrol!'

'You managed to get some!'

'About two gallons – maybe less.'

'Fabulous! Well, let's see them catch us now!'

'You know,' laughed Buzz, 'I've always wanted to drive a cab.'

'Drive it!' she laughed.

With the needle steady on seventy we were into the outskirts of Niagara Falls within forty minutes, now off the highway and onto city streets. At the first red traffic light Buzz pulled on the handbrake. 'Come on, Nicky, you take over,' and fell into the back with me.

'Well done, mate,' I said, 'Great piece of driving.'

'They nearly had us, by God. If I hadn't looked up just when I did . . .'

We were off again, driving more sedately now, Nicky picking her way through the snow-covered town with confidence, having done it many times before.

'Where are the gorillas?' she asked.

'Still two cars behind and looking mighty pleased with themselves,' I said. 'I reckon that Frank hasn't stopped grinning since New York.'

'Well, now, we'll just have to find something to make him smile on the other side of his ugly face,' she said mysteriously.

I exchanged a glance with Buzz but he shook his head and shrugged, as puzzled as I was as to how she was going to do it.

On through the town we went and out again, the houses thinning as we picked up a wider motorway, suddenly seeing in the distance a kind of toll barrier across the road. There were glassed-in cubicles and overhead signs, flashing lights indicating which booths were open and which closed, and leading up to each open booth, a line of at least a dozen cars.

'Uh uh,' I said anxiously. 'We'll have to stop.'

'They won't try anything here,' said Nicky. 'The place is crawling with cops. They'll wait until we get into Canada.'

I turned to look through the rear window. The Buick hadn't made an attempt to close up, but then, why should it? They'd got us now, knew where we were heading, and all they had to do was to follow until we had to stop.

As we joined one of the queues and began to creep forward, I gave a sigh and said, 'Nicky, love it's not that I doubt your word, but I still don't see what has changed by driving all this way. The goons are still on our tail as they were in New York, and if we spill everything to *these* cops, Frank and Charlie would still deny everything.'

'True,' she said, grinning to herself.

'And all they've got to do is follow us to Toronto and . . .'

I turned to Buzz but he was shaking his head. 'Don't look at me, mate. I don't know the answer. We're in the lady's hands.'

'There yuh go again,' she said, smiling with mock sweetness. 'That's twice in one night I've bin called a lady. You fellas really are the greatest to have around.'

She was taking it all so casually!

Creep . . . creep . . . creep. Forward we crept as the cars in line were checked by the Immigration guys and passed through, and finally we slid under the overhead shelter, drew up alongside a booth, and Nicky wound down the front passenger window.

An elderly, grey-haired official popped his head in.

'Two British tourists going to Toronto,' Nicky declared and Buzz gave a hurt cough.

'Er, one British . . . one Australian,' he corrected.

The official's cool grey eyes raked us. 'Which is the Australian?'

'I am,' Buzz stated emphatically.

'Huh huh . . . and why do you wish to enter Canada, gentlemen?'

'Well, we . . .' I began.

'Excuse me,' Nicky smiled at him, 'but is Bob Jancey on duty tonght?'

'Hm . . .?' The mention of a familiar name softened the severity of his professional countenance. 'Why sure – Bob's over in number three box.'

'Do you think I could have a word with him?'

'Sure thing. You a friend of his, miss?'

'Kind of,' she said, wrinkling her nose.

He laughed. 'Go ahead – just walk over there.'

She turned to us, grinning mischieviously. 'I won't be a moment. Why don't you show this gentleman your passports while I'm gone?'

'What a nice idea,' smiled the old fellow.

As he took Buzz's passport, I was following Nicky's progress over to box number three. She reached it and tapped on a window. A tall dark-haired young chap in uniform turned, made an expression of surprise and hurried out. And then so help me, he caught her by the shoulders and kissed her.

I dug Buzz on the arm but he'd seen it.

'Well, whadya know,' he muttered.

'You entering Canada on vacation, Mr Malone?' the official was asking.

'Erm . . . not totally. I'm playing in a tennis tournament in Victoria in a few days' time.'

'Huh huh . . . OK that's fine.' He took my passport and scanned it. 'And you, Mr . . .Tobin . . . are you on vacation?'

'Yes, purely, I can't play tennis to save myself.'

'Huh huh . . . and your baggage? In the trunk, I presume?'

'Well . . .' I glanced at Buzz. 'Well, no actually . . . we . . . you see . . .'

Once again Nicky arrived and saved us. The tall lad was with her. As she waved to us through the windscreen, the man with her said to our official, 'Er, Dave, can I speak with yuh for a moment . . .'

Our chap handed back my passport and walked off, and for a while they talked in murmurs.

'What the heck's going on?' Buzz muttered. 'What's Nicky up to? And who's the guy she's with?'

'You require an answer to all three questions immediately?'

'Fun-nee . . . aye, aye – here she comes now.'

She opened her door and slid in, called, 'See you later,' to Bob Jancey, then started the car. 'OK – here we go.'

With another wave to Jancey and one for the older official, she drove slowly through the barrier and breathed a sigh of relief as we emerged the other side. 'Well, fellas . . . welcome to Canada – the land of the free.'

With that, I expected her to plunge the accelerator through the floor boards and tear off up the highway, making use of every second headstart we could gain on Frank and Charlie. But she didn't.

Instead she lolloped along for fifty yards then pulled into the side, applied the handbrake – and cut the engine. Then she turned in her seat and gave us a comical grin.

'Want to see a *really* funny scene? Just take a look back there.'

We swivelled round.

One car in our line came through . . . then another. Then the Buick slid under the barrier. Dave, the elderly official, approached the passenger side, Bob Jancey the other, then from nowhere a motorcycle swirled in front of the Buick and sat there with folded arms. A moment later and Frank and Charlie were out of the car, arguing, gesturing, pointing to Canada, then were led quietly to one side as four more officials arrived on the scene and the demolition of the Buick began.

The bonnet rose . . . the boot was opened . . . and all the seats came out. We couldn't hear what Frank and Charlie were saying but they were waving their arms about, ranting and raving, and no one was taking a blind bit of notice of them.

'I . . . don't believe it!' laughed Buzz, 'Nicky . . .' he turned to her, 'aw, you're just too much, man. How the heck did you pull *that*?'

'Simple,' she grinned. 'I just told Bob Jancey I thought Frank and Charlie were smuggling diamonds in their petrol tank . . . and he promised to reduce the Buick to nuts and bolts and invite the hoods to put it together again. They'll be there for about a year!'

'But . . . how did you get Jancey to agree to *do* it?'

She shrugged. 'Easy – I just told him I wouldn't marry him if he didn't.'

'*Marry* him?'

'Sure,' she grinned, starting the car. 'He's my fiancèe.'

Buzz and I looked at each other and burst out laughing. 'You crafty minx,' he said. 'No wonder you were so confident they wouldn't follow us over the border. *He* was the ace up your sleeve.'

'That's my ace,' she laughed.

'Aw, Nicky, how can we ever thank you. You've really been terrific.'

'Just keep calling me young lady,' she grinned. 'For that I'd drive you to Alaska.'

FOURTEEN

Well, we reached Toronto at five in the morning, booked into the King Edward and slept the clock round, then treated Nicky to a superb dinner and very reluctantly waved her off for New York, feeling as we watched her tail-lights disappear round the corner, that we'd lost a real pal.

'What a girl,' said Buzz as we re-entered the hotel. 'I hope that Jancey fella appreciates what he's getting.'

'A bird and a half,' I agree. 'And talking of birds and a half . . . I reckon we ought to call up Fifi and Linka and explain what happened, and also get our luggage up here fast. By tomorrow I shall be distinctly unlovely.'

Up in the room, while Buzz booked the call, I was doing some earnest counting of funds and reaching the conclusion that I was about ten pounds away from being positively and embarrassingly busted – the fact of which I appraised him as he came off the phone.

'Don't worry about it!' he said, waving the problem away. 'I can let you have some.'

'Buzz . . . look, thanks all the same but I'd rather not if there's some other way around it. Let me put it this way. What are the chances of getting a job here?'

'Eh? You want to work *here*?'

I shrugged. 'Why not? Now that I'm here I'd like to stay for a bit – a couple of weeks anyway. How long are you going to be here?'

'Oh . . . about two weeks.'

'OK, well, let's say two weeks, then. What do you think about getting a job?'

'What sort of a job?'

I shrugged. 'Anything.'

A slow, devilish grin distorted his face. '*Any*thing?'

'Hey . . . what's going through that cesspit mind of yours?'

'You . . . really would be prepared to do *any*thing for a couple of weeks?'

'Malone . . . I don't trust you. You're up to no good, lad.'

He laughed. 'Who – me?'

'Yes, you, you bugger. Come on – give.'

'Well . . . it's just that I've got a pal here . . .'

'I thought you would have.'

'. . . who runs an agency called . . . "Hire-A-Guy" . . .'

'Oh-oh.'

'. . . which supplies fellas for all sorts of odd jobs . . . like . . . clearing out box-rooms, painting fences, mowing lawns, that sort of thing.'

'Go on,' I said, innately suspicious.

'Well – how d'you fancy that?'

'Firstly, Malone . . . I want to know what the hell you're laughing at.'

'Oh, it's . . . nothing. Just some stories he told me, about what happened to some of the lads while they were out on jobs.'

'Such as?'

He shrugged. 'Oh, nothing really. Look, do you want me to give him a call?'

'What – now?'

'Sure, why not? I've got his home number.'

I fingered my wallet, my exceedingly thin wallet, and thought about it . . . then gave a nod. 'OK, I'll have a bash.'

'OK,' he said, rifling through his little black book.

'Buzz...what did happen to those guys on some of those jobs?'

'Sssshh,' he said, dialling the number, grinning his face off. Then . . . 'Hello? Hello, Greg . . .! It's Buzz! Hiya, buddy . . . fine . . . fine . . . yes, in Victoria . . . sure, terrific . . .'

This old chums chat went on for a couple of minutes and then he got down to business 'Listen, Greg – I'm up here with a pal, an English guy named Russ Tobin . . . met him on the train from Miami and, Jeezus!, is *this* a story – but another time. Point is – he's broke and too damned proud to borrow money . . . wants to earn it instead. Yeh . . . nuts. Any, he'll be here for a couple of weeks, till I get back from Victoria . . . is there anything you can do for him?'

Buzz listened for a while, 'uh-huh-ing' now and again and grinning across at me, then saying, 'Yeah, good-looking slob . . . six feet . . . brown hair . . . blue eyes . . . a hundred and seventy pounds . . . uh huh . . .' Then his face split in an ear-to-ear grin. 'Hang on, I'll ask him . . .'

He covered the phone, killing himself laughing. 'You're in! He says you're just the fella he's looking for. He's got an emergency on his hands. One of the big stores here in Toronto phoned him late this afternoon, they want someone to help out tomorrow, Christmas Eve. The regular chap went down with flu this afternoon. It's just for one day but he'll pay twenty dollars. Do you want it?'

'Well . . . in a store? Sure, that sounds all right. What's the job – selling?'

'Yes, sort of. It's in the toy department.'

'Yes, fine.'

He uncovered the phone. 'Yes, he says he'd be glad to, Greg . . . no, you can give them to me . . . Simpson's, sure I know it. What time? Eight! Jeezus, that's early . . .' he gave a laugh. 'Yes, of course. OK, he'll be there. Thanks a million, Greg, see you tomorrow night, then, Ciao.'

He put down the phone, chuckling away to himself. 'Well, there you are, son – simple as that. You're to be at Simpson's store at eight tomorrow for the fitting.'

'Well, that's terrific, Buzz, I can't . . . hm? What fitting?'

'The . . . fitting – you know, for the . . . costume.'

'Buzz . . . *what* bloody costume?'

'Oh, didn't I mention it . . .' His stomach was jiggling up and down now and tears were flooding his eyes. 'You're . . . going to be . . . Father Christmas!'

'Buzz, you . . .'

'Ho! . . . ho! . . . ho! . . . ho! . . .' he gaffawed, holding his shaking belly like Santa Claus.

'BUZZ! ! YOU DIRTYROTTENSTINKING . . .'

'HO . . .! HO . . .! HO . . .! HO . . .! HAPPY CHRISTMAS, LITTLE KIDDIEWINKIES, FROM JOLLY FATHER CHRISTMAS AND GET YOUR GODDAM STICKY FINGERS OUTTA MY BEARD, YOU LITTLE BASTARD OR I'LL BREAK OFF BOTH YOUR ARMS AND STICK 'EM IN YOUR STOCKING! !'

By gum, the swine didn't realize just how prophetic those words were destined to be – but I certainly found out the next day. Never in my life have I suffered such a . . . but that's another horrifying, nightmarish story and you'll have to wait until I've recovered before you get it. Awful!

Mind you, there *were* one or two compensations to the job – like Luscious Lilly Longlegs, Santa's personal assistant, for instance. Maybe I'll tell you about her, too, *and* what happened in the stockroom.

In the meantime . . . Happy Christmas.

And tarra.

Father flaming Christmas. Laugh . . .? I thought I'd never start.